Written in Water

Written in Water

Richard Haley

ROBERT HALE · LONDON

© Richard Haley 1999
First published in Great Britain 1999

ISBN 0 7090 6350 4

Robert Hale Limited
Clerkenwell House
Clerkenwell Green
London EC1R 0HT

The right of Richard Haley to be identified as
author of this work has been asserted by him
in accordance with the Copyright, Designs and
Patents Act 1988.

2 4 6 8 10 9 7 5 3 1

FOR MARIE AND TONY BREAR

'Men's evil manners live in brass;
their virtues we write in water.'

Shakespeare (*Henry VIII* Act 4 Scene 2)

Typeset in North Wales by
Derek Doyle & Associates, Mold, Flintshire.
Printed in Great Britain by
St Edmundsbury Press, Bury St Edmunds, Suffolk.
Bound by WBC Book Manufacturers Limited, Bridgend.

ONE

The hotel was about fifteen miles south of Wetherby, situated in attractive country and convenient for the A1 and the M62. It picked up a lot of conference work and had become the sort of place where middle-aged businessmen tended to arrive with very young, very enamelled PAs. Over the years, the lights in the bar had become more and more subdued. The dining-room was as dark as a night-club. I'd eaten there alone several times and, not having enough light to glance at a paper, had had to sit and listen to women giggling as stealthy hands fondled willing thighs. It was very expensive, to keep out the sort of men who wore medallions and wanted to take off their jackets, but as most of the guests were on expense accounts it didn't much matter.

The mark was good-looking in his Italian way – dark eyes, thick, black, curly hair, a pale complexion. He'd had a good figure once, but was now getting paunchy. He looked the type who'd have a hairy chest and hairy arms. I wondered if she'd find it off-putting. I supposed the money would help, it usually did. She was hard to place; I knew she wasn't his PA. When I'd casually drifted into the bar myself he'd been already sitting with her. She could have been a call-girl, but she didn't seem quite assured enough. Perhaps she was still in learning mode.

I put her in her early twenties. Fair hair, eyes the delicate blue of harebells, bluntish rather irregular features, a gap between her two top front teeth. The words *jolie laide* came to mind. She was rather sturdily built beneath the dark-red calf-length dress, but she had a vitality and mobility of feature that gave her a powerful attraction.

'You stupid bitch,' I whispered.

They were drinking champagne at a table near the opposite wall. He refilled the tall glasses with a flourish and a rattle of ice. The woman drank very slowly though, which might be significant. Could she be a superior slapper? She might just as easily be a young exec on a training course. Perhaps she was lonely, simply wanted company. But it seemed doubtful. If she was as bright as she looked she must have realized that unknown men didn't whistle up forty-pound bottles of wine just because you had a friendly smile.

At 8.30, the head waiter stole up to the man and whispered in his ear, then led the pair into the dining-room's dim cavern, in which candles flickered in red-tinted globes. I'd seen better light in a pot-hole. When I strolled in, the head waiter was keen to sit me near the kitchen door, but a discreet fiver got me a table not too far from theirs. I made a mental list of the things he ordered, which I'd known would be the most expensive items on the menu – lobster and game – and would be accompanied by the type of Bordeaux that would itself equal the cost of the meal. Meanwhile, I ordered a single modest course from the à la carte and a glass of the house red.

I was near enough to them to pick up the drift of their conversation. He was doing his usual polished bragging act, working his prosperous business, his cars, his staff and his swimming-pool into the tale with a casual, almost deprecating skill developed over many years. It was in fact mainly true, it just sounded so totally naff when you'd worked among the old money. He then began to hint he was keen to know her better, to show her his weekend place in Norfolk. The woman smiled a lot, and talked easily, not quite picking him up on his Norfolk offer, but not quite putting him off either. It seemed a skilled balancing act and it didn't seem to quite square with her background – she was here for a personnel officers' training course.

I couldn't get a fix on her. It made no difference to the case I was on, which was to establish that the man was deceiving his wife, but if she was simply a trainee exec and considered herself mature enough to take costly food and wine from a man like Tony Ferrara, she could be in for a nasty shock. I'd seen the bastard in action; the Latin charm tended to have a very short sell-by date.

After dinner, we all had coffee in a spacious lounge, also softly lit, in which a man in a white dinner-jacket played standards on a grand piano. Ferrara had a Drambuie, the woman still toyed with a glass of table wine she'd carried through with her. She was at least a careful drinker. But it meant that Ferrara had now drunk the thick end of a bottle of champagne, a similar amount of Bordeaux and a large liqueur.

I had to sit too far away from them to hear anything else. At around ten they got up and made for the reception desk. I drifted slowly after them. He was given a key-card to a third-floor room. He wasn't asked to sign anything. He never was. His money would sort it all out. The woman didn't ask for a key-card, but assuming she'd checked in earlier she'd have got one then.

They walked off slowly in the direction of the lifts. I slipped through the door to the steps and ran up to the third floor. I came out onto a dimly lit corridor as the lift doors whined softly open. The pair emerged, he still giving out with the friendliness and the boyish laughter, which I had to admit was a class act. Even so, I could scarcely believe a young woman in the nineties would go into an hotel room with a man she barely knew. If she thought she was going in there for a nightcap, some more light chat, perhaps even a discreet pass she could easily evade, she'd got the wrong script.

But she went with him, into Room 313. I cursed. In theory this part of the assignment was over. I was free to go. He'd spent a great deal of money buying a woman dinner and taken her to his room. It was all I needed for my report.

Yet the woman seemed such a kid. She'd told him she was here on a training course and that might well be the truth. She was certainly unlike the other women I'd seen him take into hotel rooms – some definitely call-girls, others who had the look of talented amateurs, in it for the night out. They'd all somehow given the impression of knowing their way around men like Ferrara.

I glanced irritably up and down the corridor, at the range of identical doors. One of them had no number. I tried the handle, the door opened onto racks of clean bed-linen. I let myself in and left the door ajar. I could have gone home, told myself I was just doing my job, but I'd not have slept if I'd abandoned the little fool to Ferrara. I knew what the bastard was capable of and how his money could normally smooth everything over.

I quietly seethed. How could she have been such an *idiot*? I'd have to hang around indefinitely, keep on listening at his door to see what went on. If the worst came to the worst I might even have to reveal myself. I clenched my fists in frustration. Perhaps I should leave her to it after all. It would at least be a lesson she'd not forget. She'd clearly forgotten everything her mother had ever told her.

I'd imagined it would take half an hour for any real fun to begin, that was about normal, but barely fifteen minutes later the door of 313 suddenly flew open. I heard her cry 'Oh!' and saw her rush out into the corridor, her hair tousled, the bodice of her dress disordered. He was a second behind her, and made a grab for her which she only just evaded. He wore nothing but boxer shorts. I'd been right about the body hair; he was so hairy he looked like a walking fur coat.

'Bitch!' he hissed. 'What the hell's with you. . . ?'

She shook herself, like a dog emerging from a pond, and began to run in my direction.

'Hey!' he called, in that same penetrating hiss he must have perfected to meet many similar situations. 'Don't think you can just run away – I spent a yard of money down there. . . .'

He scuttled back into his room. He would have to put on a shirt and trousers at least, plus shoes, to pursue her in an hotel of this calibre. She ran past me towards the lifts, stabbed at the buttons. The lifts could be heard whining, and the soft chime of their floor-bells, but none stopped at the third floor. She looked round for the stairs, but, as in so many modern hotels, they were not easy to locate. She peered frantically up and down the corridor, began to run back the way she'd come, presumably to make her escape down a distant green-lettered fire exit. As she drew near the linen room, I opened the door and hooked her inside, putting my hand over her mouth. She struggled like a cat in a sack.

'Take it easy,' I said, in a low voice. 'I'm a friend. Don't cry out – the ape man will have his clothes on by now. He's a fast dresser, take my word. . . .'

I lifted my hand from her mouth, switched on the dim light. We heard Ferrara pound past the door then.

'Oh! It's you – John Goss!'

I stared at her. Before tonight I'd never laid eyes on her and I didn't forget faces. 'You . . . know me. . . ?'

'We all know you, or *of* you – in our business.'

'*Our* business. Don't say you're a PI. . . .'

'Sort of . . . not exactly. . . .' She smoothed her hair and straightened her rumpled bodice, grinned on the gap in her front teeth. She recovered fast; it was like the grin of a kid with a jam-jar and a fishing net. 'Girl Talk. . . ?'

'I've . . . heard of it.'

'We get it together on creeps like him.' She touched her chest between the breasts 'Wired for sound.'

'*Shit!*'

The perky grin faded and she began to watch me with an uneasiness that seemed to go with having exchanged one angry man for another.

'Who gave you the assignment? The wife?'

'You . . . don't see the wife, she does it through solicitors – Dobbs, Woolstone.'

'Look, Dobbs, Woolstone gave *me* the job.'

'Then I'm sorry, but they gave it to Girl Talk as well. It's nothing to do with me . . . John.'

'Was it *old* Mr Woolstone?'

She shook her head: 'The son.'

'Sod it!'

'He . . . said his father was on holiday and he was handling his work.'

'But he must have left details, the old lad. . . .'

'There was nothing in his diary. The son did say he could be a bit vague. He is pretty old now.'

'Vague! He can't remember the way to the Beckford Club, but I can always sort him out. . . .'

'Do you have to be quite so ill-tempered?' she said, with an edge to her voice. 'It's *not my fault.*'

'They're not going to pay *both* of us. And the young one *knows* he set you on, while the old man will have forgotten by now. Oh, bloody *hell*, that's a week's work blown away.'

'But they'll *have* to pay you, if you explain. . . .'

'If young Woolstone has to pay twice he'll do it with ill-grace, because that's what lawyers are like. And if I *make* him pay he'll not use me again and I'd be the loser in the long run.'

'I'll share my fee with you!' she suddenly cried. 'If it makes you feel any better.'

'What bugs me,' I said harshly, 'what *really* bugs me is why young Woolstone didn't send for me anyway, instead of setting on some bloody piss-artist with a recording machine strapped to her backside.'

She flushed, her uneven features distorted even further by anger, the *jolie* virtually eclipsed by the *laide*. 'You arrogant bastard! I thought John Goss was supposed to be a decent type from what people said, but you're not, you're just another macho shithead like that hairy tosser in 313.'

I flushed too. 'I can't abide amateurs, if you want the real truth. Didn't you know what you were going in that room *with*? I've seen women come away from his room hardly able to *walk*. I've seen them with black *eyes*. And he throws a bundle of money at them, and so they grin and keep their traps shut.'

'I could have *handled* it,' she cried, 'if the worst came to the worst.'

'That's what it looked like, when you were running up and down like a headless chicken.'

'I take lessons in self-defence, for God's sake.'

'Well, don't stop going inside five years.'

'*Bastard*! It's a success, Girl Talk, and that's what's really bugging you. One year, just give us one year, and they'll not want to know about dickheads like you, John Goss.'

'Except when types like Ferrara have put you all in hospital.'

She turned away, clenching her fists, her cheeks mottled with emotion. And anger had put exactly the right words in her mouth, as it often did. The best part of my own seething irritation was due to that familiar nineties spectre – relentless competition. I was only in my early thirties and here was a youngster of twenty-odd from a spanking new agency, in a position to get the *real* dirt on errant husbands, to get in close, get it on tape, no doubt to get undercover photographs with an accomplice. I'd read that it provided the sort of hard evidence that made husbands throw in the sponge: let custody of the kids go, let the house go, sign away half the pension rights. All I could do was write up reports that could be challenged, and little as I liked domestic cases, if you limited yourself to working for the professional middle class, they could be a useful earner.

She finally turned back to me as we stood in the narrow channel between the racks of clean linen. She breathed deeply and seemed to be making an effort to calm herself. 'Look,' she said, with an effort, 'could we please try to stop shouting at each other? My name's Vicky, Vicky Barker. Pleased to meet you.'

I shrugged, gave an uncivil grunt. It wasn't like me. She was trying to patch things up and I'd always been a reasonable man, ready to react to common sense. I seemed to be in a warp of ill-feeling that I couldn't break out of, because of the valuable time I'd lost on this case, because I knew I'd not be able to accept half her fee, even if she really intended to offer it, and because I could see that Girl Talk was going to be bad news for my agency, going by tonight's events.

'Look,' she said again, her harebell eyes resting fully on mine with a look that seemed more brooding than angry, 'I'll admit that I'm a bit ambivalent about Girl Talk myself. It's very well paid, but it can get chancy at times, and I also have to tell myself I'll not be young for ever. We all do. We're like actresses – the wife-cheaters do like their bits on the side young. They can get middle age and the character parts at home.'

She was still slightly flushed and she spoke slowly, reluctantly almost, as if forcing the words out against her will. She said, '*I* think we should extend into general work and I'm trying to talk the others into it. There are three of us, and one or two part-timers we can call on if we're stretched. I wondered if I could give you a meal sometime, dinner perhaps, and talk to you about how we could go about it.'

'Absolutely no chance,' I said bluntly. 'And I've never been known to buy drinks all round in a pub either.'

Even as the words slipped out I hated myself for them. Whatever the *naïveté* of her expecting me to teach direct competition how to be even more competitive, I could have dissembled, hedged, found words that seemed to offer encouragement while promising nothing. I spent my life dissembling, after all. But I couldn't break the churlish streak, it was like a heavy cold I was unable to throw off. And it wasn't simply the threat of Girl Talk; there seemed something vaguely inimical about the woman herself, and her steady blue gaze.

My words had the effect of igniting the earlier anger as if a cupful of petrol had been thrown on a still-smouldering fire. 'Oh well, stuff yourself!' she spat. 'And stuff your agency. I'll remember this when we put you out of business.'

'Goodbye, Miss Barker,' I said curtly, opening the door. 'Don't bother to thank me for saving you from being raped. I'm sure you intended to, at some point.'

As I closed the door on her, she was mouthing words I couldn't hear but could certainly guess at.

TWO

'There you go, John. . . .' Kev placed a gin and tonic on the bar in front of me.

Fenlon said, 'You look like a man who'd have won half a million if he'd remembered to send in his Pools.'

'Yes, well, I spent fifteen hours working for nothing last week, didn't I. Some stupid bitch from a Mickey Mouse set-up called Girl Talk got between me and the mark. Total write-off.'

'Leg-over?'

I nodded. 'The job was double booked. Lawyer's cock-up.'

'Girl Talk. They're not all that Mickey Mouse, you know, John. They've got them running shitless, the extra-marital ferret brigade. They go in there with body mikes and miniature cameras, and then they put it all together in a presentation pack – photo album and recording tapes. It's like handing the wife a twelve-bore shotgun.'

'I *still* think it's Mickey Mouse. . . .'

He smiled faintly. We both knew he was right about Girl Talk, both knew I'd have to deal with the competition it presented one day, but for the moment was licking wounds.

'Look,' he said, 'I've got something for you guaranteed to take your mind off Girl Talk. What do you know about a guy called Maurice Durkin?'

'The name rings some kind of a bell. Shops?'

'Crystalmarts – yes? He bought old cinemas, disused chapels, small workshops in heavily built-up areas and converted them into minimarkets. They attract people without cars – the young mums, pensioners. Everything cut to the bone, no frills, doesn't attempt to compete with the supers, but there's a Crystalmart in just about every northern town, sometimes two. He was one of the first to spot that particular gap and he's a millionaire now.'

'He's never been in trouble,' I said, 'otherwise the name *would* mean something.'

'Correct, my friend. He's cut a few dodgy deals in his time, from what I hear, but nothing that ended up with anyone sending for us.'

'So?'

'So he's gone missing.'

'I don't recall reading anything.'

'You won't have. The papers haven't picked up on it yet and his wife wants it kept that way for the time being.'

'In case he's done a runner with the PA with the melons and the square white teeth?'

'You've got it. Nancy doesn't want to lose caste with the gin and jag set. When he gets back she can give him a quiet bollocking and that will be that.'

'How long's he been gone?'

'That's the point. More than a month now. No clue, no contact.'

'And down at the nick you're all working on it round the clock,' I said, 'as you do.'

He grinned. 'We've gone through the motions, but men as wealthy as Durkin live their lives anyway they damn well want. Ten sovs to a cocktail cherry he's taken off with a woman. I'm certain Nancy thinks so too. She was a bit cagey, but I gather it's not exactly the first time he's gone AWOL. It was only for a week or so, but there was definitely another woman in there somewhere. I told her she'd be well advised to use a PI. I think your name might have passed my lips. She asked if she could leave it to me. She seems the type who leaves most things to someone else.'

'As long as she's not neurotically jealous,' I said feelingly. An incurably possessive woman had opened the Rainger case, and that fiasco still came back to haunt me on sleepless nights.

'Quite the reverse. She seems very relaxed about it all, laid back almost. I think you'll find you can get on with her a treat. Anyway, see for yourself. . . .'

He was clearly concealing a smile, and I wondered what his game was. If she had plenty of new money to spray around I'd be in line for a decent fee and expenses for a job I could do on automatic pilot, but I could also be walking into some kind of a hassle that Fenlon had already sussed out. That would appeal keenly to his sense of humour. I'd known him since childhood and I had the inside track on the way his twisted mind worked.

'Thanks, Bruce, but I'm inclined to let this one go.'

'I can't believe I'm hearing this. We're talking big people here. Connections. They've got a swimming-pool. A five-car garage. Staff. And Nancy Durkin really is someone you should meet. You *can't* let it go.'

'Just watch me,' I said, knowing now for certain there was some catch to Mrs Durkin that seemed sure to give Fenlon amusement and me aggravation in roughly equal amounts.

'Money absolutely no object,' he said enticingly. 'She assured me if I sent the right type along she'd make sure he was looked after. And you did say you'd lost fifteen hours' work last week.'

The sadistic bastard had me there. I'd had a courteous note from the Inland Revenue only the other day saying they'd be pleased to receive the second dollop of what I'd agreed I owed them any time before the end of the month (if I wished to avoid interest charges).

I drew in from the steep road that wound its way up from the valley floor before sturdy iron gates set in high walls. The name Maunan had been carved into a stone block to the right of the gates. There was a small speaker with a push-button; I pressed it.

'The Durkin residence . . .' a male voice announced.

'I have an appointment with Mrs Durkin. John Goss. . . .'

Without further word the gates began to roll slowly open, and

I got back in the Mondeo and drove across an extensive court-yard, laid in that sort of perfect, slightly glossy, pink block paving associated with colour supplements. There was a rose garden to the left that stretched to the curving perimeter wall and, to the right, the garaging, stone-built and with sufficient space for six cars not five – Fenlon had got it slightly wrong. Automatic doors stood open on two of the cars, one a Saab, the other a Porsche. The house ran along the bottom of the courtyard, green-tiled, the walls in stucco, so freshly painted in the June sun they slightly dazzled the eyes. It seemed two-storey, but I guessed there'd be further levels at the rear with the slope of the land. There were wooden tubs at the door which looked polished, filled with mixed, rather gaudy blossom. The door had a great many brass fittings – handle, letter-box, a knocker in the shape of a dog's head, and a plate that said once more the word Maunan, which I had now deduced must be the joint first syllables of the Durkin christian names.

No one had actually broken a leg to open the door in advance, but then I supposed they bracketed a PI with the man who deliv-ered the fish. The brass knocker seemed purely for effect; there was another bell-push on the side wall. When I pressed it it made some-thing that sounded like a vibraphone play the opening bars of 'Yesterday'.

A rather delicate-looking man, pale and thin, with dark straight hair opened the door. He wore green trousers, a white shirt and a green bow-tie. He seemed faintly self-conscious, and in that get-up it was easy to see why.

'Come this way, Mr Goss. If you'd like to let me have your car-keys I'll have your car garaged.'

Puzzled, I glanced back to where my car stood neatly parked near the house.

'Mrs Durkin doesn't care to see cars in the yard, sir. She believes they detract from the appearance of Maunan.'

Which was code for Mrs Durkin not liking cheap, nasty Fords in the yard in case one of her chums should drop by in the BMW and think she was feeling the pinch. Reluctantly I handed him the keys.

'Neil,' he called. 'Motor!'

A surly-looking youth, also turned out in Sherwood green and who sniffed a lot, took the keys without a word.

There was a large hall, the doors of which seemed to be covered in beige leather, mauve and white flock wallpaper and a delft rack holding expensive-looking plates which pictured small dogs in what I assumed were meant to be humorous or appealing postures. There were framed paintings of cruise ships steaming into exotic ports, and a great chandelier with dozens of lights in the shape of candles. The mauve shag-pile carpet was so thick it was like walking over wet grass.

'This way, sir.' He led me through one of the leather-covered doors and along a corridor that led to the rear of the house. It brought us to a lift, the first I'd ever seen in a private dwelling. We stepped into its mirrored interior and descended, silently and rapidly.

The door opened on to a large bright room that had been built out from the back of the house, the opposite wall of which was mainly window, with entire sections that could be slid open. The room gave on to a chequer-board tiled patio, and beyond the patio, bluely gleaming, lay a kidney-shaped swimming-pool. A woman stood at the pool's side.

'I'll advise madam you've arrived, sir, if you'd care to wait here.'

He went through an open section in the windowed wall. The woman was wearing pink pants, pink shoes, a pink and white-striped top. She had the sort of figure that could once only have been accurately described by that delightful word voluptuous. The curves were a little more rounded now, the arms a little thicker, but they evoked an earlier exotic allure as the slackening petals of a rose hint at a more compact beauty. She had brown hair expertly highlighted with fine blonde streaks.

The moment the man joined her, I heard a voice raised in irritation. 'Get him back . . . it was just the same with the bloody *leaves*. It's discoloured. . . .'

The rest of the outburst was carried away on a June breeze. I smiled. West Yorkshire is not, frankly, the best place in the world to have your own swimming-pool, not when the average seems to be one reliable summer in ten. I glanced round the large high room. A bar about as long as the one at The George ran along the right-hand wall, with around fifty bottles upside down on optics. The carpet was thick, white and wall to wall. A big-screen television stood with its back to the windows; there were bulbous, squashy armchairs and sofas in white leather, pictures of kittens and ponies, more dogs. There were planters, filled with pungent and unusual blossom that emerged from polished-looking leaves. The unmistakable and, to me, peculiarly depressing music of the James Last Orchestra was piped in softly through concealed speakers.

Mrs Durkin and the servant came slowly inside. 'I don't *care*, Brian, I could easily want a dip this afternoon.'

'I doubt he'll be able to make it today, Mrs D. We always have to book him in advance.'

'But this is an *emergency*. The sun's shining, for Christ's sake. Tell him he's got to be here before twelve.'

'Well, I'll do what I can. . . .' He glanced in my direction, not quite meeting my eyes. 'This is Mr Goss, madam.'

'Where's Neil?'

'Putting Mr Goss's car away.'

'I suppose that'll take him half an hour. Tell him to get his arse down here with some coffee. In the eau-de-nil cups, think on.'

'Very good, Mrs D.'

He made towards the lift at a half-lope. She glanced at me with a single upward toss of her head. 'Staff,' she said. 'If you want to get anything done you've got to pay them top whack and kick their backsides rotten.'

I'd more or less deduced that hefty salaries had to be the main, perhaps only, incentive for working at Maunan.

'Nancy Durkin,' she said. 'But everyone calls me Crystal. And you're John. Pleased to meet you. Let's sit on the patio, might as well make the most of the sun, we'll probably not see the sod for the next two weeks. Why can't we have more summers like that one in the seventies? Of course, we hadn't got *our* pool then, had we? By the time we got ours it was back to sun, one, piss it down, two. . . .'

She spoke in a husky tone that had a slightly rough edge to it, as if the words had travelled over vocal chords well marinated in expensive alcohol. I followed her out to an umbrella table, where we sank into great soft chairs that would convert to recliners. She was still visibly agitated by the appearance of the pool, which to my admittedly inexpert eye seemed flawless. She didn't really look a Crystal, but I could imagine she once had, could see the features as clear and sharp-edged as they must once have been, the *retroussée* nose, the chiselled lips, the smooth round chin. They were softened now, marginally blurred-looking, as if someone's hand had trembled slightly when a photograph was taken.

'They must take a lot of upkeep,' I said, 'pools.'

'Don't ever buy yourself one, Johnny, they're a pain in the neck from day one. We'd not had it a week when Jason fell in. God, two years old. . . .'

'Oh dear,' I said, shocked. 'Was he . . . did he. . . ?'

Her abstracted hazel eyes met mine and slowly focused. 'Oh, *no* he was all right. I sometimes think it wouldn't have been much loss if the little toad *had* drowned. He thinks Mercs grow on trees. "Do you think Mercs grow on bloody trees?", I asked him last week when he banjoed the *other* wing. The insurance costs as much as the sodding car if you let that one get near them.

'No, Maurice fished him out with that hook thing. The pool was his idea, but he always said he'd had it built for me. I couldn't get that together, seeing as I couldn't swim then. I asked him what he'd have built me if I'd only had one leg – a squash court? Anyway, we should have had a pool that was half in the house and half out,' she said, with another brooding glance at the calm, clear water. 'Like that place in Antwerp,' she added, obscurely.

'About your husband, Mrs Durkin . . .' I began tentatively. I'd allotted an hour to this interview, knowing that wealthy people often didn't like to be rushed, but ten minutes had already disappeared.

'Coffee, Mrs D,' the surly youth growled from the door of the pool-room.

'Well, don't just *stand* there, bring it out. And I don't see the matching sugar-bowl.'

'It got broke. . . .'

'Well, whoever broke it gets their pay docked. And it wasn't cheap, tell whoever it was.'

'Are you pouring yourself?'

'Too right. I'd like it in the cups for a change, not slopping around in the saucers.'

She sighed as he slunk off, and said, 'I'll hang some manners on that little prat if it kills me,' before he was fully out of earshot. 'I only took him on because he's something to do with Brian. I don't like to think what. You do *want* coffee? You can have a drink if you like.'

'Coffee's fine. I try not to drink during the day.'

'Oh, you've got your head screwed on. It only spoils it for the evening, doesn't it. Maurice always says you can only get successfully pissed once a day.'

She poured coffee. It may have been imagination but she seemed to bend over marginally too far, so that I had a perfect view of the upper planes of her lavish breasts below the rounded neckline of the pink and white top. A large gold disc dangled from a neck-chain, the word Crystal picked out in diamonds which seemed to flash in the sun in the exaggerated way of jewels in a children's cartoon-film.

'*I* think he's taken off with that London bitch,' she said bluntly. 'He goes up there once a month with the boys. Knowing that toe-rag he wouldn't be doing without, know what I mean?'

'The . . . boys. Your sons?'

'God, no, we've only got Jason and he's trying to be an estate agent. Only Jason would go into it when no one's buying any bloody houses. No, the *boys*. Maurice's pals. . . .'

I'd forgotten that women like Crystal tended to call their friends the 'boys' and the 'girls' even when they were shuffling round on zimmers.

'So he went to London once a month with the boys. Why was that?'

'Don't ask me, love. *They* said it was business, but they would, wouldn't they? *I* think it was a glorious piss-up and a bit of the other. I've told him – don't think you'll be climbing back in *my* bed when you're riddled with AIDS.'

It was somehow difficult meeting her eyes' rather flat gaze – I had an unnerving impression mine were only connecting with the back of her skull.

'Would you know where he stayed?'

'With the girlfriend, you can put your holiday money on it.'

'You'll not have an address. . . ?'

'No, but I've got a number,' she said, calmly triumphant. 'I found it in his diary. If Maurice just writes a number without a name you can be sure there'll be a woman involved. So I rang it, didn't I, and it *was* a woman. But she'd not say anything except hello. Dead giveaway.'

'If I could have that number it would help.'

'No problem. But what use is it without an address?'

I smiled. 'We have ways of fitting addresses to numbers. It's a London code, I take it?'

She nodded. 'That bobby said you had it all upstairs.'

'DS Fenlon?'

'I told him, I don't care what it costs, but I have to know what the silly sod's up to.'

The redeeming feature about the *nouveaus* was the urge they couldn't resist to let you know how fat their wallets were. Had Crystal been old money she'd have asked what my charges were inside three minutes and still been quivering with shock at the answers.

'Has Mr Durkin . . . Maurice . . . had any previous unexplained absences?'

She pursed her generous lips. 'He once went missing for about a week and a half. Some young totty. But he rang up in the end, didn't he, saying he wanted to think about a separation. So I said, you bloody sling your hook if you like, but it'll cost you – I'll want the house, the contents, the Roller and half the money, so you just chew on that, dickhead. He was back inside twenty-four hours and that's the last I heard about separating. But this time I've not had a muff out of him.'

'But surely he's been in touch with the office. He . . . you own the Crystalmart chain, I believe.'

'Not now, chuck, we sold out January. He wanted semi-retirement. To be fair to the lad, he's worked his cobblers off since he was fifteen. He just does his shares now and his futures; he has an office upstairs. But that bobby pal of yours, you ask me he could do with a pound of Semtex under him. All he could say was they'd put it out on the computer. I told him, that's no bloody good, it needs a *task force*, like they have on "The Bill". It's always the same, I told him, it only needs Jason to have a bit of a prang-up and they're round here like blue-arsed flies, but when an important businessman goes missing they get the office boy to diddle a keyboard.'

'I . . . think you're being a little hard on them, Crystal. It's not as if he's been kidnapped, and he *has* done it before. And . . . please don't take this the wrong way, but there's no dead body involved. If anything like that had happened the police would be thinking in terms of task forces.'

'Yes, well, Johnny . . .' she said, as her brooding gaze slid once more to the pool, whose disappointing aspect, apparent only to her discerning eye, seemed to reflect her own dissatisfaction, 'if he *was* dead I'd know where I stood, wouldn't I? We could give him a lovely send-off, like we did for his dad. Do you know what Maurice did for his dad – he had a greyhound done in flowers because his dad loved going to the dog-track so much. You know, to go on the coffin. We've got a photo of it somewhere; Maurice can never look at it without tears running down his face. I'd thought of something like that when it got to be Maurice's turn. Maybe a supermarket trolley because of how he made his money, though Mum always thinks you can't beat a person's *name* in flowers – more tasteful, she reckons.'

'I'm sure we'll find Maurice safe and sound, Crystal,' I said reassuringly, but she was still lost in that poignant and affecting scene in which a group of people looked brokenly on, in a corner of some elegant cemetery, the women in black veils, their eyes shining with tears, as whatever object was finally deemed suitable to be made up in seasonal flowers was lovingly lowered into the grave above Durkin's top-of-the-range coffin.

'They do a lovely angel too,' she said reflectively, 'down at Frank's. Do you know Frank? Delaney's Death with Dignity. And the cherubs aren't bad, but I've always thought cherubs were a bit, you know, puffy. . . .'

Durkin himself seemed to be lost in the glow of the most glittering *memento mori* Crystal's imagination could conjure up. It was beginning to seem that though Durkin's money was indispensable, Durkin himself would not be especially missed. It looked as if my job was to establish his whereabouts and condition, so that she could either sue him, bury him or give him another good bollocking.

I wondered if her irritation with the state of the pool, her rudeness to staff, were displacements for a deeper discontent. Because Crystal was a very discontented woman, despite the glittering baubles she surrounded herself with, and Durkin's disappearance seemed only a minor part of it, more a nasty scratch than a serious wound.

'Try and look on the bright side, Crystal,' I said cheerfully. 'Perhaps if you could give me some more details of the last time you saw him and a good recent photograph.'

'We'll need to go inside,' she said, giving one final troubled glance at the pool. I followed her into the big room, where the speakers had stopped relaying music that sounded as if it had been strained through a hairnet and were now putting out the anthem of men who'd made a killing from scrap-metal the world over – Sinatra singing 'My Way'. She went to a sort of edifice that climbed the wall opposite the bar – a white-wood structure with mirrors, a desk-top and drawers.

'The pool room's really my little den,' she explained. 'I spend hours in here. Now . . . photos. Here, you'd better have this one where he's in a suit – it was taken when he closed on selling the Crystalmarts. They were named for me, had you guessed? Took them for their underpants, just between the two of us, but as Maurice said, what would you expect with a bunch of Tommy Foreigners.'

He looked a composite of most of the self-made men I'd ever worked for – tallish, powerfully built, wearing a gleaming white shirt and silk tie, a chalk-striped grey suit too obviously new, too obviously the best money could buy. Hair thick, greying and wavy, strong features and a confident smile that retained all the cocky matiness of the twenty year old who'd once probably sold anything he could turn five pence on from a market stall.

She had a good memory for detail, as people who don't use their minds for much else often do, and she was able to tell me everything I wanted to know with chatty precision.

Brian, the butler who doubled as chauffeur and valet, had taken Durkin in what she called the Roller to Leeds station one Wednesday morning five weeks earlier, where he'd boarded a breakfast train to London. That was the last anyone had seen of him.

'Did Brian actually *see* him get on the train?'

'No. Your police pal asked him that. Parking's crap at Leeds, so he just dropped him off.'

'So it's possible he never actually *took* the London train.'

'He must have done, love, because the boys all met him down there.'

'How many boys are there?'

'Six, apart from Maurice. They do all sorts of deals together. We go to their places, they come to ours. They're not bad lads really, they just need watching; me and the girls are all agreed about *that*. . .'

She gave me the inner-London phone number of the female voice she was convinced would belong to Durkin's girlfriend. 'Pity he didn't take the Rolls,' I said reflectively. 'It would have made it easier. A Rolls kind of stands out – if we could have traced that it would mean we'd traced Maurice.'

'He hasn't gone in the Roller for a year or so. Brian used to drive him there at one time, till he had that do with the horses on Buckingham Palace Road. That soldier was so *rude*. He was one of those with the big helmet things and a sword. In the end Maurice had to lean out and tell him that if there was any more of it he'd get that bloody sword up his backside.' She smiled faintly. 'He has a way of calming things down, has Maurice. Anyway, Brian's nerves were never the same after that for London traffic, so Maurice started going by train.' Her eyes left mine and passed broodingly across her pool to the magnificent view of woodland on the opposite slopes of the valley. 'Mind you, they could have been telling me a tale, about the horses, so that Maurice could stay loose. I could nail him on the car-phone, you see. Once he started using the train that was it – he doesn't even carry a mobile now he's sold the business. And that Brian's in his pocket. In fact everyone who ever worked for Maurice thought he was Mister Wonderful.' She finished not on a note of bitterness but of a calm acceptance that seemed faintly wistful. She turned back to me and said in a brisker tone, 'You'll need some money up front, I suppose.'

She began to write before I could reply, in a double-size cheque-book that had a white leather binder personalized in gold leaf with the word Crystal over an impression of a faceted gemstone. 'Five all right, Johnny?'

'Five . . . hundred?'

'Well, that wouldn't get you as far as the gate, would it? Five *grand.*'

As I said, you rarely had to worry about money with the *nouveaus* – they really weren't such a bad bunch to work for as long as you didn't let yourself be overawed by the cultivated atmosphere.

'That's far too much,' I protested weakly. 'We're only talking about a trip to London probably and a few enquiries I'll need to commission.'

'Best to be on the safe side, you can always give me the change, if there is any. And don't be shy about yelling out if you need a bit more.'

'Well, thanks, Crystal, and thanks for the assignment. I'm confident I'll find him, by the way, I have a good success rate with mispers . . . sorry, missing persons.'

'I'm glad to hear it. I need to know what's going on.'

I put away the cheque and my notebook. 'I think that's all I need for the time being. I'll keep in touch, of course.'

'Now there's no need to rush off, Johnny. Why not stop for a drink and a bite of lunch – it's going on that way?'

'I'd love to, but I've got rather a full schedule.'

'You men, you're all the same, always working your backsides off.'

She seemed to be looking at me differently now we'd got the case details out of the way. I'd arrived wearing a dark-blue suit, but had slipped off the jacket when we were outside because of the hot sun, and now stood before her in a pale-blue, short-sleeve shirt, my arms and face slightly tanned from the jobs I'd been doing recently that had called for a good deal of time in the open.

'You're a well-built young man,' she said approvingly.

'I . . . suppose the job keeps me in shape, and I work out now and then.'

'Tell you what, why don't you come back this evening when you've finished your work? We could have a drop of bubbly and Monica'll make us a bite to eat. She's a cordon bleu, you know. And then we could go over it again, Maurice losing himself, just in case there's anything I've left out.'

'You're very kind, but the problem is I'm involved in a night-surveillance operation just at present. I'm afraid PI work tends to be open-ended. But thanks all the same.'

'Is it just today – your night-thingy? How about tomorrow evening?'

Just then, something stirred in a corner. It was a long, thin, rounded dog and it looked like something you put behind a door to keep out the draught. It had a red ribbon round its neck, tied in a large bow, and it growled fretfully.

'Oh, there you are, Bobo. And I thought you were up in Mummy's bedroom. Come here, darling, and we'll see if we can't find you a doggie-choc. . .'

As it began edging towards her, I seized my opportunity. 'Must dash, Crystal, I'll see myself out. I'll be in touch as soon as I have a free evening. Thanks again.'

I dived into the open lift and pressed the key marked Hall. It seemed that when the lift ascended it triggered some warning in the staff quarters; as the door slid open, Brian was standing to one side, his glance again fractionally missing mine, the keys to the Mondeo in his hand.

'Your vehicle's in the garage nearest the house, sir.'

'Thanks, Brian,' I said, with a pleasant smile. 'Mrs Durkin tells me that you don't chauffeur Mr Durkin to London these days. When you *did* drive him, which hotel did he normally stay at?'

'I . . . really couldn't say, sir.'

'Wouldn't it be you who'd reserve him a room? As his valet and butler. . . ?'

'No, sir.'

'But surely you'd drop him at an hotel?'

'I'd leave him at Claridges or the Savoy for lunch. I couldn't say whether he actually stayed at either.'

'Perhaps he stayed at a private address. With ... a friend, say. . . .'

'I couldn't tell you, sir.'

Couldn't, or wouldn't? According to Crystal he was in Durkin's pocket, the pair of them feeding her the same line to fill in the gaps when Durkin wasn't with the friends she called 'the boys'. Perhaps he was afraid to tell me anything that might get back to her that he'd lied about the first time round.

'Look, Brian,' I said softly, 'I'm a private investigator and whatever you can tell me will go no further. My brief is to find your boss. Now I have a strong impression Mr Durkin might have confided in you about things he might not wish Mrs Durkin to know. I understand all that, believe me. Now, was he *seeing* a ladyfriend in London?'

'I'm afraid you're quite wrong,' he said, 'about Mr Durkin discussing personal matters with me. I'm an employee here – my job is simply to look after his clothes, run his residence and drive his motor cars. And now, if you'll excuse me, I'm in the middle of supervising the preparation of madam's lunch.'

'All right, Brian,' I said flatly, 'then just tell me what *you* think happened to him – you must have your own ideas.'

'None at all, I'm afraid, sir. Good morning.'

I walked slowly across the glossy paving of the courtyard towards my garage, whose door began to slide almost silently open as I approached. Brian's loyalty to Durkin was going to be hard to undermine. I was certain he was covering up something. I wondered if I'd picked up on some kind of anxiety, too; his hand had trembled, I'd noticed, as he'd handed me my keys. I had definitely sensed bloodymindedness, no doubt because I'd witnessed Crystal wiping the patio tiles with him. It was an unpromising cocktail of hang-ups, and that was a pity, because getting together information that Brian could probably provide in minutes could easily take up a great deal of unnecessary time, money and effort.

I drove out past the rolling front gates and down the zigzag roads of the steep gradient that joined Beckford Road on the valley floor. It looked as if my first task in this case was going to be how did I contrive to stay clear of Crystal without causing offence. The writing was on the wall like words sprayed from an aerosol. She fancied me. A drop of bubbly, a bite of supper – my money was on it being a prelude to the double bath with the built-in jacuzzi and the gold-plated taps, plus more James Last through the speakers, or – to really get me wired – the Shadows' Greatest Hits.

I wondered, why not? She was a very attractive woman. She'd presumably been without a man since Durkin had made for the hills and it could have provided a fascinating evening. But she was also a client. Best not to get involved. It could only make things complicated, lead to embarrassment if she began to have regrets. It seemed a pity though, as I was without a girlfriend, hadn't in fact slept with a woman since I'd gone to bed in the four-poster with Laura Marsh at Larch House.

But it wouldn't be easy – dodging Crystal. She had money and she was used to getting what she wanted. That's what would have amused Fenlon – thinking he was getting me into the arms of a predatory female who was going short.

I joined the flow along Beckford Road and drove into the city. And Durkin? No problem. In the shadow of the mid-life crisis, his career over, he'd have shacked up with a brand new Crystal, facets still sharp-edged, who'd have welcomed wealthy, crisp-suited Durkin into her life with open legs.

Even if Crystal Mark One *did* sue for half the dibs.

THREE

'And he owns the *Crystalmarts* . . .' Norma said, in a hushed tone.

'Did. He sold out recently. He's more or less retired, apart from dabbling on the stock market.'

'It's not fair, it's just not fair, he can't be much over forty. What's the house like?'

I shrugged. 'Completely run of the mill. Barely as big as this office block, swimming-pool, garaging for half-a-dozen cars, no more than three staff. . . .'

'When did she actually notice he was missing?'

'Five weeks ago.'

'Had it been Ronnie I doubt I'd have bothered looking for him, not if I had a pool and six cars and someone to serve Venetian Sunsets on the patio. What does she drive on Sundays, by the way, if she's only got six cars?'

'I don't think she's actually *grieving* for him – she just wants to know it won't affect her way of life too badly, such as it is.'

'A *pool* in your own back-yard,' she said reverently, 'on a day like this. . . .'

'Music everywhere from concealed speakers. James Last. . . .'

'*James Last*,' she whispered.

'A lift from the back of the house to the pool-room. A bar with bottles on optics.'

'Don't go on, I can't handle the contrast – underpaid, over-worked, crap equipment. . . .'

'Yes, well; Crystal has problems with bolshie staff too. Made me feel I wasn't on my own.'

'Crystal!' she said. 'You call her *Crystal*?'

'She insisted. And pressed me to have a modest retainer.' I let the cheque flutter down to her desk.

'*Five thousand*! The entire case probably won't cost out at much over a grand.' She gave me a suspicious glance. 'What's going on, young Goss?'

I grimaced. 'Don't even think about it. Lovely body, shame about the black hole where the brain normally goes.'

'Well, yes, I can see you have to be very dense to end up with six cars and a swimming-pool. We had one like her in my class. Tatty, we used to call her, because of the potato brain. When I see her now her handbag's stuffed so full of twenty-pound notes she can hardly get it shut. What's *happened* to the husband, do you suppose?'

'Male menopause. New life, new woman. The usual story.'

'Any leads?'

'A London phone number. Would you give it to that Burrage chap? Tell him to try and get an address back to me before six. If he does I think I'll go to London in the morning. What's the diary like?'

'You need help, John, I keep telling you. I can reschedule but they do *not* like it.'

'On the other hand they know I'm worth waiting for.'

'Don't let it go to your head, just because a woman with more money than sense takes a shine to you. You ask me, she must have forgotten to put her contacts in.'

'Look, woman, can I bloody go to London or not?'

'I suppose so.'

'Right, I'm off. I'll call back in about five—'

'Hang *on* – I haven't given you all the messages yet. A Mrs Barker rang, wouldn't say why, wants you to return the call.'

'*Mrs* Barker? Not Miss or Ms?'

'I know my eyes are going, with having to work in such a bad light, but I've still got partial hearing.'

'Must be coincidence,' I said, opening the door. 'I'll ring her from the car.'

I took the same train Durkin had taken from Leeds station, and when the call for breakfast came I went through to the restaurant car.

'Take any table, sir,' the steward said.

I took out the photograph of Durkin and showed him it. 'This man's gone missing from home and I'm helping the police to trace him,' I said, fairly truthfully. 'Does the face look familiar?'

He glanced at it, immediately nodded. 'Very familiar. It's Mr Durkin, isn't it?'

I wasn't surprised. Durkin would have tended to over-tip and stewards remembered those telling details. 'Could you say how often you saw him? Would it be, say, monthly?'

'That sounds about right.'

'When was the last time? Roughly. . . .'

'Now you're asking. Not recently. In fact I was only thinking it must be nearly time for his next trip.'

I nodded. 'That seems to fit. Did you notice if he was alone, by any chance, that last time?'

'Take any table, sir,' he said, over my shoulder. 'Yes he *was* alone, now you mention it, and that was unusual for him. He looked worried too. It sticks in my mind because he was normally a very cheerful gentleman, always laughing and joking, even first thing . . . with his colleagues. I do hope he's all right, he really was a very nice person.'

He sounded sincere. 'Thanks,' I said, 'you've been a big help.'

A fiver slipped from my hand to his and I went back along the corridor; I didn't do breakfast. The train sped on past dark fields beneath a cloudy sky. So he'd definitely gone to London, but he'd been worried. I wasn't surprised; he knew he'd have to divide his assets if he left Crystal. Would his fortune be enough to keep two women in a similar style? It might be worth trying to find out.

From King's Cross I took the Victoria Line to Victoria Station and the District to Sloane Square. It tended to be quicker these days than taxis. From Sloane Square I walked down the King's Road and then took a left along Smith Street and a right along Smith Terrace, an angled row of small attractive houses that looked to be Queen Anne.

It was a pleasant area, once away from the bustle of the King's. You didn't have to walk very far to reach Ranelagh Gardens and the open spaces of the Royal Hospital, with beyond them the river and its views of Chelsea Bridge and Battersea Park.

The man named Burrage had provided, at a cost of thirty-five pounds, the name and address that went with the phone number Crystal had given me. I'm afraid that almost anything is available on almost any citizen if you have the price and the contacts. The house I'd been directed to appeared to have been converted into two flats, as there were two names on the bell-plate – H. Greenwood and S. Goddard. I pressed the bell for Goddard and waited for the speaker to be activated, assuming there was anyone at home. But instead, the door was suddenly opened wide. Her eyes were shining eagerly, as if she were expecting to find someone very very special out there. It came as a dreadful shock to just find me. That showed in her eyes too.

'You must have hit the wrong bell,' she said irritably. 'Anyway, he's never in before six. . . .'

'Miss Goddard?' I said. 'Sukie?'

'Who the hell are you? What do you want?'

She was seriously attractive. Long, glossy brown hair, porcelain skin, liquid brown eyes in flawless whites, teeth that seemed separately polished, full lips, a small straight nose, a figure that went with the face. She wore white jeans and a pale-green shirt of what seemed to be fine suede. I wondered, as so often before, why hostile attractive women always looked twice as aggressive as hostile plain ones.

I took out my identification wallet. 'I'm an investigator, Miss Goddard, working with the police,' I said, deciding it was a line worth sticking with. 'We're looking into the disappearance of a Mr Maurice Durkin.'

Her mouth fell open slightly and her eyes widened. 'Disappearance...?'

She went on staring at me, the hostility sidelined by what looked to be genuine shock. Which threw me a little. When she'd flung open the door, all eager and shining, I'd been certain it was because she'd confidently expected to find her favourite millionaire out there, just back from nipping along to Augustus Barnett's for a couple of Bollinger. I believe I began to take the Durkin case seriously from that point. If he wasn't with the woman who was obviously the girlfriend, who *was* he with?

'I don't understand ...' she said at last. '*Disappearance?*'

'Would you like to talk about it?' I said gently.

Her liquid, preoccupied eyes rested lengthily on mine. 'You'd better come in.'

That seemed to clinch the genuineness of her state of shock; no one invited total strangers inside these days, especially in central London, even though I had a face so unremarkable, according to Fenlon, that I could have been mistaken anywhere for a man who was a dab hand with washing machines.

She led me into a small hallway which had two further doors, both with their own locks, the left-hand one appearing to cut off the steps to the floor above, the right one standing open on the rooms of her own flat. I'd seen that kind of conversion before. The kitchen would probably have been given a dining annexe and the original dining-room turned into a bathroom. It still made for a flat well beyond the description *pied-à-terre*.

I followed her into a lofty and well-proportioned sitting-room that overlooked the quiet street. There were several decent antique pieces – cabinets, a sofa table, a Regency settee, and there were looped velvet curtains at the tall windows, and watercolours of

London parkland above the chimney-piece. The furnishings gave an impression of being included in what would be a very expensive rental.

She sat down abruptly on the settee, as if shock had almost made her forget I was there, and stared into space for the best part of a minute. Finally, she turned that impossibly perfect face towards me. Its total lack of expression couldn't have provided a bigger contrast to the animation I'd seen earlier.

'How did you get this address?'

'Mrs Durkin . . . she found a diary. . . .'

'Bitch,' she said, in a low voice. 'I suppose it was her who kept ringing up and putting down the phone.'

'When did you last see him . . . Sukie? I'm John, by the way, John Goss.'

'A few weeks ago.'

'Would it be five?'

'I suppose so.'

'Has he not been in touch by phone?'

'It . . . wasn't unusual. Neither of us liked talking over the phone . . . between his trips . . . it was too upsetting, being so far apart. We . . . waited till he actually got here.'

Which would explain the eagerness on the doorstep. This would be more or less the time for his normal visit.

She said, 'I can't understand it, I just *can't* understand it.'

'Sukie, the last time he was here, how did he seem?'

She brought her large, abstracted eyes back to mine with an obvious effort. 'Low,' she said. 'Really low. I'd never seen him like that. It had to have been that bitch. It must have got to him. All he wanted was to go his own way, they'd nothing in common any more. Oh *God*, do you think he's had some kind of a breakdown? He could be wandering about, not being able to get things together . . . you read about it. . . .'

'Did he say he was worried about things at home?'

She shook her head. 'No, but I know he was. He didn't want to talk about it – he'd said it all before. She'd try and take him for his shoelaces. He used to say he didn't know how we'd ever get together with enough to live properly. But he never really let it get to him, not till last time.'

I nodded sympathetically. But if you took the total cynic's view – mine – it seemed that that was exactly what a wealthy playboy *would* say, who wanted to give a little contrast to that agreeable life at Maunan by sampling the occasional delights of Sukie and Chelsea and La Tante Claire.

'I'll find him, Sukie,' I said confidently, from the shieldback I'd placed at the side of the settee, 'but I'll need all the input you can give me, because it looks as if you were one of the last people to see him.'

In fact she was the only real lead I'd got for the time being, and I needed to lift her out of this almost trance-like condition.

'I can't get it together,' she said. 'We weren't in touch a lot, but he'd not go off without telling me. Not Morry. We were ... we were in ... we were so *close!*'

She'd meant to say, 'We were in love' and oddly enough I believed it of her, while very much keeping my options open on Durkin. I'd seen the pattern before. I suspected she was the kind of woman who'd not look at anyone without money, but, once that crucial bridge had been crossed, tended to fall in love just as hard as her less prudent sisters, often so deeply that the love could then withstand any subsequent decline in the other's wealth – I'd seen that, too.

'Do you want to know how I see it, Sukie? My view is that he's gone off somewhere to think things through without distractions, so that he can come back and tell you he's got it all sorted out.'

She gave me a darting glance, suddenly hopeful but also dubious. 'But he could have told *me* ... John. He's told me everything else. About selling his business and concentrating on his portfolio ... trying to talk that Crystal-bitch into being reasonable.'

'Perhaps he didn't want to raise your hopes too soon. Perhaps he's rented a place somewhere to work on his finances, talk things over with a lawyer.'

Her eyes rested on mine again, almost hungrily this time, and I seemed to sense hope gaining over scepticism. I'd deliberately geared my words to encourage that result, but I wondered if I might in fact have hit on the truth. Perhaps he *was* lying low, trying to work out how to make his fortune appear less than it was, perhaps even transferring funds abroad. There wasn't much a wealthy man didn't know about shuffling money around.

'Do you really think that's a possibility? Have you known it happen before?'

'I've known just about everything happen before, Sukie, take my word.'

Which didn't quite answer the question, but she seemed to think it did and was smiling for the first time since she'd opened the door and found a nobody out there instead of Mr Wonderful. Think prettiest girl in the school, in the office, in the tennis club, think Julia and Sharon and Winona – or Tara and Sian and Helena, if you want to be patriotic – and put them in the blender. I was still trying to get used to the similarity she must have had to the early Crystal. It was always the same – I knew a man who'd been married three times; the wives could have been sisters.

I said, 'It would be a big help if you could give me a few details. How long have you known Maurice?'

'About . . . a year.'

'How did you meet?'

'I'm a sort of hostess.' Our eyes met. 'It's not really what you might be thinking. The agency's run by a titled woman and it looks after small groups of businessmen, mainly foreigners. We don't need to advertise. They want to dine in decent restaurants – Le Caprice and the Ivy and the Savoy Grill – and be taken to the top shows and then on to the best clubs. I . . . have connections.'

I believed all that too. There'd be only one way to gain access to the body of a Sloaney as attractive as Sukie Goddard and it *wouldn't* be for £250 in an hotel room.

'And that's how you met him – through your work?'

She nodded. 'He'd pulled some big stroke. He wanted a table in the Louis the Sixteenth room at the Ritz for his friends, and then Annabel's and Tramp. I arranged it all. We . . . took to each other.'

Across the classes, I wondered. Maurice, the millionaire barrow-boy, and Sukie, the upper-middle, probably not too well off, girl-about-town. She must have been an incredible draw, a Crystal who spoke beautifully and was part of London's inner circle. Durkin, too, must have had his own potent appeal, apart from his wealth, funny, sexy, a compelling hint of roughness about him that the Jermyn Street suits couldn't quite conceal, time on his hands to spoil a pretty woman now his business was sold.

'These friends of his,' I said. 'There seems to have been about six of them.'

She nodded. 'Chris, Joe, Sean and so forth. . . .'

'They all seemed to meet up with Maurice in London once a month. Why was that, do you suppose? Mrs Durkin seemed to think it was simply a booze-up.'

'It did seem to be more a fun thing than anything else. They liked to . . . well, fit everything in. But . . . I also felt they were sort of . . . celebrating something as well, something they'd all taken part in. I could be wrong – you know what business types are like, everything's a bit of a lark when they're drinking. But they seemed really wired the times I was with them. It was only once or twice, in fact. After that, Morry and I would meet later, after they'd had dinner, and go off on our own.'

I nodded. That would be in case any of his wealthy chums tried to dangle even bigger carrots before this dazzling female.

'For the past few months they've usually gone to the Café Royal. It's very central and Morry likes the food in the Grill.'

'Is that where they went on that last night?'

She nodded. 'They were all due to meet for a drink at eight. I was working, myself, into the early hours, looking after a group of Germans. He said he'd be round the following morning about eleven. We were going to have a couple of days together.' The hopeful light in her eyes began to die a little. 'He never showed. . . .'

I watched her without speaking; she shrugged. 'It had happened before. Some business problem. He made it up next time he was down. As I said before, we hated phoning each other . . . when we were miles apart. It was disappointing, but I assumed he'd had some minor crisis.'

'Would you know if he had any other contacts up here?' I said. Then added quickly, 'Business, that is?'

'Only his broker and someone from a merchant bank he occasionally had lunch with. No one else that I know of. Most of the time, when he wasn't with his friends, he was with me. Have you spoken to his friends yet?'

'No. I'll have to, of course. To be honest, I was pretty certain I'd find him here with you. That's how it usually is with men like Maurice who leave home.'

'I only wish you had,' she said sadly.

'There's one more thing it might be worth doing before I go back north. Would you help me? Are you free this evening?'

'I'm on the night club run later. I'm free till ten.'

'Will you have dinner with me? At the Café Royal.'

I'd read that they'd kept the decor in the Grill more or less the same since the turn of the century, but I was still unprepared for the sheer rococo splendour of the place, with its great gilded mirrors flanked by carvings of naked and garlanded nymphs, its ceiling paintings of more nymphs, its red and gold wall-lit ambience, through which waiters in formal dress stole, like acolytes preparing the altar for midnight mass.

'Just think,' I said, as we were shown to a table against the end wall, 'Beardsley and Wilde used to come here.'

'With Morry?'

I smiled. 'A bit before his time.'

She gave me a blank look, and I realized that Durkin hadn't liked to stray *too* far beyond the cultivated atmosphere he'd enjoyed with Crystal at Maunan.

'I think playing it very cool is the style,' I told her, as we studied the formidable menu, 'if we're going to get anyone to tell us anything, assuming there's anything to be told.'

She nodded. 'They're a guarded breed. The direct approach certainly wouldn't work.'

The food was French and delicious. It wasn't often a Beckford boy like me ate quail's eggs and gave the wine order to a waiter who actually wore a sommelier's apron. Sukie became more cheerful as the meal drew on, and though I was here on business I won't deny that it gave me a charge to be sitting on a banquette next to such a pretty woman, wearing such an elegant ivory-coloured dress, in that *fin-de-siècle* atmosphere, like some man about town who worked in one of the glamour professions and paid for dinners that cost a hundred plus several times a week.

She said, 'How did you spend the afternoon?'

'I went to see a local investigator. I use him quite a bit for missing persons, a great many of whom tend to end up in London, especially teenagers. I gave him Maurice's details, asked him to put out feelers. I doubt he'll be able to turn up anything, but it's worth a try.'

She glanced at a jewelled watch. 'Will you be able to get a train north so late?'

I shook my head. 'I'll crash down in some hotel room, get the first train out.'

'Why not stay at the flat, if you don't mind sleeping on the sofa? I'll not be in before two, of course, but I can let you have a key. There's a spare duvet in the linen chest in my bedroom.'

She was almost eager for me to go back to Chelsea. It had nothing remotely to do with fun – she was Morry's girl – it was simply because I was the single link between her and him, the sole provider of hope. It was as if she wanted to keep me close by as long as possible, like a talisman, now that she'd obviously decided I looked trustworthy and dependable and presented no particular threat. It happened a lot with me and could be deeply unsettling.

'Thanks,' I said, 'I'll take you up on that.'

'Any time,' she said, almost urgently. 'If you need to come down again let me know.'

I tried to keep my smile free of wryness. It was *never* like PIs in the novels for me. When *they* stayed overnight in Chelsea with one of the sexiest women in London it wasn't to sleep alone on any bloody sofa.

'I'm sure you're right, John,' she said, putting a hand briefly over mine, her liquid brown eyes almost as disturbingly eager as they'd been the first time I'd seen her. 'About Morry lying low and working things out. I've given it a lot of thought this afternoon. It would be difficult to do it at home with that bitch of a wife watching him like a hawk.'

'She's one tough lady, and I've met quite a few. He's got to be in some rented place, doing his sums.'

I'd thought it over too and become convinced I'd hit on the truth. After all, he'd tried to leave her once, and blown it. He'd not want to make the same mistake twice, men like him never did. He'd be back, would Durkin, his plans laid, whether I found him or not.

A young foreign waiter came to take away the dessert plates. I said very casually, 'Do you happen to know if Mr Durkin has been in recently? Mr Maurice Durkin? He comes about once a month with several friends.'

'Ah – *je regrette* . . . I'm sorry, sir, I have been here a short time only. I will enquire of my colleagues.'

He crept off. I shrugged. 'He might or he might not. Look, Sukie, did Maurice ever talk about any part of the country he specially liked? I know he doesn't have a second home, they either rent or stay in hotels.'

She thought about this as she sipped Grand Marnier. 'He liked abroad best – heat and sun. The only English place I ever heard him talk about was the Lake District. They went there a lot before he made it with his business; after that they never went again. Too wet. He said the Lakes would be perfect if they were in the South of France.'

'Cumbria's a pretty big place. Did he ever mention a town or a village? Windermere, Keswick, Coniston, Grasmere, Hawks-head. . . .?'

'He only talked about it once. I'd just been to Garda for a few days and that's what seemed to jog his memory. I *think* it was Amble something . . . does that sound like anything? Ambleton, Amblemere. . . ?'

'Ambleside?'

'Could be. If it is, that's where he used to stay. I think they camped. It would be years ago.'

An older waiter materialized at the table. 'I believe you were asking about Mr Durkin, sir?'

'Oh, yes. I just wondered if he still kept his monthly date. He's an old friend; I've been abroad for six months. Coming here this evening reminded me I must give him a ring.'

'Mr Durkin is very well known to us, sir. Yes, he still comes once a month with his group. He always seems to enjoy himself – a charming gentleman.'

I suspected that charming was a euphemism for not fully house-trained but jumbo-size tips. 'When would the last time be? If he's due shortly I'll invite myself along.'

'About a month ago, sir. He's due any day now, though he usually lets us know in plenty of time. In fact, the last time he was here he was alone. He cancelled his table for seven at quite short notice and asked for just one cover. He said he'd been a little unwell and it wouldn't be fair to his friends if he couldn't be in good spirits.'

I felt Sukie stir on the banquette and touched her hand in warning. 'Oh, I'm sorry about that. He does work under a good deal of pressure. I'll give him a ring in the morning. Thanks for your help.'

'Thank you, sir, and I hope you'll find Mr Durkin in good health. Tell him we look forward to seeing him soon.'

He went off. Sukie's eyes were wide and troubled again. 'He didn't say anything to me about cancelling. Why didn't he tell *me*? I always looked after the bookings for him, he should have let me rearrange it. Why should he suddenly cancel, the same day? I was with him up to lunchtime. They must all have been ready to set off south, the others.'

'He was having a bad day, you said so yourself. He was preoccupied with his disappearing act and all the problems he'd have to sort out. He wasn't ill, he simply had a lot on his mind.'

'If you knew him you couldn't say that,' she said distractedly. 'I was his PA up here, I took care of the detail. It was second nature for him to delegate and he liked being looked after. And he was never so worried about *anything* that he couldn't snap out of it when it came to a night out. It was as if he put his worries in a box and closed the lid on them.'

Privately, I shared her reaction. I'd known quite a few entrepreneurs and their minds were filled with compartments they could seal, it was the only way they could cope with the pressures of their complex business affairs. But Durkin didn't seem to have had a compartment big enough to contain the problem he'd brought to London with him. It had to have been a hefty one if he'd not even been able to face his monthly piss-up with the boys.

FOUR

'Can I offer you a drink, Mr Goss?'

'Thank you. G and T, please. Call me John.'

'Very well, John. And I'm Louise.'

She was rather tall for a woman, with long tawny hair and blue-grey eyes and a short upper lip that drew back slightly to expose a similar gap between her two top front teeth as that between her daughter's. She wore one of those very long tunic-like sweaters in a pale-blue cable pattern, and stone-coloured pants.

She lived in a cottage just above Daisy Edge Woods. She'd shown me into a living-room which had furniture that seemed a mixture of old and new, as if she'd inherited the oval inlaid table and the bureau bookcase and the calendar mantel-clock that stood side by side with the modern ornaments, three-piece and sideboard.

She returned with the drinks, both of which looked to be gin, put them down on a sofa-table, then sat opposite me. 'Thanks for agreeing to come. I'm sure there are much better ways you could be spending your leisure time.'

'A little telly,' I said, 'when I've quite finished writing up reports. Drinking gin with a lady has to have the edge on that.'

She smiled on the gap in her teeth. It was a nice smile. She seemed a nice woman. 'Have you just finished?'

It was 7.30. 'This is early. I spend a lot of evenings on surveillance or following people around. A good deal of my work tends to begin when everyone else is going home.'

'Like Vicky. . .'

'That's how we met, of course, when we were both on the night-shift.'

'So she said. She was very upset about the mix-up.'

I shrugged. 'These things happen, Louise. It was just bad luck.'

The case of the Walking Fur Coat had been very much pushed to the back of my mind by the Durkin disappearance. I'd written off the fee I'd known would only be paid with ill-grace by Woolstone the younger. I recalled the harsh words I'd used on that flushed and furious young woman in the linen-room with reluctance. I really wasn't the macho shithead she'd made me out to be. Perhaps that's why I was here now.

'Even so, she feels very badly about it. She couldn't really believe her rotten luck. You, of all people.'

I gave her a puzzled glance. 'You're losing me. It was just a mix-up about who was supposed to be doing the job. We were both annoyed with each other, but that was an end of it as far as I was concerned.'

She smiled again on that rather attractive triangle-shaped upper lip that never quite seemed to meet the lower one. 'I can see you haven't really grasped the regard you're held in by the PI community. Vicky says people talk about you in hushed tones since you worked on something she calls the Marsh Case. You're almost a legendary figure.'

'You could have fooled me,' I said, though I felt a cheering glow and an increasing warmth towards the woman who'd provided it.

'I . . . thought it over long and hard, John, before I summoned up the courage to get in touch.' I watched and waited, attentive but cautious. 'I'm worried about Vicky. This work of hers. I can't talk her out of it, but it seems so dangerous to me. Enticing men, getting them to compromise themselves so their wives can push for custody rights and so on.'

'I . . . got the impression she was in two minds about it herself. The trouble is, and I don't mean to sound sexist, most women simply aren't as strong as most men, and a lot of men take advantage of that.'

'That's exactly what I told her. Let me get you another drink.'

She went off to the kitchen, moving with the grace and suppleness of one who worked at keeping her body in trim. I had the uneasy feeling I could see the point of all this: the drinks, the friendliness, the flattering remarks. And the answer was still the same.

When she came back, she said, 'The trouble is, she can make more than twenty pounds an hour at Girl Talk. They can virtually guarantee a result in the wife's favour. They're very successful. It gives her a good lifestyle; she has her own flat and car and she's only twenty-two. But it's not simply the money, she enjoys the challenge and the sort of cloak and dagger aspects.'

'What does your husband—?' I abruptly cut myself off. I'd committed the mortal sin of the nineties – assumed *anyone* still actually lived with a spouse any more.

She smiled, not sadly. 'Her father's been long gone. We married too young. Getting a decent financial settlement was . . . well, traumatic. It gave Vicky rather a chip on her shoulder; she had to live through the fall-out. The wives she does the decoy work for sense her sympathy; they trust her to sort things out for them.'

I'd known Vicky Barker had hang-ups from the moment I'd dragged her into the linen-room. I had them myself and you can tell.

'I wondered . . . oh, this must seem so intrusive . . . I wondered if you could possibly throw any work her way? The sort of work where she just *follows* people or does traces, or whatever. Anything but chatting up those frightful men.'

I'd guessed right. First Vicky, then Vicky's mum. Yet I had a feeling they'd not collaborated on this. The stroppy kind of woman

Vicky was, when she'd once been turned down, wouldn't want a mother going in to bat for her. It didn't matter – I had to stifle the idea as firmly the second time as I had the first.

'I'm a one-man band, Louise,' I said flatly. 'I do everything myself because that's the only way I seem able to work. It means putting in crazy hours, but that suits me, to be honest.'

She nodded, with no impression of reproach in her calm glance. 'I think I knew that would be your reaction the moment I saw you. I understand, really, you know your business best. I hope you'll forgive me for asking you here. She's really all I've got. I'm not a possessive mother by any means, but I felt I had to do anything I could to encourage her away from Girl Talk.'

I sighed inwardly. I'd now learnt more about the Barkers than was good for my conscience. A decent woman living alone, her only daughter doing a very dodgy job. I'd spent half an hour getting entangled in the family web; I could easily break loose, but I'd be taking fragments of the web with me.

'Louise, I didn't mean to sound unsympathetic. In fact, I could do with help. The trouble is I need someone with general experience and Vicky won't have the experience till she's been with a general investigator.'

'Say no more, John.' The calm manner hadn't altered by a flicker. 'I always knew it would be a long shot.'

'Well, look,' I said, striving not to sound as reluctant as I felt, 'I won't promise anything, but I'll talk it over with Norma and see what we can come up with. I must admit Vicky has a good manner – she put on a clever act at the Grantley Hall and acting's an essential part of PI work.'

'If you can do anything, John, anything at all, to help get her away from what she does now I'd be eternally grateful. But please don't make problems for yourself.'

But I would be. I didn't want to think about taking *anyone* on, either now or ever, but if Vicky ever tottered out of an hotel room looking like a couple of the women I'd seen go in with Tony

Ferrara I'd find it difficult to live with myself. I forced a cheerful smile. 'I'll . . . do what I can.'

'Thank you, thank you so much.' She hesitated then, gave me an embarrassed glance. 'Oh dear, I don't know how to say this. The thing is, she's such a strong-willed madam, so touchy. If you *can* offer her any work could you make it sound as if you really want her to help you out? Oh dear, this is *dreadful* . . . if she thinks you've any other motive, that you're sorry for her or doing her a favour, she'll not . . . she'll. . . .'

In other words I'd need to wear kid gloves to inveigle her into doing work for me I'd sooner do for myself in the first place. 'I know what you're trying to say, Louise,' I said, unable to conceal the wryness this time, 'I did once have dealings with her.'

'It would be such a weight off my mind if you can help,' she said simply.

She pressed me, without much difficulty, to have another drink. She was a schoolteacher. Like me, she read a lot and liked watching old films. An hour passed very quickly.

'I'd better be going, Louise.'

'Heavens, can that be the *time*!'

There were few nicer compliments. She got up and gave me a smile that seemed faintly appraising and which probably reflected my own. We were after all singles, very much alert to the signs and nuances.

'Perhaps . . . I could invite you for a meal some time, John. It's been lovely talking to you.'

'I'd like that,' I said. 'Very much.'

I got in the car, smiled, shook my head. It had been some time since a woman had shown an interest in me and now, within a few days, I'd had two invitations to dinner. I supposed a man who'd just been given a £5,000 retainer, offered a champagne supper, access to a pool and almost certainly to Crystal's remarkable curves, would have to know which side his bread was buttered on.

I was really looking forward to seeing Louise again.

*

'The Durkin home . . . er, house . . . er, residence.'

'I'd like to speak to Mrs Durkin. The name's John Goss.'

'Hang on.'

It sounded like the young man with the nasal problem, on whom Crystal was keen to hang manners. There was a lengthy silence, a good deal of clicking and then Crystal's irate voice saying, 'Well, put yours down, dozy devil, and then I can bloody hear him. Hello, Johnny, how are you doing, love?'

'Hello, Crystal. Not a lot to report so far, I'm afraid. I got a name and address for that number you gave me and I've been to London to check it out.'

'What's she like?' she said darkly.

'Oh . . . youngish . . . some sort of a tourist guide.'

'I can guess where she guides them as well. What does she *look* like, Johnny?'

'Prettyish, I suppose. Nothing special.'

It was the instinctive guarded line I gave most of the wives who paid me to follow errant husbands. The girlfriends were – with certain fascinating exceptions – invariably knock-out compared to the wives, but I tried to spare them further ego damage.

'Pull the other one – with his kind of money he'll not be going out with any Jo Brand lookalikes. Anyway, what did you get out of her? I suppose she is his bit on the side,' she said resignedly.

'I really think she's more of a PA. She books the meals he has with the boys, hotel rooms and so forth.'

'Johnny love, I *know* what personal services she'll be providing for Maurice, so don't prat about, there's a good lad.'

I smiled. It was refreshing to deal with a total realist; I was used to dealing with women who really did want to believe the euphemisms.

'All right, Crystal, but the truth is she hasn't seen him for five weeks either.'

'Go *on*.'

'No, really. I spent a couple of hours with her and I'm convinced she's as anxious to know where he is as you are.'

'I'll bet she is. It's bloody marvellous, isn't it? You know, Johnny, that first Crystalmart we opened, I used to work fourteen hours a day helping him get it off the ground. It hasn't always been beer and skittles, not by a long chalk. And now some young London totty who's never done a hand's turn thinks she can walk away with the lot. Over my dead body.'

'Look, Crystal, would you know if Maurice took his passport with him?'

'No chance.'

'You sound very sure.'

'I am sure. Because I keep them, don't I, locked up in my little drawer, and I'm the only one who has the key. I can do without that bugger nipping abroad on the sly. If he'd got the world to go at we'd have no chance.'

'Good. As you say, it narrows it down dramatically. When was the last time you went to the Lakes?'

'Not since we got on our feet. Must be fifteen years. God, if you think it pisses it down in Yorkshire just go up there for a few days ... how did you know we used to go?'

'His ... London friend mentioned it in passing.'

'Do you think he might be up there?'

'It's an angle.'

'We did go a lot when we had nothing,' she said reflectively. 'We had a battered old caravan we towed. I could take it or leave it, but Maurice loved it, walking round the lakes and watching the boats. But we both lost interest when we made our first couple of grand.'

'Where did you stay?'

'Nearly always near Ambleside. It's central, you see. You're bang up to Lake Windermere and it's easy to get to the other lakes. Mind you, I always used to say when you've seen one of the sods in the pissing rain you've seen the lot.'

'Right, I'll think about that. One other thing, Crystal: I need to talk to Maurice's friends – the six who go to London with him. Do you think you could warn them to expect me and let them know what it's about?'

She sighed. 'You'll get naff-all out of that lot, Johnny. If there's one thing they can give lessons in it's keeping shtoom, especially if they think there might be a totty involved.'

'Don't worry, I'll be speaking to them man to man. Promising it'll go no further. I spend my entire life getting people to talk.'

'You've never been up against the magnificent seven.'

She had a valid point. You were combining the Yorkshire temperament here with men who'd made it their way, and getting any kind of information out of them could be slightly harder than tearing limpets off a rock with your finger nails.

'Tell you what,' she said, 'they're starting with the barbies now the weather's acting right in its bloody head. Ray Challis is having a do tomorrow night as it happens. Trust Maurice to go walkabout now the fun's starting. I'll take you as my guest. They'll all be there.'

'That sounds ideal.'

'I'll tell Ray who you are and ask him to have a quiet word with the boys. As far as everyone else is concerned you're just a business friend of Maurice's.'

'Excellent.'

'Get yourself up here tomorrow night for eight and we'll go from here in the Roller.'

'Will do.'

'And by the way, Ray Challis is Maurice's closest friend, and *his* mouth's as tight as his arse.'

'Vicky?'

'Who is this?'

'John Goss. Remember me?'

'I wish I could forget.'

'Look . . . Vicky, I've been thinking about what you said the night we met in the linen-room.'

'What, about you being an arrogant bastard?'

'Ah, now that's where I think you might have got me wrong.'

'You could have fooled me.'

It wasn't easy trying to maintain a friendly tone through gritted teeth, but I persisted, for Louise's sake. 'I owe you an apology,' I said. 'I was out of order. It wasn't your fault the Woolstones set us both on. I realized how unfair I'd been to you when I'd chilled out. Anyway, I've thought things over and if you're still interested in general work I'm prepared to give it a try.'

'What . . . does that involve?' she said guardedly.

'Would you like to go with me on the occasional job? Just watch and listen. I think they call it shadowing in the business world.'

After a silence she said, 'You made it very clear in the linen-room you didn't do anything for nothing, so what's in it for you?'

I closed my eyes, drew a deep breath. 'If it worked out I'd consider using you as an agent.'

'You're definitely wanting a recruit?'

'My PA tells me I've got to have one or begin turning work away.'

'And you think I might be suitable?'

'That's what we'd have to find out. Obviously,' I said carefully, 'we'd have to put our past differences aside and make a fresh start.'

I'd promised Louise, so I'd go through the motions and give her a little training. But that would be that. It wasn't just the spiky temperament, it was something more inimical, something that had made me uneasy around her in the linen-room which I couldn't pin down.

Another silence and then, 'All right,' she said coolly, 'I'm interested.'

It wasn't quite the reaction I could have expected from someone said to regard John Goss in an almost legendary way, but I was getting used to it. Suddenly she added, 'I'm taking a day off tomorrow, if that's any good. . . .'

'All right. I'm aiming to go to Cumbria. I need to spend an hour in the office and I could pick you up around nine. It's quite an interesting case, a very wealthy missing man.'

'I'll be ready at nine,' she said, then gave me her address. Finally she added, with obvious reluctance, 'And . . . thank you, Mr Goss.'

'See you in the morning,' I said, with a cheerful grimace. 'And call me John.'

She had a flat in an attractive modern two-storey block on the northern outskirts where the city gave way to farmland. It was set a little back from the road and she must have been waiting for the car to draw in, as she came out directly, wearing a slightly strained-looking smile.

'Hello, Vicky.'

'Hello . . . John. Will this gear be all right?'

She wore a blue and white-checked shirt and lightweight denims, and as she got in she tossed a pale-blue canvas jacket on to the back seat. 'Ideal,' I said truthfully, 'for what I have in mind.'

As I waited for her to sort out her seat-belt before letting in the clutch, I glanced at the short fair hair and the harebell-blue eyes, the bluntish irregular features and the gap in her teeth she'd inherited from Louise, the *jolie laide* attraction that if I forced myself to be objective I could accept was almost as appealing in its own way as Sukie Goddard's flawless beauty. Plenty of other men seemed to have thought so, the ones she'd smiled at invitingly in hotel bars and whose lives from that moment had never been the same.

It was another bright June day. We were both silent as I put my foot down on the fast by-pass routes that brought us to Gargrave, the first of the villages and small towns that were strung out along the open rising country that took us north by north-west to the Lakes. The tourist season wouldn't begin in earnest until the schools broke up and it was pleasant to drive without delays beneath a high sun that gave drifting cloud an incandescent edge.

Beyond Gargrave, I began to explain the case to her, assuming she'd accept the unwritten rule of PI work that nothing went further than the two of us, not even to Louise. 'I've got little to go on at present and could just be pratting about,' I told her. 'Sukie swears she doesn't know where he is and I believe her. But she said he once talked about Ambleside and the wife confirms they went there a lot before he became wealthy. It seemed worth a look round.'

'You mean, checking out the hotels?'

'I doubt he'll be in an hotel. You can be found too easily in them and he'll certainly know that. Our best bet is the estate agents. There are an awful lot of second homes up there that people rent out when they're not using them.'

'Simply ask estate agents if they've rented a property to him? Will they tell you?'

'If we play it right. We can pose as a couple trying to find your uncle. That's why your clothes look OK. We'll seem like ordinary tourists.'

'But if he is up there perhaps he'll not be using his own name. . . .'

'I think he will, you know. He'll probably want to keep what cash he's carrying intact. He'll have used his Gold Card or his Amex, ten to one, and you can't use false names with those.'

She nodded in a preoccupied way, her mind seeming to be in learning mode. She reminded me of myself a decade ago when I too was developing the habit of lateral thought. Then she said slowly, 'If he hasn't contacted his wife and he hasn't contacted his girl-friend, do you think there could possibly be a *third* woman involved?'

I gave her a glance of reluctant admiration, as we moved rapidly along an arrow-straight road through sweeping Dales country open on every side to the sky. I'd considered the possibility myself, unable for obvious reasons to discuss it with either Crystal or

Sukie. 'I've known it happen,' I said. 'And it could explain why he was so worried. Two women, two relationships to sort out, and a new girlfriend in the pipeline.'

'At least he can't go abroad.'

'But money buys everything, including a replacement passport. He could be lying low while he sorts things out. Mis-pers are normally routine. They're nearly always middle-aged men or penniless youngsters, and the sorts of things they do tend to follow a pattern you soon learn to get the hang of. This case has a little more interest than usual because we're up against a wealthy man with a lot upstairs. I suspect that at least one of his friends will be covering for him, and if we draw a blank in Cumbria they're my next port of call. They'll all be together tonight at a barbecue at one of their fancy houses.'

'And you're going?'

I nodded.

'What shall I wear?'

'Ah . . . I'm afraid it'll just be me and Mrs Durkin.'

'But surely she'll not mind if I tag along. If you explain. . . .'

'I'm afraid she will.'

'Why – does she fancy you or something?' she said, with peevish accuracy.

'That's beside the point,' I said evenly. 'It's not her party and she can take only one guest. I can't include you in everything, Vicky.'

The bridges I'd thought we were successfully rebuilding seemed to have crashed into the river again. She was as touchy as an adolescent. She sat in a brooding silence, her lower lip jutting pettishly.

About seven or eight miles from Windermere, we crested a rise that gave that first magnificent view of the lake, the largest in Cumbria. It lay blue and glittering diagonally to our left beneath the woodland of the western fells, with a scattering of yachts gliding slowly over its rippling surface as gracefully as swans. I'd been here often in my youth and childhood with my parents – for some reason, as the car had come in sight of that first great sheet of water, my late father would begin to sing about lemonade springs and big rock-candy mountains, and I seemed to hear his soft, hoarse voice now as we sped along the dappled winding roads that led us rapidly by the side of the gleaming shoreline.

'Can I help you?'

'I'm sorry to trouble you, but we're trying to find out where my wife's uncle is staying. He wrote to her with the address of a house he's renting, but she's managed to leave the letter behind.'

'Well, you shouldn't rush me,' Vicky said, with a helpful giggle, her earlier irritation suspended in the cause of the amateur dramatics. 'Rush, rush, rush,' she told the young woman at the counter, 'you'd think we were going to work instead of on holiday.'

'He's renting a house in the Ambleside area,' I went on, 'and we wondered if you might have handled the letting. Mr Maurice Durkin. . . .'

Her glance passed from one to the other of us, but we looked exactly like the standard tourist article who hired boats and pony trekked and made with the fell boots up Helvellyn.

'Durkin,' she repeated. 'Let me have a look. . . .'

She tapped the keys of a VDU and studied the screen. She shook her head. 'Sorry, can't help you. No Durkins on the books.'

'Thanks all the same.' We walked out on to the street. It was the last agent.

'What now?' she said.

'Back to Windermere. It's bigger than Ambleside and they'll probably have lettings for a wider area.'

'If you don't mind me saying so, I'd have thought Windermere was the logical place to begin the search anyway. It was on our way. Did you have a special reason for coming to Ambleside?'

I did mind her saying so, even though she was right. It *would* have been logical to try the bigger town first. But I'd had Ambleside fixed obsessively in my mind, and I was a human being, and the two towns were only three or four miles apart . . . and I wondered how soon I'd be able to give this graceless bitch the elbow.

'I sometimes act intuitively,' I said evenly, 'when a more considered approach probably would save time.'

I could feel her eyes on me as I drove, but I refused to meet them. I wished I were alone, half pretended that I was.

'Perhaps his name won't be *with* an estate agent. Perhaps he got an address from a private advert in one of the papers,' she said, in a tone that might have held a trace of conciliation.

'It's a good point,' I admitted, 'but it all seems to come back to the rush he was in. I doubt he'd have had time for that. My feeling is – if he's here – that he drove up from London, possibly overnight, and made direct contact with the property people. But my instincts could easily be on the blink again.'

I wished I'd not added that final sentence. It was snide, and though some of the things she said irritated me I didn't think she was being catty, just brash. I glanced peripherally in her direction; her mouth was set once more in its sullen pout.

In Windermere, I parked on a side road and we made our way along the main street, calling on estate agents and going into our little act of exasperated husband and scatterbrained wife. To be scrupulously fair I had to accept that I'd have found it a much harder task without her.

'Durkin . . .' a middle-aged woman with greying hair and rimless glasses said slowly, 'now the name does ring a bell. . . .'

She, too, began to do the business with the VDU. 'Yes, we do have a letting for a Mr M. Durkin, but not in Ambleside.'

'It may not *be* Ambleside,' I said, as calmly as possible. 'He said he'd prefer Ambleside, but would probably have to take what was available.'

'The property's just beyond Near Sawrey. A detached house overlooking Esthwaite Water. Four Winds, they call it.'

'Near Sawrey – would that be across the lake, on the Hawkshead Road?'

'Your quickest route's the Bowness Ferry.'

'Thank you very much.'

Vicky said, 'Would you mind telling us how long Uncle Maurice is booked in for? We might be able to talk him into letting us come again. He did mention it in his letter, but I've forgotten that as well. Memory like a sieve.'

Once again, I had to give her marks for sharpness. That had been going to be my next question.

The woman flicked to another screen. 'He's taken it to the end of the month, with an option to extend for a further fortnight.'

As we walked back to retrace my car, Vicky said flatly, 'Well, it looks as if you've won.'

'It's what experience in this business is all about,' I said equally flatly, and with a gathering reluctance to go on explaining my methods to a woman whose hang-ups seemed to leave her incapable of accepting any kind of teacher-pupil relationship in the right spirit. 'When someone goes missing, and there are no obvious leads, always find out if there was some part of the country they favoured for holidays. If they were happy there they often go back when they're in some kind of mental state, as if the place itself can give them peace of mind. I've tracked down several mis-pers in exactly that way. But, let's not count our chickens. . . .' I opened the car doors to relieve the heat build-up. 'Before I ring Crystal we need to be sure the guy's actually there.'

'What makes you think he won't be? He's booked till the end of the month.'

'Perhaps it was the shortest booking he could get to secure the place he wanted. It's pretty isolated across there, and the money wouldn't matter. I don't know,' I said in a low voice, more for my own benefit than hers, 'there's something about this case I can't get my head round. It has an odd feel. I told Sukie Goddard he was probably sorting out his affairs, with a view to leaving Crystal, but if, say, there was *another* girlfriend, he might have needed a base while *she* made arrangements to go away with him, and perhaps by now they've cleared off, possibly abroad.'

We got in the car. Though it could be assumed the town of Windermere would actually be at the side of the lake it was in fact about a mile away, with the smaller town of Bowness closer to the water. We now drove down to it along a road surprisingly busy despite the main season not being due for several weeks.

'What if it was a business thing,' she said, 'Durkin doing a runner? Wasn't that why they were supposed to meet in London once a month, to talk about business deals?'

'I think we can safely rule that out,' I said. 'This case has *cherchez la femme* written all over it. They were all womanizers, not just Durkin, and the story that they went to London to talk business away from the daily pressure was a line they fed the wives. A bit of business might well have been involved, but the main reason was the piss-up. A regular dinner-date at the Café Royal and then on to the sorts of nightclubs the average punter can forget about.'

'I've known a lot of businessmen,' she said, with the dogged scowl I was getting to know so well, 'and keen as they are on sex, business has the edge, especially when they're in the middle of a big deal. Perhaps it was some kind of a stroke that screwed up.'

I stifled a sigh. I'd had to consider that too, especially as Sukie had mentioned what seemed to be an occasional celebratory aspect to the Café Royal dinners, and men frequently *did* do a runner because of money problems. But those kinds of men had invariably had their hands caught in the till. 'He's a millionaire,' I explained patiently. 'Even if he'd lost a hundred grand in some investment that went belly-up it wouldn't begin to compare with what his women could take him for.'

'It just seems a bit blinkered to set your mind on it being simply a woman when it *could* be business.'

I breathed in slowly. 'It could be *anything*. I just happen to think, all things considered, and after ten years of tracing mis-pers that it's most *likely* to be woman orientated.'

I didn't think I could handle much more of this. I'd not expected or wanted her to sit in silent awe of the man said (though only by Louise) to be so highly regarded in the PI community, but I had looked for a shade more respect, a rather more unquestioning acceptance of actions and opinions that were guided by considerable experience. But she'd had problems through being fatherless at a vulnerable stage, and according to Louise it had made her strong-willed. I was beginning to think that that was Louise-speak for bloodyminded.

We came out on to the lakeside at Bowness. It had almost a sea-front atmosphere, with its piers and tackle shops and lines of hire-craft. We could see the blue lake stretching north from here, past Belle Isle, against a soaring background of fawny-green fells. The sprinkling of yachts now seemed like duckling against the mother-bird of one of the great tourist vessels that floated majestically southwards, always known as steamers, but now almost certainly diesel-driven.

I branched left from the lakeside road and drove then in a loop to the ferry crossing, about half a mile to the south and at a narrow midway point in the lake's eleven-mile length.

'Sod it!' I muttered, as we drew to a halt behind a tailback of traffic, and almost abreast of a sign that indicated that if cars were queuing at this point it would take forty minutes to board the ferry. 'She was wrong, Mrs Rimless Glasses, it would have been quicker to go round. The season in this place is getting to be wall to wall.'

We spent the time grinding forward for a few minutes, then sitting it out as the ferry made its crossing, picked up on the opposite shore and returned. The road took us gradually on to a long narrow spit of land. To each side of the spit the shoreline made a deep bay-like curve. These had been turned into marinas and were crammed with moored cruisers and yachts. At this stage the air became filled with a peculiarly disturbing, almost sinister ringing sound. I saw that it was the breeze that made the rigging tap against the metal masts of many of the boats. The word tocsin came unbidden into my mind, and when I remembered it later it was as if the sound really had been a warning of the labyrinth the Durkin case was set to take me into, to which I didn't respond.

After a silence that must have lasted fifteen minutes, she suddenly said, 'That night in the linen-room . . . you said I'd not thanked you for saving me from being raped.'

'I said a lot of things. We both did. It might be better if we put it behind us, as I said yesterday.'

'He'd not have raped me,' she said bluntly. 'He might have managed to give me a black eye, but he'd not have raped me.'

I looked at her in the again stationary car. The long silence had helped to feed my illusion I was alone, able to think my own thoughts without interruption, able to do my work in my own way without being questioned or second-guessed. I'd been indulging in a little elation that I'd pinned down Durkin's bolt-hole, might soon, when we were across the lake, be able to wind up the case. It was as if I'd been shaken out of a pleasant dream, and I spoke with a resignation I found impossible to conceal.

'All right, Vicky, he'd not have raped you.'

'Well, he *wouldn't*. I'd have found a way out. And if he'd caught me I'd have known what to do.'

'All right, I'm convinced.'

'But you're not. You think if you'd not been there I'd have been a stretcher case.'

'You're wrong. I don't think *anything* about that night any more. And next time I see some bloody woman in a rumpled dress running out of an hotel room with a human ape behind her I'll know there's nothing I have to do because women don't need men any more, and it'll save me three or four hundred sovs.'

'*Oh!*' She abruptly opened the door and got out. 'I'll see you at the ferry.'

'You'd better, because I don't intend to lose my place.'

She slammed the door and marched across the road to stand glaring at the moored vessels that gave out their endless ringing sound. But, as we began to edge forward again, to let another handful of cars on to the ferry, I could see her through the side mirror, a lonely and forlorn-looking figure in her check shirt and denims, her short hair ruffling in the breeze. I felt sorry about my outburst then. I had to remind myself she'd never had a father who'd sung about lemonade springs as he'd driven eagerly into lakeland.

As the ferry drew in for what would be my crossing, the door softly opened. 'Thanks . . . John . . . for pulling me into the linen-room. I mean it. He'd not have raped me, but he could have hurt me badly. I'm sorry you lost your money. I did say I'd share my fee. . . .'

'Oh, Vicky, I don't want your money. It wasn't your fault. And I *do* believe he'd not have raped you. I think he'd have had to kill you first.'

'It was important to me that you believe it.'

We left it there, but it seemed to mark the onset of a more companiable mood between us. When the car was in position on deck, we both got out to look at the life of the lake as the ferry's grooved side-wheels began to winch us to the opposite shore between submerged parallel hawsers, which seemed to drip a shower of diamonds in the sunlight as the wheels drew them from the water. Yachts swept within yards of us, sails bellying in the breeze, and the trees on the advancing slopes could be seen in pin-sharp detail, as if the air had been scoured clean by a Mediterranean mistral.

'Nice place to hole-up in,' she said.

'Seems a pity to drag him back to whatever he was running away from. That's usually the downside of nailing a mis-per.'

The ferry crunched against the opposite ramp and we drove off along a road that skirted the lake and then wound up the densely wooded hillside to the open country above. We drove past the villages of Far Sawrey and Near Sawrey, silent and peaceful in the noon heat, and then came to Esthwaite Water, and to the right, on rising land, the house called Four Winds.

It was large and square and had a gaunt, raw-edged, slightly rundown look to it. The woodwork could certainly have done with a coat of paint. It was stone-built with a roof of the tough grey slate of the region, yet it gave an impression of inhospitality and draughtiness. There seemed also an eerieness about the small lake it overlooked which, when shrouded in its normal mists, must have appeared almost forbidding. I wondered if Durkin longed for that house he'd had built, with its pool and its thick carpets and its valley landscape.

'Spook-eee . . .' she said, with a slight shudder.

'Fancy being a damsel in distress?' I said. 'We're losing water from the radiator and could he let us have a kettleful till we can get to Hawkshead.'

'What if he comes out with me?'

'I'll have the bonnet up. I'll blather my way through, don't worry.'

'What if he doesn't answer the door? What if it's some woman he's with?'

'If there's a woman there then he's sure to be there too. The job's a good one and we can ring Crystal.'

She left the car and pushed open one half of a pair of iron gates, set into a stone archway. It was in need of oiling and whined loudly. I watched her walk up the rutted tarmac drive, then got out and lifted the bonnet. She'd studied Durkin's photograph on the way up and would know him the moment she clocked him. That's all it needed. I gazed at the orderly tangle of cables and hoses in the car's insides. I was almost certain now there was going to be a third woman involved. A bundle of energy like Durkin wouldn't need to spend five weeks in isolation to sort out his finances.

About three minutes later she came back down the drive. A group of cars, recently released by the ferry, passed between us and she waited for me to cross, framed in the gate's arch and shaking her head. I went over. 'It seems absolutely deserted,' she said. 'I rang the bell, knocked . . . zilch.'

I closed the gate behind us. 'The noise it makes will be our warning if he comes back from a walk or whatever. And we stick to our story – radiator leaking.'

The lengthy, neglected drive ran between dense hedging bushes to the right and a stand of cypress trees to the left. At the end of it stood a stone-built garage. It was unlocked. Inside there was a newish Ford Granada. That, too, was unlocked.

'He's a wealthy man,' I murmured. 'Used to other people locking up things.'

In the glove compartment there was paperwork with the Hertz heading and the Buckingham Palace Road address. It was completed in Durkin's name and signed by him. The hiring was overdue by three weeks, but he could have extended it by phone and credit card.

'This *must* mean he's around,' she said.

'Or that someone's picked him up.'

We walked along the front of the house. The trees cut off a great deal of light, adding to the general gloominess of the place. The main door was panelled and heavy, but had standard locks.

'We could get in at a pinch,' I said. 'I've got keys in the car that would probably open them.'

'Why do we need to get in if he'll be back soon?'

'I don't think he will be back. I think he's moved on again. Don't ask me why, it's simply a gut reaction.'

I felt a keener sense of elation then. There was a lot of satisfaction to be gained from solving a case quickly, a great deal more from solving one that presented a genuine challenge.

We moved round to the back of the house, through deep patches of oily shade. The silence was profound – it was a time of day when even birds become subdued.

The large rooms at the front of the house looked to be what estate agents called reception; at the rear we could see into an equally roomy kitchen, which had an outside door, and a dining-room with french windows.

'What a *mess*,' she said.

The dining-table was littered with plates, each bearing the remnants of a meal and a fork, and giving an impression that one person had eaten a series of scratch meals and simply left the plates where they lay.

I had cupped my hands round my eyes and held my hands against the french window to get a clearer view. The window suddenly gave with the slight pressure. Not only was it not locked, it wasn't even properly closed. But it had been a long time since Durkin had needed to involve himself in the minutiae of life.

'I can't resist an invitation like this.'

She watched me pensively. 'He *could* come back. . . .'

'It's a chance I'm prepared to take. My job is to find him, and not being police I can cut corners.'

'What if he's had a heart attack . . . or something?'

It was a valid point. He was a man on the verge of middle age who'd lived hard. She was very uneasy. I wondered if she saw a body slumped in an armchair, or worse, perhaps even hanging from a bannister. I'd seen both those things in my time, and the frightful way the bodies had smelt had had even more impact than the way they'd looked.

'Tell you what, why don't you keep watch from the car? Then, if you see him coming back, you could give me a toot.'

'No,' she said stiffly, with her old scowl, 'I don't honestly think he's coming back either. I'll go with you.'

The tough words were belied by the pallor in her cheeks, but I opened the french window fully and went quietly inside, with her so close our bodies almost touched. The room was furnished, as were most second homes, with pieces that looked as if they'd either come from the saleroom or been discarded from the main home, but they were in decent condition, if dusty – a welsh dresser, a sideboard, a drinks cabinet. The littered dining-table itself was of dark oak, with ten chairs of varying styles, all now untidily positioned, as if Durkin had eaten one rough and ready meal, abandoned the plate, and simply moved on to another place for the next.

There was equal squalor in the kitchen – draining-boards stacked with encrusted pots and pans, an overflowing waste container, scraps of toast trodden into the carpet, a dozen smeared whisky tumblers on the kitchen table.

'*What* a shock it must have been,' I said, 'to have to come down in the morning and find exactly the same mess as when he'd gone to bed. It rather looks as if he was very much on his own.'

We passed through to the living-room, where more smeared glasses stood on an occasional table and newspapers and paperbacks littered the floor in front of an elderly television.

'Papers!' I said. She gave me a startled glance. 'We need to find the one with the latest date. That could give us an idea of when he left, assuming he *has* left.'

We scrabbled about among the mounds of newsprint – all *Daily Mails*. The last date we could find was about three weeks earlier. 'On this basis,' I said, 'he was only here a fortnight.'

The other main room had a more formal air. There were bookcases and an upright piano, and a baize-covered table in front of the long casement windows with playing cards and board games. There was also a writing table against a side wall with paper and blotter, but the blotting paper was pristine and the wicker waste-basket disappointingly empty.

The additional rooms on the ground floor were a neglected-looking study and a cloakroom, neither of which contained anything to alter the picture of Durkin's stay at Four Winds which was slowly emerging, that of a man living alone in a muddle while waiting impatiently to move on elsewhere.

It left only upstairs. She was still pale and had scarcely spoken as we'd crept round the silent shadowy rooms, as if afraid I might detect a wavering note in her voice. 'Sure you don't want to wait in the car?' I said. 'It seems there are two chances: he's either left, or he's lying up there dead, as you suggested.'

'Don't be wet, John,' she said, almost roughly. 'I'm supposed to be shadowing you. And I'm *not* scared.'

She suddenly ran up the stairs ahead of me. I followed with a wry smile. I had to admire her spirit even as I hoped she wasn't going to get the shock of her life up there.

But Durkin wasn't dead, just absent. When I reached the top of the stairs she'd gone into one of the back bedrooms and now stood in the centre of it. It was clear from the mess it was in that this was the one he'd used. I quickly checked the other rooms, all of which looked undisturbed, and then returned for a detailed study of this one. There was a double bed with a disordered duvet on top and a pair of crumpled silk pyjamas. In the large linen-fold wardrobe there was one of his expensive suits and a sports jacket and cords. There were shirts, ties and socks in a drawer. At the side of the wardrobe stood an expensive fabric suitcase, empty except for underwear, a toilet-bag and a pair of unused trainers. At the side of the bed there was a pair of maroon velvet slippers embroidered with a gold M – a present probably from Crystal.

'He must have gone in what he stood up in,' she said, calmer now that there'd been no unpleasant sights to witness. 'And must be coming back sometime.'

'Except that he's probably so used to having his bag packed and put in his hand that he simply forgot to do it. In any case, he can simply buy what he needs. He didn't forget his document-case – that would be the most important possession to a wealthy man. But it looks as if he left in a hurry,' I said, glancing at the armless spoon-back chair that lay on its side in the middle of the room, the bedside rug that looked to have been kicked aside, the drawers that hung half open. 'Why was that, I wonder?'

There was a phone on a bedside cabinet with next to it a small flowered note-pad, a twin of the one next to the phone in the hall. 'Now then,' I said, 'what have we here?' The top note on the pad was blank, but there were faint ballpoint indentations on it. I held the pad to the light, ran a finger over the grooves. 'No good,' I said. 'But I've got some gear in the car that might bring it up.'

But I heard movement behind me, and turned to see her dragging the cabinet away from the bed, which had a solid base. She picked up something from the space between the two and began triumphantly smoothing out what looked to be the crumpled missing notelet. 'I *thought* I could just see something down there. He must have memorized what was on it and thrown it away.'

'Well done!' I said. Her cheeks went from pale to pink. Before I'd have left the room I'd have routinely searched inside, behind and underneath every article of furniture in it and would have found the notelet myself. But I wasn't about to spoil her moment, even though she'd spoilt quite a few of mine.

There was a word and a figure on the notelet: Veronica – 8.

'The third woman!' I said jubilantly, and couldn't stop myself adding, 'So that knocks business worries on the head.'

I dialled 1471, of course, but Veronica, whoever she was, didn't seem keen to make it too easy for us, as she'd put a block on her number being recalled. I wondered why.

FIVE

'Good evening, sir.'

I handed Brian the keys to my car. The Rolls was waiting in the yard. 'Neil,' he called. 'Motor. . . .'

The sullen youth who sniffed a lot appeared from one of the garages, sniffing. He still wore the green house clothes, but Brian was dressed more grandly in black jacket and peaked cap.

'Johnny!' Crystal cried, bursting into the hall with its doggie plates and leather-covered doors. 'Lovely to see you.' She kissed me on the cheek as if we were now very old friends, as Brian, standing behind her, gave me a smile of faint but unmistakable derision.

Costly scent hung around her and she was dressed in a white linen suit with a boxy jacket, her brown, highlighted hair newly washed and set. I wondered how Durkin found the energy to play the field when he had someone as powerfully attractive as Crystal at his own poolside.

Brian opened the door of the Rolls for us. I suppose if you could define serious money by a smell it had to be that of a Rolls' leather and walnut interior. 'Now then, Johnny,' Crystal said, a little breathily, 'what have you been up to?'

'I went up to Cumbria this morning and made a check of rented accommodation in case he was up there. I drew a blank, I'm afraid.'

I'd decided not to tell her the truth just yet. She might rush up there herself, and if Durkin saw her before she saw him he might bury himself so deep we'd never dig him out. And I had a strong feeling he was still up there, with the Veronica woman.

'Not to worry, Johnny,' she said, giving my thigh a reassuring squeeze. 'See what you can find out from this lot. It won't be easy, think on, they're all as close as a crab's backside.'

Brian had turned left outside Maunan and driven further up the hill to the moorland plateau, purpling and hazy now in the evening light, where he again turned left to take the skirting road.

'The boys, Crystal, they're all in business like Maurice was?'

'Not all, love. Four of them are. But one's an accountant, Chris Denholm, and one's a solicitor, Bill Ackroyd. They both did work for Maurice when he had the Crystalmarts. He saw they were sharp lads, helped fix them both up with their own shows.'

That meant a group of high-powered entrepreneurs had a tax consultant and a legal expert virtually in-house. Handy, especially if they were helping Durkin sort out his affairs right now.

'Would you say the boys were as well off as Maurice?'

'Not according to Maurice. He reckons they'll all be nicely into their second million, but he passed that post a while ago.' She rested a warm hand on my thigh again. 'But they all *owe* Maurice, Johnny, one way and the other, Ray Challis more than any of them. Early on he had a building contract that went cockeyed; he'd have banked if Maurice hadn't bunged him a hundred grand. He always had big pockets for men he thought could make it. That's why you'll be lucky if you can get anything out of the sods. And it's just not on. Honestly, I don't think I'd have come if it hadn't been to help you.'

She suddenly flushed, clearly brooding about the effect on her caste status of a husband on the loose, whom she knew as well as I did was with another woman. 'They'll be loving this,' she said darkly, as if confirming my thoughts, 'the wives.'

As the whispering motor swung off the road, an automatic gate was already rolling open. We drove into the usual extensive yard, stuffed with costly motors; beyond it ran a perfect expanse of lawn, dotted with maples in blossom, their leaves looking hand-painted.

'You can go, Brian,' Crystal told him. 'I'll ring when we've had enough. If you're sending Neil, for Christ's sake make sure he has the full monty on this time. White and red trainers do *not* go with a chauffeur's peaked bloody *cap*.'

Brian's eyes skirted past mine, but not before I'd given him a little smile to match the one he'd earlier given me. He backed the Rolls carefully out on to the road, Crystal warily looking on. 'You need to watch these automatic gates,' she said. 'Colin Blacow nearly had his Daimler cut in two when theirs went funny. That dog's never been the same. . . .'

A small, stocky, roughish-looking man with a military haircut came out to greet us, dressed in black trousers, white shirt and a bow-tie. 'Hello, Mrs Durkin, nice to see you again,' he said in a hoarse voice, his breath smelling slightly of beer and tobacco. 'They're all out the back. I'll take you through.'

'Right, Charlie, how are you doing, cock?'

He led us into the usual large, newish house, though it wasn't quite as grand as Durkin's, and along a lengthy hall that gave glimpses of the usual shag-pile carpets, leather suites and flock wallpapers, through a fun room with its own bar and optics, and out to a circular pool. The piped music was that old but deathless favourite 'Tijuana Taxi'.

There were about forty guests, a handful swimming, the rest sitting or standing round the pool with their drinks. A long table, laid out with buffet food, adjoined a large and elaborate barbecue. Behind the barbecue, in red Bermuda shorts and a vari-hued T-shirt, stood a tallish, well-built man with trimly cut grey hair, strong features and horn-rimmed glasses. He was paunchy but powerful-looking. He was grilling steaks and chicken thighs, while chatting to a handful of guests standing nearby.

The party was in full swing now and our arrival caused little or no stir, except among a handful of women standing to the left of the pool. They gave Crystal friendly waves, but one of them smiled in a way that held a definite hint of scorn.

As we took our drinks from the tray Charlie proffered, I said, 'The man at the barbecue – Ray Challis?'

'Right on, love. And those are some of the boys' wives. The one who looks as if she's been sucking a lemon is Cecily Challis. Little Miss frigging West Yorkshire Nineteen Seventy-six. She's loving this, you know, Maurice going walkabout. Well, she wants to keep all her fingers crossed it never happens to her, because Ray's got a wandering dick, just like Maurice. Come on, I'll introduce you to him.'

We skirted the pool's curve to where the burly man stood deftly flipping the grilling cuts of meat. 'Hello, Ray love – looks like a nice do.'

'Crystal . . . darling.' He put down his long-handled fork and turned to kiss her warmly, perhaps a shade too warmly, even if they were close friends. I caught a glimpse of Cecily across the pool, who now smirkless looked coldly on. 'No news of Maurice?' Challis added, in a low, concerned tone.

'Not yet. It can't go on, Ray,' she said, in a voice that held a note of accusation. 'I need to know what he's up to, where I stand. You know. . . .'

'Of course you do, pet. I've not heard a word from him either. Or the boys.'

She didn't believe him and neither did I, even though he had the look of a man whose word, in any other circumstances, I'd have had no misgivings about accepting.

'This is John Goss, Ray, I rang you about him.'

His eyes rested steadily on mine, then he gave me a large strong hand. 'Pleased to meet you, John. I believe I know the name. Didn't you sort out that spot of fraudulent conversion for Rodney Greaves?'

I nodded. The glasses and the portly figure gave him an appearance of slight benignity, but the eyes were shrewd. I knew the type well. A go-getter, hard-working, hard-driving, corner-cutting, tough but usually fair. I realized disconsolately that if he did know anything of Durkin's whereabouts, Durkin would be able to sleep with an easy mind. 'I'll catch you later, John,' he said, in a friendly, almost confiding voice. 'I'll do anything I can to help Crystal sort it out . . . we all go back a long way. In the meantime, please help yourself to the buffet and drinks.'

Crystal led me away. '*Are* you hungry, love?'

'Very. I've had a single sandwich all day.'

'I'll sort you out a nice steak. I'll eat later, when I've had a couple.'

If she remembered. She forked a steak from a warmer on to a paper plate for me, added a roast potato, some mixed salad and a crusty baguette. I was ravenous, and it seemed sensible to eat now and then concentrate on the job in hand.

'See you later then, Johnny,' Crystal said, walking purposefully off towards the group of wives. I sat down alone at a small white-painted table. A couple of minutes later, a woman holding a plate and glass stopped at my side. 'Mind if I join you?'

'Please do.'

She was a smallish, rather fine-boned woman with soft, wispy fair hair, a slightly sallow complexion and dark-blue eyes. She wore a white, short-sleeved silk blouse and a pale-blue cotton skirt. She smiled. 'I doubt the others will want to eat for another half-hour or so, and I get so hungry. . . .'

I also smiled. 'My problem too.'

'I'm Guinevere, by the way.'

'John Goss. How do you do.'

'And you're a friend of Crystal's?'

'A . . . friend of both the Durkins. I used to do a bit of business with him. I happened to be in the area and she invited me along.'

'I rather thought she was lying low. What do you make of his disappearance?'

'I really don't know what to think. It's difficult for me to take a view when I knew him mainly in a business sense.'

'Perhaps he couldn't face another summer of poolside parties.'

There was a note of contempt in her voice. She gazed impassively over the circle of glittering water in which bathers splashed and shrieked with laughter, raucously encouraged by the people round the side, as coloured lanterns in the ornamental trees began to light up against the darkening sky.

'I gather pool parties aren't much to your taste.'

'Nor to yours, I fancy. Sitting alone, actually eating at this unfashionable hour. Can he be a kindred spirit, I asked myself.'

I chuckled, and we ate for a while in silence. 'Have *you* any views,' I said, 'about Maurice's disappearance?'

'As a matter of fact, yes. I think he's gone off somewhere to think things through.'

I glanced at her; she seemed a shrewd one. 'About leaving Crystal,' I said warily, 'for someone else perhaps?'

'Oh ... that.' She gave what seemed to be a resigned shrug. 'Affairs are part of the country with these people. But with Maurice I think there's more involved than another woman.'

She gave a brooding glance to a group of men huddled together across the pool. I wondered if she was married to one of Durkin's friends. She spoke well and seemed as somehow out of it as I was myself. None of the women drifting past our table, clinking with jewellery, paid her much attention. She pushed away her empty plate, sipped a little wine.

'What do you think he's up to then,' I said, with the same chatty wariness, 'if it's not another woman?'

She gave the sort of Mona Lisa smile that sometimes means a woman has the inside track, and just as often means she's pissing you about. 'So you can tell Crystal?'

I shrugged. 'My only interest is idle curiosity.'

'Whatever happens he'll leave old airhead Crystal well-provided for.'

'I rather think she'd make sure of that.'

'He would anyway. He knows he couldn't have built up the Crystalmarts without her. But apart from that he's quite incapable of a mean action,' she said firmly. 'We *all* owe him. If he'd not given Chris so much help we'd not have a great big house and a great big pool of our very own.'

Her voice held a curious mixture of gratitude and bitterness. She'd be the accountant's wife. Perhaps she liked the affluence, loathed the lifestyle. We weren't really getting to why she thought Durkin had split. She gave me another of her Giaconda smiles. 'I used to think Maurice was the same as all the others,' she said, almost tenderly. 'Interested in nothing but business. It was only when he sold out, had time to spare. . . .' She glanced at the pool, empty of bathers, and now glass-like and lit by submerged lamps. 'Not long after he sold out he came to a party at our house. At the height of the fun he went missing. I tend to go discreetly missing myself till they've all reeled home.' She was making no attempt now to hide her distaste. 'I found him in my little study, reading *Far from the Madding Crowd*. He'd never had time to read before, he'd always been too busy, and he'd not had much schooling. After that I threw my bookshelves open to him. He seemed to swallow books whole, up in his own study when Crystal thought he was working on his portfolio. I think he began to change from the day he first read Hardy, though it might be more accurate to say he began to find himself at last.'

She became silent for a moment. Across the pool I saw Crystal hook up yet another glass of champagne from Charlie's tray. There seemed to be a coiled and aggressive stance to her body, and she was talking to, or at, Cecily Challis, who still seemed to be smirking.

'One day, Maurice told me he had this recurrent dream. That he was back at school completing his education. He would be in a classroom in one of his business suits among fifteen-year-olds. Very Dennis Potter. He said every time he had the dream he'd wake up with a depression that lasted half the day.' Our eyes met. 'You asked me what I thought he was up to: I think he wants to remake himself.'

'Into what?'

'I believe that's what he's thinking through, wherever he is.'

I suspected she knew. I wondered if she was yet another of Durkin's women. 'Anyway,' she said, almost dreamily, 'that's what *I* think he'll be doing, in some hotel – contemplating his renaissance.'

I nodded sympathetically. It all sounded very worthy, but I could have told her there was a Sloaney in London who could out-bimbo Crystal, who now seemed to have been displaced by a lady in the lakes called Veronica.

'Oh dear,' she said, 'there seems to be some sort of upset with Crystal and her chums.'

Crystal and the wives were moving unsteadily in the direction of the buffet table. One of them seemed to be trying to calm Crystal down, two others walked protectively with Cecily.

'Bitch!' we heard Crystal hiss, as they came into earshot. 'You're bloody loving it, aren't you? Well, if you can't say anything help-ful you want to keep your big flapping mouth *shut!*'

'Will you tell her I don't know what she's on about?' Cecily said to her minders, as if Crystal herself was at the other end of a phone line. 'Will you tell her I can't think of anything I've said that could possibly cause offence?'

'It's not what you frigging say, it's the way you say it. And that bloody face you pull, as if you've just seen your big fat arse.'

The women were now near the barbecue range, where Challis stood talking, his cooking completed. Cecily said, 'Will you please tell her I'll not be insulted in my own place?'

'Your own *place* . . . you'd not have a place like this if it hadn't been for Maurice baling Ray out. You weren't smirking then, were you, and you weren't smirking when Maurice ditched you for me twenty-odd years ago.'

'Oh! Will you tell her to find her toy-boy and get *out!*'

Challis looked on impassively; he had to have heard. He seemed to be one controlled man. I could see no sign in his body language of how this really affected him, and I knew them all. '*Girls* . . . *girls*,' he said, with a wide smile, 'this is supposed to be fun night.' He put a fatherly arm around each. 'We can't have this. Now come along, kiss and make up. You know Crystal's under a strain, Cess.'

'Will you *please* tell her I'll not be insulted like this, Ray, at my own poolside in front of *guests*!'

Cecily was another maturing beauty. She wore a dark-green crinkle-effect dress and had dark, glossy hair, pale-green eyes and a soft wide mouth. Like Crystal her figure was thickening but in good shape. 'Look, Cess,' Challis said, in the same gentle tone, 'you know Crystal wouldn't fly off the handle if she wasn't so worried about Maurice.'

'Will you please tell her I don't know where her bloody husband is? He's never been interested in *me* since she got her hooks into him. It's not the first time he's done a runner. Can you blame him, having to get in bed with her every night?'

'I'll knock you in that pool in a minute. You *know* where he is. You *all* know where he is.' Crystal's furious gaze passed from the Challises to the group of men across the sheet of water, whom I took to be the close friends, out of earshot and still huddled in conversation. 'Well, *he'll* find him, he's the best in town, and when he does I'll not forget what marvellous sodding friends you all turned out to be.'

SIX

'I think I'd give that a seven,' Guinevere said, with a chuckle, 'on a scale of one to ten. Yes, definitely a seven.'

The fracas was over, the warring women now sitting sulkily with their friends again. Burly Challis had seemed to absorb the ill-feeling into himself, like an air-conditioner drawing off heat.

'That wasn't unusual?'

'God, no, not with that lot. They get off on it. I'd say that stuff about Maurice baling Ray out was off limits though, even for Crystal. But Ray takes it all so nobly. He's a very guarded man.'

I could only dismally agree. I wondered if he was guarding Durkin with the same care.

'They're like schoolkids,' she said, 'the *arrivistes*. The primal instincts of the playground still apply.' She sipped from a second glass of wine. 'But who am I to talk? I'm an *arriviste* myself now.'

That earlier discontent. Both the voice and manner seemed to hint at a former background of discreet dinner parties, of afternoon tea on lawns not gouged out to sink swimming-pools.

'It all comes back to Maurice,' she said softly. 'Unless you really knew him you'd not understand. Low-interest loans to get them all started; pace-setting, with his house and cars and servants; such a generous man with his money and time. I sometimes wish he'd not been quite so generous.' There was a hint of sadness in her tone. 'It's been a lot of fun for the men, but it's tended to leave the women staring into space in our state of the art kitchens.'

'But now you're convinced he's planning a new life.'

She smiled. 'Delicious, isn't it? How will they cope without him? Ship without a compass.' She rose to her feet. 'And now even I must circulate.' She gave a faint shudder. 'I've enjoyed talking to you. You have the sort of face that invites confidences. Sympathetic but discreet.'

I also smiled. Trouble was, she'd not confided half enough.

'By the way, I have my own ideas why you're with Crystal, and I'm positive it's nothing to do with being a toy-boy,' she said, and with one final cryptic glance she walked off to mingle.

A strong hand clamped my shoulder. 'John,' Challis said, 'now you've eaten, let's talk. I'd like you to meet Maurice's friends. The close ones. The other people here are mainly business contacts.'

I got up. 'I was hoping to catch you all together.'

He led me beyond the circle of water to the end of the paved area, where a wall with an openwork pattern of ornamental stone gave the usual remarkable views of the valley's opposite slopes, where house lights now flickered beneath a clear sky in which shone a sliver of moon.

Here, beneath a cherry tree set into a square of soil between paving stones and hung with coloured lanterns like exotic tropical fruit, was another round table, at which sat the five men who, with Challis, made up Durkin's inner circle.

Challis said, 'This is John Goss, boys, the private investigator Crystal's hired to try and find Maurice. This is Chris Denholm, John, Bill Ackroyd, Joe Speight, Sean Doherty, Tony Ferrara. . . .'

Tony Ferrara. The man at the Grantley Hall Hotel Vicky and I had both had in our sights. I felt unpleasantly surprised that anyone, even this raunchy bunch, could regard a slimeball like Ferrara as a friend.

But I gave him exactly the same cordial glance I gave the others, as my trained memory fixed each face to its name. The men nodded in turn, though not extending hands, and gave me brief wary smiles. The wariness wasn't unusual, people tended to be as watchful of PIs as they were of plainclothes policemen. But it could mean they were anxious not to let anything slip, assuming they had anything to let slip.

They were now being served plates of food and glasses of wine by Charlie, and I had a chance to study them as this went on. I became convinced that some of them were uneasy, not just wary, especially the two professional men, Denholm and Ackroyd. Denholm was slender, with sleek brown hair and sharp-edged rather delicate features, and was dressed in a stone-coloured linen suit. Ackroyd had coarse, untidy fair hair, blue eyes and reddish cheeks, and wore spectacles that had come to be known as granny glasses. He had a studious, almost donnish look, an impression enhanced by the crumpled, if expensive, safari-style shirt and grubby white chinos.

The other troubled-looking man was Ferrara, the second-generation Italian woman-molester. There was none of the confident charm about him tonight I'd seen at the Grantley Hall. His hairy body was concealed in a new white cashmere turtleneck and black silky-looking pants. The usual gold bracelets spangled his wrists, but there seemed to be a faint but definite film of perspiration on the pale face beneath the thick, black, curly hair.

The other men were more relaxed, with Challis totally at ease. 'Look, John,' he said, in his quiet, confiding voice, 'we'll do anything in our power to help. We know it's bugging Crystal, well, you saw the way she flew off the handle just then.'

'Ah, sure, he'll be back, your man. He's done it before, for the love of God. Faith, I can't see why Crystal started all this, John, no disrespect to yourself. If he's taken off he'll sort the money out for her, and that's what she's really worried about, she's had enough boyfriends of her own.'

It was Sean Doherty, probably third generation Irish, yet talking as if he'd just landed. He was as dark and pale as Ferrara and yet, with his green eyes, thick eyebrows and smooth round face, there was a set to his features, impossible to define, that could only be Celtic. He wore a green silk shirt, modern and collarless, a white linen waistcoat and white pants.

'The last time he went missing it was for less than a fortnight,' I pointed out.

'But he had the Crystalmarts then, so he did. He *had* to get back in good time then because the business wouldn't run without him. But he's his own man now, he'll not be after having the same pressure on him.'

Challis, at my side, had paused in his eating, and was watching Doherty steadily. It could mean anything or nothing. He drank a little of his red wine appreciatively and said, 'We'll lay our cards on the table, John, we'll not piss you about. Maurice likes the gals and Crystal's possessive, even though she likes her own bits on the side. So we tend to be secretive about him in front of her.' He glanced at the others in an unhurried circular motion of his large grey head. 'Apart from that we're in two minds about Maurice skipping. We don't like to see Crystal upset, but if he wants to leave her we don't want to interfere. You see, we all owe him, every manjack of us. He's one very special guy; we love him like a brother. And the bottom line is we want for Maurice what he wants for himself.'

He had a way with words, which seemed to be why he did the talking, and the sense was clear – if they did know where he was they weren't keen to let on. But if I couldn't get a lead out of them it meant going back to Cumbria and needles in haystacks, assuming he was still in the haystack. I thought fast.

'I hear what you're saying, Ray,' I said carefully, 'and I understand. Let me put it this way, if one of you *could* give me a lead, and it helped me find him, I can give you my word he'll never know where the information came from.'

Challis put down his fork and sat back with a relieved expression. 'Well,' he said, 'now you're talking our language. Right, boys? That's what was bugging us. We didn't want old Maurice thinking any of his pals had put the finger on him.'

'He won't, I can guarantee it. Look, Crystal's main worry is the financial side. I'm hired to find him and tell him that. Once I've done it I tell Crystal where he is. If,' I added delicately, 'he decided to move on again, there's nothing I can do, is there?'

It was twaddle, but I had to meet cunning with cunning, and perhaps they really did love him like a brother.

'Well, that really puts our minds at rest. You have a very professional approach, John,' Challis said, glancing at the others again in that benign but watchful way. They didn't look like men who'd had their minds put at rest; in fact, the unease seemed stronger, as if it was transmitting itself to them all. The silence at our table was enhanced by the cheerful talk and laughter elsewhere. It seemed to be a silence that held a warning, inexplicable but powerful, that reminded me of the tocsin ring of rigging which had tapped against masts at Bowness.

'Very well, John, how can we help you?'

'I gather you were the last people to see him. You met once a month in London. Would you mind telling me why?'

'Officially, business: unofficially, a lads' night out,' the man called Joe Speight growled. He too was a heavy and strongly built man, dressed in the usual costly leisure-wear – cotton shirt, mohair sweater and denims. He had auburn hair turning pepper and salt, pale-blue eyes, a bulbous nose and thick, red lips. He had the short-fused look of a man who'd kicked many a backside in his time.

'Business?'

'Just business. We all have contacts up there.'

'It was convenient to set aside one day a month, John, when we could all do our bits of business and then meet up.'

Sukie had felt there was more to it than that, that they were there for some joint venture, but if that was so they weren't saying. I wondered why.

'We'd have dinner at the Café Royal, John,' Challis said. His confiding tone hinted he was slipping me a choice nugget of information. He touched his nose. 'Not a word to the girls.'

'And ... you were there the night he disappeared?' I said cautiously.

'We were.'

'And after dinner, what then?'

'We went on the town. Annabel's wasn't it, Sean? Maurice went off on his own. He ... well, he had a girlfriend. We saw him into a cab in Upper Regent and....' He shrugged. 'We've not seen him since.'

'This girlfriend. Would you have an address?'

'We haven't even a name. Maurice was a bit possessive.'

'He had to be with you, you crafty old bugger,' Doherty said. 'I tell you, John, Ray was always trying to poach Maurice's girls. He'd tell them Maurice worked for *him*, and then what are they after doing – they swap Maurice for Ray!'

There was a ripple of decidedly forced laughter. Challis shrugged with a little sheepish smile, that didn't quite reach the eyes that rested steadily once more on Doherty. 'Maurice played the same trick on me,' he said, 'many times.' He glanced at one of those oddly cheap-looking metallic watches that rarely cost less than six thousand. 'John, I'm sorry to rush you, but we've got a whole raft of people we need to talk to before the night's out.'

Which meant they were going to tell me nothing that would help me find him. What they *had* told me was that they were involved in a cover-up. They said they'd eaten with him, the maitre d' said Maurice had dined alone.

'Don't neglect your guests, Ray,' I said agreeably. 'Would each of you be kind enough to think about that last time you saw Maurice? Did he say *anything* that might give me a lead, however trivial or unimportant it seemed? If you'll do that for me I'll be in touch with each of you over the next twenty-four hours.'

They didn't like that. They didn't like it one bit. The uneasiness seemed to increase as palpably as a change in temperature. It said it all – only Challis did the talking. 'You know, John, I think I can save you legwork,' he said, bang on cue. 'Tell you what, I'll get the boys to drop by here tomorrow night and we'll have a bit of a brainstorming session. If anything comes up, I'll ring you.'

'That could be helpful,' I said, with careful ambiguity. 'And thanks for your time this evening.'

'We'd like to get the thing sorted, one way or the other.'

I got up. There was a sense of relaxation and relief. Hands reached for wine-glasses over neglected plates. 'Oh, by the way,' I said casually, 'the lady dancing with the tall man in the plaid trousers . . . I feel I know the face. Would I be right in thinking her name's Veronica?'

The word produced a silence so intense, in the murmur of small talk among them, that I might have switched off a radio. I'd even wrongfooted the nimble Challis. Two or three seconds passed with them sitting like men in a science fiction film in which time stood still.

'I think you must have a crossed line there, John,' Challis finally managed to say. 'I had to give my own memory a bit of a jog, I only see her now and then. That's Dottie Spencer, wife of one of Sean's suppliers. Right, Sean? There's no one called Veronica here tonight.'

But Ferrara's hand was trembling as he put down his glass, and the others remained motionless, their faces stained with the differing primary colours of the lanterns above their heads, a sight that now seemed peculiarly sinister. 'My mistake,' I said breezily. 'Well, I'll be in touch.'

I walked round the pool to sit with Crystal, who was now alone. The other wives had joined those guests who'd begun dancing in the patio area to old chart-toppers.

'Park your bum here, Johnny,' she said with her usual delicacy, thumping the chair at her side. 'And tell me what you've screwed out of those sods,'

She'd had a lot to drink, but could handle it. She seemed quite unscathed by the emotional scene she'd had with Challis's wife.

'Nothing that'll help.'

'I knew you wouldn't. Not about their precious Maurice. God, you'd think he belonged to *them*, not me.'

Drunk or sober, she could get it together. They'd lied about the Café Royal and they knew who Veronica was. I was certain I'd learn nothing more until I could get them away from Challis, each of them.

The night was into overdrive now, the patio almost filled with lurching bodies, the air throbbing with the heavy beat of the disco music, shrieks of laughter and men singing out of tune. The still pool lay like a great gleaming gemstone, as if symbolizing the dreams and triumphs of men who'd done it their way. Beyond it, the friends of Durkin were still huddled together and standing near the water. From eye-corners I could see Tony Ferrara gesturing again and again in my direction.

'Drink up, love, you're a long way behind,' she said, with the peculiarly sexy lisp alcohol induces in some women. 'What were you talking to toffee-nose Guinevere about?'

'Oh, just about Maurice,' I said casually. 'She was concerned about him for your sake.'

'Can't get that one together.' She glanced balefully to where Guinevere sat, alone and clearly bored. 'Her and Maurice were always *talking*. Couldn't understand it, because Maurice doesn't go in for much talking, not with women anyway, not when he has his mind set on a bit of the other, don't I know. He once went missing at her place, and I thought I'd catch him at it, but he was just sat talking with Queen Tut. I keep thinking he's been a bit different lately and I can't help wondering if it's anything to do with her. Stuck-up bitch. Just because her family once made a few bob in the wool trade. Not real money, like me and Maurice, but talk about side. Here, Charlie, get Mr Goss a G and T, cock. A big one.'

'Right you are, Mrs D,' Charlie said, bowing deeply.

It was ironical. Most women married to a Jack the Lad would have been relieved to find him alone with a woman simply talking.

But that wasn't what the men in Crystal's circle did, and it disturbed her much more than finding him with a pair of bare legs round his neck. I was beginning to realize she was a lot sharper than I'd first given her credit for.

Suddenly, there was a great crash of water.

'Oh, God!' Crystal said. 'Do they *ever* stop acting the giddy goat, that lot.'

Tony Ferrara slowly surfaced in the pool, glittering rings of disturbance expanding from his body, thick black hair plastered to his skull, his beautiful clothes ruined. Water up to his chest, he stood staring in silence at the five men on the poolside. Then his lips began to move, but the words couldn't be caught from where we sat because of the music.

'Oh, come on, Tony, it was only a joke,' Challis shouted, as if wanting to be heard. 'You know what the mad Irishman's like when you get him going.' He directed his benign smile in the direction of the patio, where a number of the dancers had stopped mid-lurch to watch the fun.

'Sure, I'll be after buying you a new rig-out,' Doherty called down. 'I get carried away, you know me . . . come on, old son.'

But the smile looked forced, as if got up for the onlookers, and couldn't quite conceal a coldness. As did the smiles of the others.

SEVEN

'Come in, John.' She wore a pale-green summer dress, calf-length and with a scooped neckline. But when she turned to take me inside I saw that the reverse of the dress had a laced slit through which I could see her smooth, lean back. That mixture of the rather demure and the decidedly sexy was very much to my taste. It was nice to see her long tawny hair again too and the triangular top lip that never quite met the bottom one over the gap in her front teeth.

'G and T?'

'Please.'

The bottles, mixers and glasses were already in place on a side table. Towards the rear of the room the small dining-table was also prepared, with place-mats, napkins and cutlery; there was no separate dining-room. One main room and kitchen downstairs, probably two rooms and bathroom up – it was tiny but I felt at ease here after the great gaudy houses on the valley slopes, after Crystal and Co.

She handed me my glass with a smile. 'Good health.'

'Likewise. And thanks again for the invite.'

'How was your day?'

'Best forgotten,' I said. 'How about yours?'

'Let's ban shop talk, shall we?'

There was nothing I'd rather do; it would get my mind off the Durkin case, which was getting heavily obsessive.

'I've seen Vicky a couple of times, by the way.'

'She rang me. I'm very grateful. The sooner she's out of that frightful Girl Talk the better, as far as I'm concerned.'

'I took her on what you might call a field trip. She did very well. I'm trying her out on the office side now, see how she copes.'

'I'm so pleased. I'm afraid she can be rather trying at times, rather abrasive,' she said warily, as if guessing I'd already found out. 'And I'm afraid she often gives an impression of not having much to learn. But at bottom . . . she can be very uncertain and insecure. It's a lot to do with her father remarrying, with feeling rejected.'

It was all I needed with a case like Durkin to headbang my way through, a dysfunctional apprentice. 'She's a bright kid,' I said truthfully. 'If PI work's what she wants she should do well.'

'Thanks again, John,' she said, with a warm smile.

She poured me another drink as the sun slanted over the small enclosed garden beyond the lattice window, and then we sat down to a starter of melon, eaten with some chilled Anjou rosé. With Vicky now sidelined, we lost ourselves luxuriously in the sort of talk we'd had the night we met – books, films, current affairs – and we were hungrier for it than the food we ate, as singles often are. She finally glanced at her watch with that endearing shock of surprise I remembered, and went off to the kitchen for the next course.

I smiled, sipped some wine. What a riveting contrast to the expensive glamour I'd known on the hillside, and those strident, jewelled women who drank too much and had too much time to spare. It seemed like the corniest of morality tales, the rich women on the hill not appearing to enjoy life as much as their poorer sisters in the valley, yet Guinevere had hinted at the emptiness of their lives.

And Louise did seem to have the better deal, with her work and her hobbies and her modest outings. She was focused, you sensed a life under control. She had a quality of calmness I found irresistible at this stage of my life, following the trauma of the Laura

Marsh case. She was like a friendly nurse, skilful at dressing wounds.

The main course was omelette with a ham and mushroom filling, served with sauté potatoes and a mixed salad. Then there was a little Camembert and some fruit.

'All rather simple,' she said.

'Perfect for a summer evening,' I said. 'I hope you'll let me return the hospitality – that's if you dare risk my cooking.'

'I'd love to, and I suspect you'll be rather good in a kitchen.' Her smiling eyes lingered on mine. Another hour rapidly eclipsed itself as darkness filtered across a clear sky. And then, in a rare moment of companiable silence, she said, 'Can I speak plainly, John?'

'That sounds faintly ominous. . . .'

She shook her head. 'I find that a few cards laid on the table as soon as possible can save an awful lot of embarrassment later on. I'm . . . talking about the possibility of you staying the night. . . .'

She hesitated, and I sensed a nervousness in this calm woman for the first time. She moistened her top lip with the tip of her tongue. I didn't speak, having always found it best not to when I was uncertain what was being implied. 'You see,' she went on, 'if you'd *like* to stay the night I'd like that too. But if it's not what you had in mind then I'd still like to see you for a meal or a drink. The . . . the important thing is to sort it out before there are any misunderstandings.'

I began to smile. 'That was a masterpiece of tact. And yes, I'd love to stay the night. And I'd like to go on having the meals and drinks as well. The full card, in fact.'

She smiled too, on the gap in her teeth, and I sensed a feeling of relief that hinted that the self-possession, assured as it seemed, might be a veneer. And at this point I think it was less the idea of lovemaking than the simple fact that I wanted to stay with her that counted. I wondered if I detected in her something of the same vulnerability it was impossible to miss in her daughter, and was perhaps due to similar feelings of rejection by the man who'd once been at the centre of their lives, but in Louise skilfully concealed by intelligent maturity.

'There is a little more,' she said, with obvious reluctance, touching her lip with her tongue again. 'I feel I ought to point out that I'm not really looking for a partner, or a live-in lover, or whatever the jargon is, but . . . but more a sort of. . . .' She found it difficult to define the appropriate degree of closeness.

'Loving friendship?' I offered tentatively.

She nodded, again relieved. 'I do hope you don't mind all this frankness, but . . . simply so we both know where we stand . . . John. . . .'

Again I seemed to see Vicky, an older Vicky with the jagged edges almost perfectly smoothed off. There was a gentle doggedness in her determination to say what she felt must be said, a dissembled clarity in her unwillingness to accept any favours, and yet behind it an unmistakable impression of a kind of longing to replace something of what she'd once known.

'Louise,' I said softly, 'I very much appreciate the frankness. To be honest, as you probably know from Vicky, my own lifestyle rather precludes living with anyone. I'd like a no-ties friendship with you very much.'

'Then that's settled,' she said sitting back, as relaxed once more as she'd been earlier in the evening. Her smile widened. 'The thing is, much as I'm used to being on my own, I do love company, a meal, a glass of wine. I'm rather fond of sex, too. . . .'

'Well, according to Henry Miller sex is one of the nine reasons for reincarnation.'

'What are the others?'

'He said they were unimportant.'

She began to giggle. 'I walked into that, didn't I?'

And so we stacked the dishes in her little washer and went up to the bedroom, which was white and airy and smelt of clean linen. We had a nice time. We both tried to be generous lovers, were both grateful, I think, to have found a partner willing not to encroach too oppressively on the ways of life we'd had to devise for ourselves. My last relationship had been so traumatic that I'd been celibate for six months, and I'd almost forgotten, or deliberately blocked out, the intense pleasure of running a hand over a breast or the curve of a hip or the baby-skin of an inner thigh, to feel fingers that delicately touched and guided, to hear those soft explosions of breath in the silent darkness.

But later, she had whispered, her voice seeming to come from a distance, 'Do you think it might run?'

'I'd like to think so.'

I detected a hopeful note. Her arms had seemed to tighten around me almost reluctantly, as if she wanted to give, but was wary about the amount she should give, as if she'd once given so much as to leave herself defenceless.

And somehow I felt that if we went ahead, became an item, I'd not really be able to regard it as the semi-detached relationship she'd been so careful to stress was what she wanted. I could sense a yearning for a little more than that, could foresee a closeness developing between us almost of its own volition, the special closeness of the walking wounded, skilled in providing a particular type of sympathetic comfort.

I wondered if I minded. Decided almost immediately that I didn't. Because I knew that if I didn't think I could accept what the relationship might become it would be better to end it now. But I felt I could. I certainly wanted to.

Shortly after, she fell asleep. Contentedly, I hoped. Me, I never slept well at the best of times, and with Durkin on my mind. . . .

They'd fished Ferrara from the pool, kitted him out with some of Challis's clothes, which had hung from him, and he'd abruptly left. Had they hurled him in the pool because he had something on his mind he wanted to get off? He went to the top of my list.

The party broke up soon after, and I went back with Crystal to pick up my own car, the Rolls now driven by Neil, more or less correctly dressed, down to shoes instead of trainers. But Crystal had other ideas, about me transferring from her car to mine. Murmuring, 'Nightcap, Johnny. My room, it's got its own bar,' she yanked me into the house and up in the lift to a vast bedroom with mirror-panelling, sheepskin rugs, a chandelier and a king-size bed.

I was tempted, she was a very attractive woman. She wanted to pour me a drink from a cocktail cabinet embedded in the wall, but I was genuinely thirsty, and craved spring water. It wasn't something she found much use for, but she directed me to the fridge in Durkin's study, which was beyond a connecting dressing-room. 'Take your time, eh, chuck, and I'll be making myself comfy.'

The study had everything: a large rosewood desk, a personal computer, a fax, a television, a wall-safe and the fridge itself. I wondered how Durkin could bear to leave this remarkable nerve-centre unattended for so long, wondered if he fretted for it, when he'd spent so many mornings here, working on his equities. She must be quite something, this Veronica, perhaps brains as well as beauty to help him shape this supposed new life.

I tried the safe, but it was locked, of course. I wondered if its contents would give any clue as to where he'd be. I helped myself to sparkling water from the fridge, my mind slowly filling with thoughts of Crystal's sumptuous curves. She was clearly not going to let me go without a determined struggle so I might as well give in gracefully.

But when I returned to the film-set bedroom she lay on her back on the great bed in a short rose-coloured nightdress, one leg crossed over the other, her arms spread as if waiting to clamp some-one to her. Fast asleep.

So that was it. I went down in the lift, but this time no one waited in the hall. I wondered if the staff had gone to bed; I needed my car-keys. Would Brian be assuming that if I was in madam's bedroom I'd be there all night?

I opened a door off the hall I'd seen staff use, entered a short corridor, lit by dimmed wall-lamps. A door to my left stood ajar. I heard Brian's voice, and he was on the phone.

'Yes, Mr Challis . . . I understand . . . No, sir, nothing . . . Yes, he did, but I bore our conversation in mind . . . Yes, sir, absolutely . . . Well, thank you, sir, but there's really no need . . . Yes, sir, very good . . . Yes, he is. . . .' Brian chuckled. 'Yes, you're right . . . I understand . . . Yes, and goodnight to you, sir.'

The phone went down. I tiptoed back to the hall door, opened and shut it noisily, and called. 'Hello . . . hello?' Brian slowly emerged, face pale and glistening, hand trembling on a whisky glass.

'Ah, Brian,' I said, in a friendly tone, 'I'm glad I found you. I need my car.'

'Ye-yes, sir, of course. I'll get your keys.' His lips also trembled; he'd been badly thrown. Because he was in it too, as I'd half-suspected. He'd been telling Challis he'd told me nothing, had confirmed that I was upstairs with madam, and been promised a backhander for keeping his mouth shut.

I could have gone for the jugular with what I'd picked up, could have wrung out of him what he knew. I had nothing to learn about scaring the shit out of the Brians of life. But when I'd gone he'd only be back on the line to Challis. And I didn't want Challis to know I knew they were all covering for Durkin. Not yet.

He led me silently out to the garages. 'I'm getting nowhere, Brian,' I told him. 'None of Mr Durkin's friends seem to have the remotest idea where he could be. It makes things very difficult.'

'I'm sorry to hear that, sir.' Our eyes met beneath the garage lights. There seemed a gleam of relief in his, combined with the usual sneering pleasure he tended to take in seeing me at a disadvantage.

I drove down into the valley, thinking of the treat I'd missed. Poor Crystal. She should have learnt by now that it was fatal at her age to close your eyes when you'd had a few. Even for a second.

*

I smiled in the darkness. I'd missed out on Crystal, but I'd been rewarded with Louise, whose invitation had been waiting on my answerphone when I'd got back from Durkin's place. She slept quietly at my side: I wished I could.

This morning, all Durkin's friends except Joe Speight were 'out of town' when I rang. And he said he was too busy to see me. Tongue in cheek, I told him he either saw me or he saw the police, as Durkin was now a police matter and I was working with them. It worked.

He owned a gigantic furniture warehouse on the city boundary. It was like a hangar and you walked through a maze of linking units arranged to resemble living-rooms, kitchens, bedrooms and bathrooms. He stood belligerently at its centre, surrounded by minions.

'Take him in the office, Roland. I'll see you when I'm free, Goss, I've got a business to run. Ray Challis said we'd meet with him and he'd tell you if we came up with anything.'

'That was his idea, not mine.'

Flushed, angry and decidedly worried, he strode off, and a cowed young man led me to an office suite at the centre of the maze. Women input VDUs in an outer office, and I was taken to an inner one, furnished as lavishly as Durkin's at Maunan. A woman sat at a circular glass-topped table in a corner of the room. 'Sit down here, love. Remember me from Ray's barbie? I'm Joe's wife – Dora.'

'Hello again, Dora.'

She wore a silver-grey silky trouser suit, and she, too, must have been very pretty when young. She had an olive complexion with short dark hair, dark eyes and an oddly babyish nose, which must once have been very appealing but would one day look faintly grotesque as it didn't seem to be ageing in line with her other features. She'd smiled warmly in greeting, but her face had then relapsed into the expression of discontent I was beginning to associate with most of the wives in the Durkin circle.

'I'm a director,' she told me. 'I help Joe with the confidential stuff now and then. A little bird tells me you're a detective.'

'Mr Durkin,' I admitted. 'I'm trying to find him.'

'I wish he'd run away fifteen years ago and never come back.'

'That sounds as if you don't like him very much.'

'Like him! We don't just *like* him, we all love him. The way he looks at you, the way he *talks* – God, gift of the gab isn't in it. He has the boys mesmerized. Have some coffee. . . .' She poured me a fragrant cup from an automatic percolator. 'He can talk anyone into anything, and that's the trouble. He'd not be riddled with ulcers, would he, that poor devil out there, and blood pressure.' She glanced at a clutch of closed-circuit screens where Speight could be seen striding about his little empire with his band of salesmen, waving his arms. Her eyes became heavy. 'It's all down to Maurice. He was a manager at the Co-op once, Joe, furniture department. We were doing quite well. We'd go to the Fleece on Saturdays and if we'd got a bit of money to the front we'd have a nice meal at the Ring O' Bells. But then Maurice talks him into setting up on his own, lends him a fistful of money. We've got everything we want now, and I wish he was back at the Co-op because none of it'll mean anything when the poor sod's killed himself trying to keep up with Maurice.'

I'd rarely heard words spoken with such sadness. Her unhappy eyes met mine again. 'If they know where he is, John, they'll never let on. I sometimes think they care more about Maurice than about us. Without him they'd none of them be where they are now, you see.'

'Ray Challis did admit they loved him like a brother.'

'Known him all their lives, apart from Chris and Bill. They played five-a-side in Clifford Park as lads.' She glanced through the half-glazed panel to the outer office. 'Here comes Joe now. Try not to upset him, love, he's been under a lot of stress lately.'

As she went out, he came plunging in. Sweating, glowering, and, without Challis to hold his hand, even more uneasy. I wondered if the stress he was under lately was due to his business or Maurice Durkin.

'Get on with it,' he said curtly. It was difficult to associate this red-faced bully with the nice man from the Co-op who'd enjoyed a few jars at the local.

'*Have* you given a little thought to the last time you were with Maurice,' I said, curtly polite, 'and what he was talking about?'

'Yes. I heard nothing useful. I wasn't sitting next to him.'

'Ah. Who were?'

His flush deepened frighteningly. He couldn't handle the lies like Challis. 'Ray and . . . Sean . . . I think.'

'I can check that out with the others.'

His forehead began to bead with sweat. 'I can't be certain,' he said hastily. 'It was *usually* Ray and Sean.'

It was difficult deciding who'd sat where at a dinner that never took place. I'd wrongfooted him. I went on fast. 'You and Maurice go back, I believe.'

'So what?'

'It means a long, close friendship in my book.'

'So?'

'If you're so close I think you'll know where Maurice is. I think he'll have told you.'

'Well, he didn't. Can I get back to running this place now?'

'All right, tell me *why* he's gone.'

'It's his bleeding life, mister.'

'Come on, it's a woman, isn't it?'

'It doesn't have to be.'

'What else could it be?'

'That's what Crystal's paying you to find out.'

I wasn't giving him time to think and he was already flustered from the trap I'd set on the Café Royal seating plan. 'This woman. . . .'

'It doesn't have to *be* a woman.'

'Just give me a name I can work on.'

'It's nothing to *do* with a frigging woman!' he suddenly cried.

'Ah. We're getting somewhere.'

But he turned abruptly away and bent over, waving his hand as if trying to repel a wasp. The door flew open then and Dora rushed in, her face crumpled in alarm. 'Hang on, Joe, I'll get your pills.' She wrenched open the door of a cabinet. 'I think you'd better go, John, I did ask you not to upset him.'

Back at the office, Vicky had been and gone. 'I'm sorry I couldn't introduce you formally,' I told Norma. 'As I said, I'm simply going through the motions for a friend.'

'The kid's a worker, I'll give her that,' she admitted guardedly. 'She never stopped. Good manner too.'

I glanced at her. I didn't really wish to know that. 'What did you give her?'

'She suggested she rang the top-grade Cumbrian hotels, to see if Durkin had checked in anywhere. It seemed a good idea.'

'No luck, I suppose.'

'None. She did a thorough job though. Played the PA to the life. She thinks it might be worth going back up there.'

'No point in just swanning around. I'm pretty sure he's still in the area, but we need a lead.'

'She thinks if you retraced your footsteps . . . she's got it in her mind she saw something that needs to be looked at in a different light, but can't think what it could be.'

She wasn't being sarcastic, seemed impressed even.

'It's too tenuous, Norma, and anyway I'm convinced his pals have the answer. There's more to it than this Veronica, by the way; I managed to screw it out of Speight. In fact, he let slip it was nothing to do with a woman.' I told her the story. 'They're all running scared, apart from Challis, and he may be just a good actor.'

'Can it *possibly* be a money thing?'

'They're all millionaires, Durkin almost certainly multi. Money on legs. And none of them have any form or you and I would know about it.'

'If there's more to it than running away with Veronica and it seems unlikely to be money, what else can it be?'

Norma's final words went round and round in my head until about three, when I finally slept the kind of disturbed sleep that went with this kind of case. Louise's radio-alarm woke me at seven. She put out a hand and silenced it with a sigh, then hunched herself up in bed, still naked, and smiled down at me. 'Give me about five minutes and the bathroom's yours. What's your usual breakfast?'

'Strong, black, just the one sugar.'

'Thank heaven for that. Had it been anything to do with a frying pan I think something would have just died.'

I grinned, took her hand. 'Thanks for everything, Louise. I've enjoyed it. I'll ring you very soon. We'll either go out for a meal, or if you're feeling adventurous we can eat at my place.'

'Whatever. . . . I enjoyed it too, John.' There was a look of tenderness in her eyes as she kissed me on the cheek. 'I'll look forward to it.'

As she closed the bathroom door, I took the mute off my mobile. It began to ring seconds later. 'John? It's Bruce. Can you make it to the George for one? Something's come up on Durkin. . .'

EIGHT

Fenlon drank sparingly from his half of bitter. 'What have you got on him?'

'Zilch. Nothing that helps the case anyway. I tracked him to a rented house on the western side of Windermere, but some woman seemed to have picked him up and he'd disappeared again. In a hurry.'

He nodded slowly. 'So what line are you taking?'

'He has six close friends. I mean, close like a coat of paint. They all owe him, one way or the other. I'm certain some of them know where he is, if not all.'

He gave me a sudden sharp glance. 'That's interesting. That's very interesting. You think they may be covering for him?'

'I'm certain of it. And certain there's more to it than him legging it with a woman, though a woman's involved. And they've got to be in the know, they're all as jumpy as Torville and Dean, apart from one called Challis, who seems to have majored in self-control.'

'You could be right, John.' He lit one of the small cigars meant to wean him off cigarettes. All they seemed to do was make him cough. 'You know the Seven Arches?' he said, when he'd finished coughing.

'Down by the Aire?'

'Right. Where the canal crosses the river on an aqueduct. There's a lot of woodland, and some of the toms go down there with the posher punters, who don't like pigging it in trick-pads. They can charge extra, so they don't mind. A young tom called Tessa King bought it at Seven Arches. Head smashed in.'

'And. . . ?'

'Her body's just turned up. It'll not be easy pinning a date on the death, even roughly, but the last time she was *seen* alive seems to be around the last time Durkin was seen at all. She lived round the corner from Dresden Place. When she was reported missing, all any of the other toms could remember was that she got in a big car. They only take a number if a mate's a bit uneasy about a punter, and King wasn't. However Cheyenne's back on Dresden, so called because her name's Anne and when she went on the game she was very shy. She was away when King went missing, so she wasn't questioned. By coincidence she's a snout of mine to do with that fat slob at the Unicorn receiving. I mentioned King's body in passing and she said she saw the pick-up too, and it was a bronze-colour Rolls with a personalized number plate.' He watched me. 'Part of which was MD. . . .'

'That's *his*,' I said, in a low voice. 'I've been in it.'

'Agreed. I checked it out.'

'Christ, I *knew* the sods were running scared. But why a *tom*, he could have the best crumpet in town? Any town. . . .' My skin began to tingle with an excitement I'd not known in months.

'Now, let's go very canny,' Fenlon said. 'We're talking wealthy, reputable citizens here. Can you really believe they'd put their names on the line for a mate who may or may not have whacked a tom?'

'Definitely; the things he's done for them. Four of them have known him all their lives. If he *was* traced, and he had had something to do with a tom buying it, I daresay he'd be on his own, but I'm certain they'd do everything they could to make sure he *wasn't* traced. You might have to write Lord Lucan across your file, Bruce.'

'You've got me worried now,' he said. 'A street-wise fat cat with a bunch of wealthy pals, and even you stumped for a lead. . . .'

'Do you . . . want me to back off,' I said, 'the way things are going?' After the Rainger case, I trod warily with the police.

Our eyes met. 'I don't think so,' he said slowly. 'We're still waiting for the autopsy and SOC reports. The only people who know about the Rolls are you, me and Cheyenne.' He had another good cough. 'What I'm saying is, if I let this information loose at the nick they'd be all over Durkin's place like the SAS, his pals would twig, and they'd have the bugger on the first flight to Argentina.'

'His wife's sitting on his passport. That could be one of the things holding him up, assuming he's still in the Lakes.'

'Just carry on, John, for the time being. You might be able to screw something out of them, however small, we can work on. If the lads go in at this stage I'm certain we can forget it. The big plus now is that they don't know you know about a dead tom. It's a hell of a card to have up your sleeve.'

'How long have I got?' I said, trying to conceal my pleasure.

'We'll play it by ear. The local Press will have picked up on the body, but they'll need a name to give it full coverage. In any case, nothing can be linked to Durkin without our information. What really matters is nailing the sod, even if only to show that fat cats get the same justice as everyone else, if he really has gone for her with half a brick. We've got to bear in mind that her buying it and Durkin legging it could be coincidence – it happens. We'll keep in touch. We . . . never had this chat, of course.'

'Of course. . . .'

'How are you getting on with Nancy Durkin, by the way?' he said, with a faint leer.

'It's Crystal to her friends.'

'I'm not surprised, she dazzled both *my* eyes. If I had to choose between her and Julia Roberts I'd be in agony.'

'You could leave the decision to Crystal,' I said feelingly. 'All you'd need to do is lie back and think of the European Union.'

'You jammy sod!'

Grinning, I told him about Vicky helping out at the agency and her mother being the new woman in my life.

'Can this mean Vicky's mum's even sexier-looking than Crystal?'

I shook my head. 'She's quite plain, lives very modestly just above the woods. Makes a mean ham and mushroom omelette though.'

As so often before, he found my attitude incomprehensible.

Norma said, 'Vicky's in your office. I've been taking her through the routine work and showing her how to do a detailed invoice. She's one sharp kid. Had you thought seriously about offering her a job?'

'Can't cope with *two* paid-up members of the awkward squad.'

'There are all your messages. You've got to have help, John.'

It would be half the battle if any possible recruit had Norma's approval, but there was something inimical about Vicky I'd sensed at Grantley Hall, and it wasn't simply her scratchy manner.

She was sitting at my desk, absorbed in an accounting tabulation.

'Hello, Vicky. You've got a free afternoon, I take it.'

She nodded without looking up. 'The evenings are the busy time for Girl Talk, as you can imagine. How's Durkin going?'

'I've had some news.' I told her what Fenlon had told me, adding, 'This is for your ears only.'

'I know, I know,' she said brusquely. 'Fenlon thinks he did it?'

'Could be. It may seem strange to you, a wealthy, good-looking guy like Durkin, who could have his pick, consorting with a tom.'

'No, it doesn't. Some men I could think anything of.'

She was young to have a layer of cynicism as sturdy as my own. But, in fact, it was me having difficulty getting it together, Durkin and a kerb-edge hooker, when I thought of Sukie and eyes you could drown in; Crystal, too.

I said, 'Have you had much to do with toms?'

She watched me suspiciously. 'Quite a lot. We paid one of the better ones to show us how to pick up men in hotel bars. Why?'

'Does she work Dresden Place?'

'Has been known to. Why?'

'Could you contact her again? Casually. They gather at the Unicorn mid-afternoon. Buy her a couple; I'll give you expenses. See what she can tell you about Tessa King. Say she was an old friend.'

'How would that help with Durkin?' she said bluntly. 'We're supposed to be trying to find out where he is, not why he did it.'

I breathed deeply. 'I want to know for certain if his motive for legging it had anything to do with Tessa's death. I once worked on a case where I took too much at face value and I don't want to make the same mistake. I just can't see Durkin with a twenty-pound hooker.'

'I think I'll just be pratting about. *I* think we should go back to the Lakes. Did Norma tell you?'

'There's no *point* unless we've got a lead,' I said, with a curtness I couldn't control. 'And I'm certain we didn't miss anything.'

'We did, you know,' she said, almost to herself. 'I wish I could explain it. I dreamt about it last night, crossing the lake on the ferry and finding that bit of paper with Veronica on, and I suddenly felt I almost had an answer. And then I woke up, and I hadn't.'

I gate-crashed Mamma Patti's. I knew it was no good ringing or trying receptionists – the 'boys' were permanently out of town. I waited till there was a build-up at the reception desk, then simply slipped through a door marked STAFF ONLY and kept on walking till I traced Ferrara's office. I didn't bother to knock, just walked in. It handed him a nasty shock. He dropped a newspaper and sat staring up at me from behind a vast desk, white circles gleaming round the pupils of his dark eyes. His wife also became very still, where she was standing at a table in front of the window, holding what looked to be a menu card.

'Hello there, Tony, Mrs Ferrara,' I said brightly. 'Thought I'd call by for a chat.'

'Who let *you* in here!' he cried. 'You don't just walk in my office unannounced.' He grasped a phone.

'Put it down, Tony. I didn't bother going through reception. I knew you'd be away till a week next Tuesday.'

'Get out! Get out *now*, otherwise I throw you out.' He rushed round his desk.

I held up a warning finger. 'You should know I'm rather a strong man who works out regularly.' I also wanted to add that knocking around eight-stone call-girls would be inadequate training for mixing it with me. Even so, he made a grab for my lapels.

'Stop it, Tony, *stop* it!'

It was Patti Ferrara, and he stopped it. 'He can't just come barging in here, Patti,' he said. 'I can't have that!'

'Sit down, Tony,' she said, almost wearily. 'Mr Goss is in now, and he's right, you'd not have seen him. What do you want, Mr Goss?'

Trembling with anger, Ferrara stood for several more seconds, then did as he was told. I suspected that was normal. Patti was a dumpy woman, half his size, but I was certain he'd never tried using her as a punchbag. His face was acquiring its familiar sweaty sheen.

'Tony knows, Mrs Ferrara. Can he help me in finding Crystal's husband? Did Maurice give him any idea why he was leaving home?'

'You'll have to see Ray Challis,' he cried. 'That was the deal.'

'His,' I said, 'not mine. Now, how about making it nice and easy for me and telling me what came out of the meeting at Ray's.'

'Tony . . .' his wife said. Just the one word.

'We . . . couldn't come up with anything. Not a thing.'

'You astound me.'

'You've got your answer, now get out.'

'Do you know what I think, Tony? That you were all at Challis's to make absolutely certain you were all telling the same story. That is, if you didn't want to get thrown in swimming-pools.'

'That was an *accident*!' he screamed. 'I don't have to take this shit!'

Patti came forward from the window. She was plump and homely-looking, but her features had the same Italian cast as Ferrara's, the black hair now stranding with grey. She had none of the glamour of the other wives, and there was some further quality she didn't seem to share with them that I couldn't quite pin down. She was the Mamma Patti whose title in coloured lights graced each of the short-order restaurants they owned in the area.

'Tony . . .' she said again, putting a hand gently on his shoulder. He perspired a little more, glancing nervously from her eyes to mine.

'You don't think he's done something wrong, Tony?' I said evenly. 'Crystal thinks he's just gone off with a girlfriend.'

'It *is* a girlfriend,' he croaked, his hands shaking so badly he had to hide them beneath his desk.

'You see, when I spoke to Joe Speight about it, he thought there was more to it than that.'

'See Challis if you don't believe me! For Christ's sake, see Challis. We're all certain it's just a woman. The London one.'

Patti sighed, her eyes meeting mine in resignation. She knew all about other women, because she'd had Ferrara checked out, discreetly through solicitors, by Girl Talk and me.

'It's already a police matter, Tony,' I said, 'and if he's done something wrong you could be seen as accessories, you boys.'

'It's a *woman*, it's a *woman*. Christ, how many more times?'

'Tony,' his wife said gently, 'you'll give yourself a nervous breakdown if you go on like this.'

I wondered if it was stress that made him knock toms about, the same stress that made Speight shout and bawl at staff. I'd always felt Ferrara was the softest target if I could get close to him.

'You see,' I said carefully, 'there might be blowbacks on your business, Tony, if you and the others were mixed up in anything.'

'Tell him to go away, Mamma!' he cried, the whites of his eyes flaring like those of a frightened horse. 'Tell him to go away!'

Perhaps calling her Mamma had been a Freudian slip. Or perhaps a mother figure had been what he'd always needed, even when young, as some men did who found the adult world too difficult to cope with.

'Tony,' she said, stroking his thick curly hair, 'you're a Roman Catholic. He was a good Catholic boy,' she said to me, over his head.

'Please tell him to go away, Mamma,' he almost whispered.

'You'd better go, Mr Goss, he'll only get in a state.' But she gave me a slow wink. 'I'll see you out.'

'See you later then, Tony,' I said, 'when you're calmer.'

We left him slumped at his desk. She touched my arm in the corridor and indicated another office. It was smaller than Ferrara's and not as grandly furnished, but I didn't think she bothered about status symbols. 'Sit down, John. I can call you John? Call me Patti. I want to help. We owe Maurice so very much.'

'He . . . helped you financially?'

'He said I made the best pizzas outside Italy. We just had the one parlour, but Maurice said we should expand. He helped us buy the second; after that we bought our own. He taught me . . . *us* about finance, cash-flow, and, of course, I'd always been around kitchens, knew my mother's recipes by heart. I'd cook for Tony and the others when they'd been out kicking a ball around.' She gave me a sad smile. 'We're very successful but it doesn't always bring happiness.'

Not when you had a husband who not only played around but was also a waste of space. I'd grasped in nano-seconds that Patti was the driving force here. It was odd. It turned the normal situation on its head, in which Durkin bank-rolled the husbands to success, and the wives seemed doomed to boredom. In this case it was Patti who'd had the entrepreneurial flair, and Ferrara the incidental winner. The result, in terms of human unhappiness, looked to be exactly the same.

'I'll talk to him,' she said quietly. 'We . . . Catholics . . . we can't live with anything on our consciences. We get into the habit of confession from childhood.' Her eyes were heavy in a fleshy, suddenly haggard face. I suspected she'd had more confessions out of Ferrara than the parish priest himself. 'Leave it to me, John, I'll get some answers for you.'

'Thanks, Patti,' I said, with a heartfelt sigh of relief. 'I'd like to get this thing sorted out for everyone's sake. Just by the way – does the name Veronica mean anything to you?'

She thought carefully, shook her head. 'We once had a waitress called Veronica, but that must be ten years ago.'

'Messages,' Norma said importantly.

'Hold on, Norma. You know about this link between Durkin and a dead tom now, I take it.'

'Vicky filled me in.'

'Well, even if Durkin did it, which I doubt, and even if his chums *thought* he did it, why are they all running so *scared*? I mean nothing much will happen to them, even if the police think there's been a conspiracy. It's incredibly hard to prove – look at the Lord Lucan case, how could *he* have disappeared without some kind of help?'

She thought about this. 'We are talking *nouveaus* here, not your old money. Unsophistocated. Perhaps they just think they *might* go to prison if he's done the poor girl in and they know about it, and they're covering for him.'

'A lot of ifs,' I said dubiously, 'but you could be right.'

'Messages. Mrs Durkin wants you to take her to Sean Doherty's barbie this evening, and Mrs Ferrara, of the *restaurants*, said she'll see you at the barbie and tell you what you want to know.'

'*Great!* Why didn't you tell me right away?'

She looked up at the ceiling. 'Is Mr Doherty the one who sells the caravans?' she said, in hushed tones.

'That's right, and when he's had a couple he does Terry Wogan impressions.'

NINE

Doherty's pool was harp-shaped, of course. Otherwise the house was just as large and florid as the others, where it sat high on the valley wall, just below the moors.

'I might have a lead, Crystal,' I told her. 'I'll say no more at this stage. Don't want to raise your hopes.'

I saw the irony of the words the moment they were out. Raise her hopes for what – that I might be finding a tom-killer?

'Good lad. You gave me the right vibes from day one.'

She was dressed as lavishly as usual in a white, cotton-voile blouse that had a high collar and flounces, and tight pants of very fine denim, flower-embroidered, that resembled costly curtaining.

'I'll be glad when it's sorted,' she said. 'A bloke keeps ringing from London about Maurice settling his buying account. I told him he could settle it out of his back pocket, for Christ's sake, when he gets home; there must be a hundred grand in the current account. But I can do without the hassle, chuck.'

I listened with half an ear. It had been another sunny day, but had now clouded over, and the guests were crowded into the pool-room. The friends of Durkin were huddled together near a circular, central bar. They eyed me in a tense silence, the sort you get in rough city pubs just before glasses start flying through the air. I smiled warmly at them; only Challis smiled back.

'Have you seen Tony and Patti, Crystal?'

'They're always late, love. She's married to the business.

Someone has to be with that idle pillock. Give them an hour. And look, Johnny, I've a bone to pick: where did you *go* the other night?'

'But you were asleep when I came back from the study,' I said innocently. 'It was obvious you were worn out with all the worry.'

'You should have given me a *shake*,' she said, her husky voice dropping a little. 'It was just a little cat-nap till you got back.'

A strong hand squeezed my arm. 'Nice to see you again, John,' Challis said warmly. 'A word, if you don't mind, old son, with me and Sean. Shan't keep him long, Crystal dear.' The strong hand steered me firmly out of the pool~room and into a small room nearby, which had leather armchairs, a square knee-high table, a sideboard and decanters, a desk. Doherty's study, I supposed.

'Sit yourself down, John,' Doherty said. 'Will I be after freshening your drink?'

'I'm fine, thanks.'

He added a lavish measure of Scotch to his and Challis's glass, and we all sat down in the half-light of wall-lamps, me between them. In the darkening night, his deserted pool could have graced any of the more superior Benidorm hotels.

'I'll not piss about, John,' Challis said softly. 'I said *I'd* be getting the boys together to see if we could help you find Maurice.'

I'd been expecting it. 'I'm sorry, Ray, but I like to use my own tried and tested methods.'

'I don't like your methods, John. It comes back to me that you talk as if Maurice might have got himself the wrong side of the law.'

'And so he might. It's one of the reasons people leg it and I have to bear it in mind. No need to take it personally.'

'But we do, John,' he said gently. 'Maurice just isn't the type to have trouble with the law. Remember his Smithy Street minimarket, Sean? Some guy was smashing the windows, John. An ex-employee with a grudge, sacked because he was useless. Maurice knew it was him, but wouldn't even report it – he didn't want the lad to get a record. So me and Sean put our heads together and Sean had a word with this guy, and after that – no more broken windows.'

I felt fear touch my spine like a cold hand as he smiled warmly on. I suspected he was telling me in coded language how Doherty, or more likely one of his people, had taken a young tearaway up a backstreet and kicked him senseless. If Challis was the brains of the group, it looked as if Doherty could supply the muscle, when necessary. A one-man Sinn Fein fronting a one-man IRA.

'Let me top up your glass, John,' Doherty said. This time I let him. 'You see, Ray has more of a special thing about Maurice than any of us. He didn't just save Ray's business, he saved his life.'

'True. We were swimming in the river,' Challis said, 'and there was a strong current that day. It swept me off. But old Maurice could swim as well as he does everything else, and he was there for me, dragging me to the side. You never forget a thing like that, John, never. I suppose *that's* why I take it so personally when people start talking police around a fine guy like Maurice Durkin.'

Silence slowly gathered in the little room until we could hear faint music and laughter. Hands trembling slightly, I considered the message. It was a stark one. Durkin may or may not be on the run, and they may or may not know, but they'd go to the wire to cover for him. Loner that I was, I had to admit to a sneaking admiration for such indestructible loyalty. Doherty patted my knee with a large square hand. 'Crystal's taken the mother of a shine to you, John. Why not just go through the motions and enjoy the ride, know what I mean?'

More code, it seemed, for if I wanted to hang on to my teeth.

There was a tap at the door and Cecily Challis came in. 'Barry's on the phone, Ray, couldn't get you on the mobile. Says it's urgent. And Maureen says Alan can't find the Martini, Sean.'

'Right, pet,' Challis said, 'we're about finished in here. Catch you later, John.'

They went off. Cecily gave me a friendly smile that didn't quite mask the discontent most of the wives seemed to share. I said,

'Have Tony snd Patti arrived yet, Cecily?'

'Haven't seen them. Could be buried in the crush. I *hate* it when we can't go on the patio. You're a private detective, aren't you?'

I smiled wryly. 'Trying to find Mr Durkin.'

'Well, *he'll* not tell you. Talk about close, they're like a married couple, those two,' she said in a low voice, gazing petulantly at the glowing pool.

'Ray and Maurice?'

'They've *always* been best friends. It's like one of those marriages where people are crackers about each other, but jealous as well, and always wanting to be top dog.'

'It's not the impression Ray gives. He seems so calm, controlled.'

'He is, about everything except Maurice.' Her pale-green, luminous eyes rested on mine. 'He·didn't want to take that loan, you know, when his business was going down the lav. Not from Maurice. Pride. That's how they were. In the end he'd only take it at fifty per cent over three years. He worked seven days a week. "I'll show the bugger", he used to say. "I'll show him". As if Maurice had insulted him by *offering* it. You see Ray wanted to be the one baling *Maurice* out. But Maurice always had the luck.'

'Lucky in his friends anyway,' I said feelingly.

It no longer surprised me, the way the *nouveau* wives would let it all hang out. And I already knew about the extent of the closeness. She was comparing it to a prima donna relationship, and I'd known plenty, and they were rock-solid because they never got dull.

She gazed once more at the pool, her long, dark hair sleekly perfect, her brocade dress and ruffle-neck blouse crisp and new. 'You know, John,' she said unhappily, 'if me and Maurice Durkin were trapped in a burning house I think Ray would rescue Maurice first.'

The moment I returned to the crowded party room, a hand plucked my sleeve. 'Have you a moment, John?' It was Guinevere.

'Of course. But I must see Patti Ferrara first.'

'I don't think they're here yet. They're often late.'

'This late?'

'It's quite possible. I'll . . . not keep you long.'

I followed her back along the corridor to get away from the noise. 'What's on your mind, Guinevere?'

'It got me worried, John, when I learnt you were a detective, working for Crystal. I couldn't understand him not contacting her. That's just not Maurice. He might not have told her where he was, but I was certain he'd be phoning her. To . . . to prepare her. . . .'

'For what?'

'In the strictest confidence. . . '

'You have my word.'

'That he'd be wanting a divorce . . . to marry me.'

She watched me with a rueful smile, sensing my incredulity. I'd seen two of Durkin's women and they were both drop-dead gorgeous. Guinevere was attractive too, but she was like an English flower almost lost to sight among the exotic hot-house blooms surrounding it. 'You're in shock, aren't you?'

'Of course not. A little surprised. . . .'

'I know about his many girlfriends, John. He was going to put all that behind him.'

'But . . . if you're going to get together, didn't you think it odd that he was never in contact with *you*, let alone Crystal?'

'No. He always said when the time was right he'd simply go, stay in an hotel somewhere, and think it all through without distractions, not even phone calls. You see, he's a kind man and he wanted to leave Crystal completely secure. It would need a lot of planning. But this long silence . . . not even contacting Crystal . . . it's worrying.'

I sighed inwardly; how right she was. 'I know it must seem very odd,' she went on, 'Maurice and I. I suppose it all started with the books. We began to meet secretly. He was bored rigid without the business. The . . . new direction I mentioned the other night . . . it was politics. Mine's a political family – I have an uncle an MP. I rather fired him. He's such a persuasive talker, has such charisma, well, you'll see. And he's always had the luck. I'm certain he'll make it, he has so much to offer. He wants me at his side. I was the catalyst, I suppose, if that doesn't sound too grand.'

And her simple skirts and tops, her voice and manner, would be the perfect assets in an MP's wife – they were never going to be around swimming-pools. I believed everything she'd told me, could just see a man with Durkin's energy and charm, at screaming pitch with parties and cruises and games of golf, snatching at the chance of a new career which offered the open-ended hours he'd always known. The sad part, from where I was standing, was that the make-over didn't seem to have taken, not only did Magic Maurice appear to be involved with five women, if you included Veronica, but one of them was dead.

A man passed us with a woman in a red dress. 'Hi,' he said indifferently. Guinevere watched them go off into one of the rooms further along the corridor. It was Chris Denholm, her husband.

'His latest popsy,' she said. 'He doesn't bother concealing them any more; he believes his money will always keep me quiet and looking after his house and family.' She looked back at me, heavy-eyed, stroked her wispy hair. 'We were so happy once, John. We stopped being happy the first year he made a hundred thousand. I used to think Chris was a man of ideals and Maurice just loved the goodies, but now I think it's the other way round. It's all so strange . . . and sad.'

Poor Guinevere, it seemed the sadness and strangeness had barely begun. The strangest part being how could a man fired with entering public life even *think* of driving his Rolls on to Dresden Place, even if he had nothing to do with Tessa King ending up dead?

She took my arm. 'What do you think,' she said anxiously, 'about him not being in touch?'

'Look, Guinevere, I've got to be honest with you. It could be a good news, bad news situation. I'm virtually certain which part of the country he's in. Very soon I hope to have a firm lead on exactly where to find him. But . . . well, he could be in trouble.'

She gasped, her mouth fell open. '*Trouble*! What kind of trouble? A nervous breakdown . . . something like that?'

I shook my head. 'Not that. But I can't be specific because I simply don't know for sure. I just feel he *might* be. This silence has been too long, as you say, with no contact with either you or Crystal.' Or, I could have added, Miss Fabulous of Sloane Square.

But then she began to smile. 'Oh, John, I simply don't care what sort of trouble he's in as long as he's in one piece. You see, you don't know him. If you did, you'd know there was no sort of trouble Maurice Durkin couldn't get himself out of.'

Did that include breathing life back into a tom who'd only been seen in a very dead condition since climbing into his Rolls?

As I returned to the party, Crystal took my arm in a crab-like grip. 'What's Talking Tessie been on about this time?' she demanded. 'Never says much to us girls, but get you or Maurice inside ten yards of her and it has her gob going like a fiddler's elbow.'

'Oh, she was just asking if there was any news on him.'

'She must be missing the talking. I'll get to know what they talk *about* one day.'

I was learning more about my client than I'd really wanted to know. For her, it looked as if it might all be bad news. If Durkin wasn't in serious trouble he'd be leaving her for Guinevere. Despite the open marriage, I suspected she cared about him an awful lot, as everyone seemed to. I liked Crystal, didn't want to see her hurt.

'Have you seen Patti or Tony yet, by the way?'

'No, and for God's sake take a break. You'll knock yourself up.'

'I am here to work, you know. I just need to see Bill and Chris. They're the only ones I've not spoken to yet.'

'You'll probably find Chris with that tart's ankles round his neck. Girl with the red dress and the big bazookas. He two-times

Guinny rotten, you know,' she said, with a malicious grin. 'No wonder she has to make do with talking. Don't be long, pet. You'll be able to have a few drinks then. I'm taking the booze a bit steady myself.'

I thought, don't ask.

But I found both Denholm and Ackroyd in an annexe to the dining-room, heads together. The girl in the red dress was in the dining-room itself, piling a plate with the more expensive items of buffet food.

'Good evening, gentlemen.' I abruptly pulled out a chair and sat down at their table. 'So glad I've caught you together.'

Denholm's hand shook so badly a little of his red wine spilled from his glass and ran over his fingers like blood. Shock also mottled Ackroyd's reddish face. But he recovered fast. 'Ray Challis . . .'

'I handle my own enquiries, Mr Ackroyd.'

'I can't talk now,' he said, in a precise, authoritative tone. 'Ring my PA – I might have a five-minute window next week.'

'You can stuff your window, right now will do fine.'

'Forget it, we're talking business here.'

'How to swing a two-for-one deal on the girl out there?'

Denholm leapt to his feet. 'Take that back, you ignorant sod!' he cried, in a slurred voice. 'Take that back or come outside.'

'Sit down, Mr Denholm,' I said mildly, laying my strong hands on the table, 'and keep your face intact for another day.'

Drunk as he was, some distant warning voice told him he was too slender, too delicate-looking to mix it with a man like me. Muttering to himself, he finally sat down again. I watched them in silence. After Ferrara, I'd seen these two as the softest targets. Perhaps I'd not have needed to bother with them had Ferrara got here. But he hadn't, and it bugged me. I decided on a direct approach.

'Where is he?' I said bluntly. 'You do know, don't you?'

'We're not his keepers,' Ackroyd said in a controlled voice. But he couldn't control the sweat glands that made his forehead glisten.

'But you're his *pals*. You flock together. He helped you all to make it, laid out money to start you off. Big money, they tell me.'

'We don't owe him a *penny*!' Denholm almost screamed. 'We paid it all back, the loans. They weren't gifts.'

The near-hysteria was puzzling. Suddenly his face crumpled in a grimace of pain. It meant Ackroyd had kicked his ankle. Hard.

Another silence. They'd have had the Challis warning to tell me nothing. I wondered if they'd had the sort of warning I'd had, with the implied threat of what might happen otherwise lying beneath the genial words like shards of glass embedded in a tablet of scented soap. They were a scary couple, Challis and his enforcer, but I had friends where it counted and I'd learnt to watch my back. They'd only get me off this case now, the way it was going, if they knew how to separate the two components of a bi-metallic strip.

'Who's Veronica?' I said suddenly.

Denholm's hand twitched so badly this time that he knocked his wine-glass over, where it fell across his plate and flooded the food like beetroot juice. Ackroyd's face was so damp his granny glasses were slipping down his nose. He removed them, so that his eyes now looked unfocused, adding to an appearance of intense alarm.

'You see,' I said calmly, 'you react so strongly to certain buzz-words that I *have* to ask myself if Maurice is in trouble, you know, the really, really deep-shit kind. . . .'

Denholm looked ill. His sharp-edged features were so pale they seemed to carry a tinge of green. He picked up Ackroyd's glass and drank shakily from it, spilling some of that too down his new summer suit, where it added another stain to those already there.

'If you don't stop harassing us, Goss,' Ackroyd said harshly, 'I'll make sure no lawyer in this town ever uses you again. Don't think I can't, and that would mean half your livelihood gone overnight.'

'Threats, is it?' I said, in the same even tone. 'Well, let's see what

I can come up with. I wonder how the Law Society and the ACCA would react to being told about certain members covering for a missing millionaire, who might just have been a really naughty boy.'

That seemed to do the trick. They both stared at me now as if in a catatonic trance. I didn't need to tell them anything about being disowned by their bodies. In a nutshell, kiss of death.

'Right,' I said, 'shall we have a nice little chat now?'

I felt a hand on my shoulder. 'Ah, John, me boy,' Doherty said cheerfully, 'you are a one for the talk and the questions, and no mistake. But can't you see, the lads are in no *mood* for the crack; they're what you might call *reserved* types, the pair of them. Will you not be after joining the fun on the patio, it's warm enough for dancing, at least. Crystal's feeling awful neglected, so she is.'

I glanced over my shoulder. His green eyes were emerald-hard above the whimsical Val Doonican smile. Denholm suddenly bolted to the window, flung it open, and was noisily sick over one of Doherty's best rose-bushes.

As the Rolls whispered us back to Maunan, I said, 'The Ferraras never showed then, Crystal.'

'Maureen rang their place in the end, pet. Just the answerphone. Funny, they've got a live-in housekeeper. I hope it's not Patti's mother, she's not at all well. Poor Patti, she has enough to do running the business, and that useless prick round her neck.'

I needed to think, but Crystal's hand rested warmly on my thigh, and I first had to work out how to avoid being shortly clamped against her more than friendly bust. It seemed the easier option would be breaking out of a sealed mailbag at the bottom of the Thames wearing handcuffs. Such irony. Two nights ago I'd been very willing, but there was Louise now. Yet it wasn't as simple as that either. The truth was the Durkin case was getting to be sexier than sex.

Beneath Brian's derisive eye, I was yanked off once again to that vast bedroom and a large gin pressed into my hand. Sinisterly sober, Crystal poured herself half a glass of champagne. Little chance of her nodding off tonight. She sank down on the bed and thumped it encouragingly. 'Come on, Johnny love, take the weight off your feet. You push yourself too hard, you need some relaxation.'

The bed gave me an answer. It was one of the lowest I'd seen. It crouched on ornate gilded claws barely a foot off the ground. Looking eager, I flopped at her side, to give a roar of pain the moment I was sitting.

'Johnny,' she cried, 'whatever's the *matter?*'

'Oh *God*, my back's gone again!' I began to writhe in simulated agony, clutching my spine. 'It must be with your bed being so low.'

'It'll go off in a minute or two, won't it?'

'No chance,' I gasped. 'I've got a special board at home. I'll have to lie on that for a few hours.'

She fought a long, hard battle. She'd get Brian to find a bit of board; she'd massage my back with vapour rub; she even hinted that we could just, you know ... but I groaned so convincingly that in the end a sneering Brian was sent for to help me out to the Rolls, my own car to be delivered in the morning. As the Rolls pulled away, she gave a forlorn half-wave from the front door, looking like the only kid on the street who'd not been invited to the picnic.

Fifty yards down the road, I said, 'Pull in to the side, Brian.'

He braked and did so, then turned on the courtesy light and glanced round, clearly hoping to see me doubled up in extreme pain.

'There's nothing wrong with me,' I said, without explanation. 'I want you to get my own car, but first I need a word. The night before Mr Durkin went to London that last time, did he take out the Rolls?'

'I can't remember, sir,' he said too quickly, his lips already quivering with the same agitation that seemed to affect almost all the men close to Durkin when questioned about him.

'Funny,' I said, 'you're his chauffeur. It must have stuck in your mind that he wanted to drive himself, especially as he likes a drink or two.'

'He often drove himself. It's weeks ago. I just can't remember.'

'Only a little over *five* weeks ago, Brian.'

'I don't know if he went out that *night*!' he suddenly yelped, with what seemed the same alarm I'd seen in Denholm and Ackroyd.

'We're talking about the night before he disappeared, Brian,' I said. 'And you remembered his movements the following morning very precisely.'

'It was my night off!' he cried. 'Neil was on duty. . . .'

'You've just made that up, Brian, haven't you?' I said gently. 'But I can check with Neil in the morning.'

I was getting used to the sight of glistening foreheads. He passed a hand distractedly through his neat dark hair. 'I'll get your car,' he whispered hoarsely, leapt out of the Rolls and ran back towards Maunan.

I slept about as fitfully as I usually did, but that had to be balanced against getting no sleep at all had I been locked in the arms of an energetic, alcohol-free Crystal. Just before leaving for the office, I keyed out the Ferraras' number. A woman answered.

'Could I speak to Mrs Ferrara?'

'She's not here, I'm afraid. Who's speaking, please?'

'My name's Goss, a friend of hers. She has something for me.'

'There's . . . been an accident, Mr Goss. Mr Ferrara's been badly injured. He was taken to Casualty last night. The BRI. . . .'

TEN

She'd had him transferred to Scarsdale House, a private hospital on Beckford Road, set in several acres of immaculate lawn, and barricaded by dense woodland. The reception area could have graced a five-star hotel, and I sat on a comfortable sofa in deep silence among planters filled with glossy exotics. A softly spoken young nurse then took me along corridors until we came to where Patti Ferrara stood outside a door. She looked to have aged twenty years. Silently, she pushed open the door on a small room. Ferrara lay on the bed, in a drugged sleep, his head thickly bandaged. His eyes were bruised and swollen, his nose was protected by some kind of rigid dressing and his left arm was raised on a pulley. The bedcovers were suspended over a frame, which indicated strapped-up ribs and damaged or broken legs. There were drip-feed stands and a heart monitor. It wasn't possible to feel pity. I remembered women on two separate nights limping from hotel rooms he'd taken them to. I wished I could let them know the good news. It couldn't have happened to a nicer slob.

I clasped her trembling shoulders. 'Who did this, Patti?'

'Mugged. . . .' She made a noise between a gulp and a sob. 'In the . . . the Mamma Patti car-park. Last evening . . . *baseball bats!*'

'For his money? His Rolex?'

She shook her head, tears rolling down swollen cheeks. She'd clearly not slept, the crumpled black dress she wore was yesterday's. Her eyes finally met mine and she shook her head again. We both knew. 'You'd better go, John,' she said, in a strangled tone.

'Patti, you must tell me what you know,' I said gently. 'He did tell you where Maurice is, didn't he? And why he's gone.'

'Go away!' she suddenly screamed. 'If it hadn't been for you and that bloody Crystal. . . .'

'Patti, you must tell me. There's something very serious going on around Maurice.'

'He'll not tell *anyone* now,' she cried. 'And neither will I.'

I picked up the car-phone, keyed out. 'It's me, Norma, I had a call to make. I'm on my way down now.'

'Mr Challis is anxious to see you. He's the one who builds those lovely Challis estates, isn't he?'

'God, don't start that again. Is he at his office?'

'He's at home. He'll be there till eleven.'

'I might as well go directly.'

'Vicky's calling at lunchtime. She wants to see you.'

I was already on the valley road, and so I returned once more to that prime area on its northern slopes. The gates to the yard stood open, and Challis himself came out to greet me, taking my hand in both of his. 'John, great to see you again!' he said, as if it were weeks since we'd last met, not hours. 'This way, old son.'

He led me up a wide staircase and past lavishly furnished bedrooms to a large, square home-office overlooking his pool and the valley's opposite slopes, their ridge blue-tinted, trees sharply defined in the sunlight. He smiled his benign horn-rimmed smile. 'My nerve-centre,' he said, glancing round at the gleaming rosewood, the state of the art equipment, 'for controlling my little empire.'

Which he'd not have had had it not been for Durkin, his closest friend, whom he loved and hated and would lay down his life for. Or so I'd been led to believe. It could be true, I supposed. But I was beginning to stir up so much near-panic among the friends that I'd begun to wonder, however much they loved Durkin, when they were going to decide they'd done enough for him. Unless, of course, taking the cynical view, they were somehow involved in what Durkin could be on the run *from*. Were shielding him because they had to.

Challis brought a tray from a nearby table which held a cafetière and cups and saucers. 'Help yourself to milk and sugar.'

'Thanks. What can I do for you, Ray?'

He sighed. 'We're getting our lines crossed, John, aren't we? You know, some men would leave home for a chance to bed Crystal. And you're just the type she goes for, tall, well-knit....' I wondered if I detected a faint wistful sadness in his eyes, remembered that tender kiss he'd given Crystal at his party. Perhaps he was one of the men who'd leave home. He sipped coffee. 'And then, no sooner do you, me and Sean have our little chat, and we think everything's sorted, when Sean finds you scaring the shit out of Chris and Bill, implying *again* that Maurice might be on the run. I tell you, I had my work cut out calming Sean down. He might seem an easygoing guy, but he has a tendency to flip, especially about Maurice.'

I didn't need convincing, I'd just come away from viewing what was left of Ferrara. 'Look, Ray, I'm sorry, but I keep being told how to run my own investigation, and I can't see why. What I can see is that apart from you all the friends seem extremely uneasy.'

'Can you wonder, when you keep banging on about the police and Maurice being in trouble?' he said calmly. 'There aren't too many people who can control themselves like you and me. Look, John, I'm going to level with you. I'm not going to say I don't know where Maurice is, and I'm not going to say I do know, but I'll give you my word he's in no trouble. But I really don't want him pestered till he's good and ready to come home.'

'And he is *coming* home?'

'Definitely – in his own time. And do you know why I really asked you here? Because I'm very impressed by the way you work. You really do give the job a hundred per cent, and I'm delighted to have seen you in action. I'll tell you why. I've got building sites all over the north, and we have a lot of expensive gear kicking about – JCBs, HGVs, dumpers, fully furnished show houses. Theft, vandalism, it never ends. I need a guy to co-ordinate security, someone I can trust completely. You're that guy, John, and I'm offering you the work. It's a big job and I'd be paying top whack.'

'It . . . sounds very interesting.'

He gave me a warm smile. 'Think it over. You're wasting your valuable time on Maurice, believe it. You can go on scratting around, if you like, but it'll make no difference in the end. And this job of mine could be where your career really takes off, you can't get your head round the amount of business the lads could throw your way.'

He knew I knew what his game was, yet I also felt he genuinely wanted me on the team, was genuinely impressed by my tenacity. It was as if he had that benevolent urge, perhaps like Durkin himself, to develop a talent he felt he'd spotted, to encourage and enrich me, until one day perhaps I, too, would be taking my place at that boisterous table in the Café Royal Grill. And I couldn't resist another twinge of envy for what seemed to be the genuine camaraderie of Durkin's people, for what could still be their inde-structible loyalty to Durkin himself, even if it led Challis and Doherty, probably basically decent types, to arrange the Ferrara mugging. I always had to bear in mind a closeness going back years, and Durkin's remarkable generosity.

'I don't know what to say,' I said. 'I have a distinct impression a chance like this only comes up once in a lifetime.'

'You'd be right. Think it over, John, and get back to me. Come on, I'll show you out. We're both driven men.'

I wondered if this was my last chance. Either let Durkin go, with the sweetener of joining the inner circle, or baseball-bat time for me too.

'Tessa King,' Vicky said, as I opened the door to my office, where Norma had sat her again. 'There's a definite connection to Durkin.'

She spoke brusquely, but I remembered she'd thought it would be a waste of time even if there was.

'Really . . .' I said dispiritedly. She gave me a suspicious glance and turned to a note-pad. 'She used to work a check-out at the Smithy Street Crystalmart, but she was doing an occasional trick on the side. Rita, my contact, says Durkin was potty about her, even talked about leaving his wife for her. Anyway, she left and went on Dresden full time. She was an unusual type, liked the life on the Place, but was difficult to get to know well. She was a sort of free spirit. She once told Rita she'd left the minimarket because of Durkin getting heavy. Just didn't want it, being his totty with a flat and a fancy car and loads of clothes. Rita thought she was out of her tree.'

'I'm not surprised. . . .' I'd always been certain there had to be something different about Tessa for Durkin to be linked to her.

Vicky went on, 'She'd go out with him now and then, but wanted to stay loose, sleep around, go off on her own for a weekend if she felt like it. That's how things were when she was picked up in Durkin's Rolls.'

'But they didn't *know* it was Durkin's Rolls,' I broke in, 'the toms. Not according to Fenlon. All they remembered was a big car.'

'They wouldn't tell the Bill much, according to Rita, not unless Tessa had asked someone to take the car's number, and she hadn't. Most of them knew it was a Rolls, and knew about her and Durkin, too.'

I nodded, chastened. So much for Fenlon's certainty that the only tom with the inside track was Cheyenne. 'There's more,' she said. 'It was Durkin's Rolls, but Durkin wasn't driving.'

'Go on,' I said, startled out of my gathering apathy.

'They all knew Durkin from the days when she did go out with him now and then. Rita could describe him: well built, grey hair, strong features. The guy driving had dark hair and was smallish and wiry.'

I moved to the window, gazed absently at the graceful buildings of the old quarter. 'Did Rita say what Tessa looked like?'

'She wasn't a beauty or obviously sexy. Brown hair, slender, a bit street-urchin. She just had this incredible personality: intelligent, very very funny and sort of wild. Completely her own woman.'

An original? Had that been the pull for him? A woman who didn't give a toss about anything, including his money, his status, even Durkin himself. Nothing made a woman more desirable than being out of reach. I'd seen what it could do to men. They could reach a stage where, if they couldn't have her, they didn't want anyone else to.

'That's about the story,' Vicky said from behind me, her voice seeming to come from a distance as I stood in a dejected silence. 'Well, thank you, Vicky,' she said then angrily. 'It must have taken ages getting it all together. Thanks a bunch and well done.'

I turned to her flushed face, smiled wryly. 'You're absolutely right. I'm sorry. I'm preoccupied. You've done a tremendous job. It's not your fault I dislike the message. Thanks a bunch and well done.'

Her flush deepened, but now she looked both pleased and contrite. She was a bright kid, no doubt about it, simply needed handling. And I just didn't have the time for walking on eggshells and remembering to trowel on the praise.

She said, 'What's . . . wrong with the message?'

I sighed. 'Oh, I feel I almost know the guy. He comes across as such a decent type. He's been a dreadful Jack the Lad, but I've never known of anyone to be so generous with their time and money.'

I told her of the many things he'd done for his friends, how he'd even saved Challis's life. 'Well,' I said, 'this business with Tessa could be why they're all rallying round. And how could they *know* she's dead – if they do know – unless Durkin had told them, or they were somehow involved; she's not been officially identified yet. We still can't assume he did it, but it's looking very bad.'

She gazed at me incredulously. 'John, with what I've dug out it's got to be open and shut. A millionaire crazy about her, and his car picks her up, probably driven by one of his pals. The next day he legs it and the next time she shows she's a body in Punters' Paradise.'

'Is that what they call it? Oh, Vicky,' I sighed, 'part of the reason I can't see Durkin as a tom-killer is that I just don't want to. But . . . people do get obsessed. . . .' I should know, if anyone.

'Where do we go from here?' she said tentatively.

'You tell me. My gold-plated lead was Tony Ferrara.'

'*Tony Ferrara!*'

'Of *course*, you've met the sod, haven't you? Well, he's also a Durkin pal, and I nearly screwed Durkin's hidey-hole out of him, but then, surprise, surprise, he got so badly mugged he's in an ICU.'

She began to grin. 'Really? Black eyes, severe bruising?'

'You name it; it's either stitched up or in two pieces.'

'Oh dear, oh dear, oh dear.' She began to giggle. 'I must remember to send him a get well late card.'

I smiled too. 'But it silenced him, and I'm positive one of the friends did it. That's what seems to be going on around Durkin.'

We sat for a few seconds in silence. 'When you were talking about the other friends,' she said, 'I caught the name Denholm. He's as well known as Ferrara in places like the Grantley Arms.'

'I can believe it. Woman-chaser, near alcoholic. . . .'

'What if,' she said slowly, 'I were to check out the places where he goes – there aren't many – and see if I can't hook him. Late evening he usually does business with some call-girl or other. But I'll come friendly and free – he'll like that.'

'You're ahead of me.'

'Wait till he's smashed, go to a room with him, ask him how Durkin is these days. Say I went out with him for a while, saw Denholm at one of the parties. He might just let something slip about Durkin to an outsider. I've had an awful lot of experience in getting men to let things slip.' She grinned on the gap in her front teeth. 'And I'd be wired for sound, of course.'

'It's a very long shot.'

'What other kinds of shot have you got?'

It could be worth a try. Men often did talk to hookers, and assumed it would go nowhere, especially when they had things on their minds. But I was meant to be weaning her off enticement work.

'It could be dangerous – they'll know now about Ferrara looking like something they dug up in the Nile Valley.'

'I can handle it, for Christ's sake,' she said irritably. 'I've done self-defence.'

I was tempted. Denholm was now the weakest link, and though he talked tough was of slender build. 'Well, if you're sure about it. . . .'

'Of course I'm sure. So that's settled,' she said firmly. 'And if this doesn't work can we please go back to Cumbria? Try retracing our steps? I wish I could explain. I just feel if we went back. God, that name, Veronica – it goes round my head. I've even tried anagrams.'

Her preoccupied eyes met mine. Again I felt the uneasiness I'd known in the linen cupboard that night. I couldn't define it, it was like saying you'd seen a ghost or had *déjà vu*. I shivered slightly.

'I'll think about it.'

'Great!' she said, grinning again, and taking it as unqualified agreement. 'I'd better go tart myself up for the hunt. See you.'

'She's a pro, John,' Norma said, as I skimmed through work outstanding. 'You want to snap her up. I mean, that stuff she got out of the Rita woman about Tessa King, it's masterly.'

'She's good, agreed, but by God she's stroppy. Runs rings round you. She also has a dysfunctional background. It means telling her exactly how good she is every verse end, and life's too short.'

'I just get good vibes about her. The same ones I had about you the first day you came through the door, despite your cocky grin.'

Her words were the key. They suddenly made sense of the complex feelings I had about Vicky Barker. Explained the *déjà vu*. Could it be that in a business where I was seen as top of the heap I'd met someone with the potential to be as good as I was? Her approach was faultless, she had hunches she couldn't stop living with and she went for objectives like a bird-dog. Which meant the uneasiness she'd always given me was professional jealousy, pure and simple.

'I'll think about it,' I said, hedging again. 'I must go. Look, Norma, I've tried this number, no luck. It's Sukie Goddard, Durkin's London friend. There's an outside chance he's been in touch with her and I don't want it to go by default. Would you keep trying?'

'If she answers I say I've got a wrong number and ring off?'

'Right, then get me on the mobile and I'll contact her. If I think she's covering for him, too, I'll give her a strong hint what he might be on the run for. This other number belongs to the man who has the upstairs flat in the house – I got his name when I was there. If you can't get through to Sukie, try him and ask if he knows if she's away. It's bugging me a little, her being unavailable. And if she's taken off with Durkin it adds another angle still.'

'Will do.'

'I aim to be at Crystal's place towards evening. I might do a Plan A at some stage. I'll let the phone ring three times and cut off. Will you ring my mobile then?'

She smiled. 'Aye, aye!'

'Johnny! Why didn't you let me know you were coming? How's your back?'

'Much better. All it needed was an hour or two on my board.'

'It must be a hell of a board, you crawled out of here like a tortoise with a wooden leg.' Faint traces of suspicion still lingered in her hazel eyes.

'Sorry I spoiled the evening, Crystal. I'm just here to have a quick word with Brian.'

'God, talk about dog with a bone. Tell him what he wants to know, Brian. We'll have a drink when you've finished, Johnny, and you'll be staying to dinner. Tell Monica I've a guest, Brian.'

'Very good, Mrs D.'

Brian had the look of a man who'd had a bad crossing on a Channel ferry. 'Come to the staff parlour, sir,' he said reluctantly.

'See you later, Johnny; you know where I'll be,' Crystal said, making a jabbing motion towards the ceiling seven or eight times to clear up any possible doubt.

I followed Brian's green-clad, slightly crouched figure to his cosy den, which had a three-piece, a television, a stereo-system and a table with drinks tray. He didn't ask me to sit, had begun to tremble again.

'I've told you everything, sir, I really don't know why you keep going on like this.'

I brought my face very close to his. 'Look, you little toe-rag, you know bloody well who was in the Rolls the night before he went missing, don't you, because it was *you*.'

I'd seen corpses with more colour. 'You went to pick up a Dresden Place tom,' I said, eyes three inches from his, 'called Tessa King.'

He couldn't get a word out, but his body language did the talking – the staring eyes, the quivering lips. I poured Scotch into a glass, handed it to him. He almost drained it. I wondered if he'd any idea she was now dead; news of the body had reached today's evening paper. 'I don't know where he *is*!' he suddenly cried, eyes moist with what looked like tears. 'I've *never* known, not after London.'

'I believe you.' I'd always been certain Challis wouldn't trust him with that information. 'But we're talking Tessa King here.'

There seemed a pleading glance in his brimming eyes.

'Look, Brian, you didn't tell the police the truth, did you, when Mrs Durkin first sent for them?'

It had to be why he was so upset, because he'd told the police half a story. He couldn't know about the killing; he'd be in a mental home by now.

'I just didn't want to get him in any *trouble*.' He gave a sudden sob. 'If . . . if he'd decided to try again with Miss King.'

He began to cry. It was a sad sight, but I'd seen several men cry before, all decent enough types who'd put a single foot wrong.

I took his arm. 'You love Mr Maurice, don't you?'

He suddenly grasped my hand, began to sob uncontrollably. 'Everybody loves him,' he said, his voice sounding almost like a mew. 'If . . . if you knew him you'd understand.'

How many times had I heard that? 'But you care for him in a special way, Brian, don't you? You'd do anything for him. I understand, believe me. But I do have a duty to madam. Now tell me exactly what happened and I'll cover for you, both with madam *and* the police.'

He took out a handkerchief, mopped his wet face. Then he looked at me directly and steadily for the first time, and there were the beginnings of trust in his swimming eyes. 'He . . . went out in the Saab that night. He was very . . . nervy, had a lot on his mind. I'd . . . not seen him that way since he'd gone out with her . . . the last time. . . .'

'Tessa? When she worked at the Crystalmart?'

'He'd . . . well, he'd been obsessed with her, sir, but I thought it had blown over a year ago. Anyway, he went off in the Saab and then Mr Challis rang. He . . . er . . . confides in me a lot, sir, like Mr Maurice does. He said Mr Maurice was in a terrible state and had to see Miss King. He asked me to try and pick her up and take her to a spot called Seven Arches.'

'I know it. Why didn't Mr Maurice pick her up himself?'

'Mr Challis said he was afraid she'd not even speak to him. She . . . well, she just wanted to live her own life, you see, sir. You must find it hard to believe when she could have had Mr Maurice.'

I smiled faintly. 'People are full of surprises.'

'Anyway, Mr Challis asked me to go to Miss King's flat and ask her if she'd just agree to see Mr Maurice once more so he could say a final goodbye to her.'

Some goodbye. 'And she agreed to that?'

'There's a clearing at Seven Arches, sir, where young women of a certain type. . . .'

'I know all about the clearing, Brian.'

'Mr Challis said that I should let Miss King out at the track end of the clearing, and that Mr Maurice would be at the other end and he'd flash his headlamps three times to show he was waiting. When I saw the headlamps I had to drive straight off because Mr Maurice was feeling very self-conscious about it all, with having struggled so hard to get over Miss King. I . . . I could understand that, sir.'

'Why take the Rolls, Brian? You could have taken a more discreet car.'

There was a flicker of pride in his eyes. 'The Rolls is my little perk, sir. I can always use it myself if Mr Maurice doesn't need it. Force of habit, I suppose.'

I nodded. 'I see. And that's the full story?'

'As God's my judge, sir.'

Poor Brian. I wished I could spare him the frightful future shock of knowing he may have carried Tessa to her death. It should never have happened to a decent, hard-working gay, mad about his boss.

'All right, Brian, you've been a big help, and I'll keep the heat off you if you swear you'll not tell anyone else what you've just told me until I say so, anyone at all.'

'You have my word, sir. I'm sorry to have been so uncooperative earlier.'

'That's all right. I know all about divided loyalties.'

'Come in, Johnny love.'

The great bedroom was full of evening sunlight, and she sat in front of a dressing-table that took up half a wall, combing her long, high lighted, brown hair. She wore a pale-blue towelling bathrobe, and from the general softness of her opulent body it was clear little was being worn beneath it, if anything.

'Dearie me,' she said calmly, 'you've caught me fresh from the shower and not even changed. Get anything out of the fairy? I never did, not when his precious Maurice was involved and off tottying.'

'No luck. I hoped to find out where Maurice had been the night before he went missing, but he didn't know. Said he went off alone.'

'He'd be with gabbing Guinny, you ask me. God *knows* what they were always chuntering about, their heads never stopped bobbing. Still, better their heads bobbing than their bums, I suppose.' But she didn't seem too sure. 'I tell you,' she muttered, 'there were times when I thought that bitch might be at the bottom of it all somehow, even if it was only her mouth she opened and not her legs.'

How sound her instincts had been. I was glad she was a tough lady and a realist, because it seemed that whatever happened she'd be in a no-win situation. And I was certain she'd miss that man of hers very badly, even though she played around as much as he did.

'Let's have some champagne, pet,' she said. 'Perhaps you'd like to do the honours with that wire thing.'

Two bottles of Krug chilled in a silver pail, almost lost to sight among vases of freshly cut flowers on a side table. I carefully uncorked one and poured into funnel-shaped glasses. By this time, with her usual flair for scene-setting, she'd drifted to the bed and lay propped against the ornate headboard. She thumped the silken bedspread. 'Come and take the weight off your feet, love.'

But what had happened to the bed itself? I stood motionless before it, and bewildered. Last night it had been so *low*. It had now magically grown until it reached the middle of my thigh.

'Can't have you doing your back in again,' she said, in a kindly tone. 'I got the odd-job man to raise it a bit.'

'Oh, Crystal, you shouldn't have bothered.'

'You were in agony, love. I really felt for you. Anyway, I think I prefer it higher. Seems easier on the knees.'

I sipped the costly wine, genuinely dismayed by the trouble she'd gone to to get me horizontal. I'd begun to like her a lot, and I'd once fancied her, but the calm Louise seemed to have pushed her aside almost without effort, simply because she was more me. I sighed inwardly. I didn't want to hurt her, but apart from anything else I really was busy, trying to fit in routine work around Durkin.

I said, 'Can you point me to your en-suite, Crystal. Must be the bubbly. . . .'

'Maurice always says it runs through him too. It's that bit of mirror there, Johnny – you touch the little diamond engraving.'

I did so, and a section of the mirrored wall glided back, closing when I was in the bathroom, which had a bath that seemed only marginally smaller than the pool, and from the array of levers I saw that it could do much more exciting things to your body than merely leave it clean. There were two handbasins, a stereo, a television and a wall-phone. But I took out my own phone, keyed Norma's home number, and let it ring three times. Then I stowed the mobile and quickly returned to the bedroom, where Crystal had thoughtfully arranged for a great deal more of her fragrant cleavage to be on display. Within seconds my phone began to ring. 'If that's mine I can't think where I put the bloody thing,' Crystal said. 'Think I'll ignore it. . . .'

'It's mine. Excuse me a moment. John Goss. . . .'

Norma began reciting nursery rhymes very slowly. 'I can't believe I'm hearing this, Norma . . . But this is the second time. Surely there's someone in the building . . . Norma, I'm having a client meeting with Mrs Durkin, I *can't* just drop everything . . . I thought you had a spare . . . Oh *God*, give me half an hour. . . .'

I found it hard to meet Crystal's eyes. She sat frozen into immobility, pupils white-edged. 'I'm dreadfully sorry, Crystal, my PA can't get out of the office building. They lock the main doors at seven and the caretaker goes home. The stupid bitch has forgotten her key.' I hit the palm of one hand with the fist of the other, in a creditable impression of anger and frustration.

'Can't she ring the caretaker?' she cried.

'He's new. She doesn't even know his name.'

'But there'll be a fire door.'

'That's locked too. Irregular, but we've had break-ins.'

'Oh, Johnny,' she wailed, 'do you have to go right now?'

'She gets panic attacks. She's not a young woman.'

'You'll come back when you've let her out. . . .'

'Wouldn't be worth it, Crystal, it'll take me ages to calm her down. She's an old fool, but she's been with me since I began. I'm really dreadfully sorry.'

Crystal couldn't work it out, but her powerful instincts were telling her it was exactly the same thing she'd had when people were covering for one of Durkin's affairs. She couldn't pin down its age or its breed or its pedigree, but she knew there was definitely a pup in there somewhere, and that once more, despite her careful planning, someone had contrived to sell her it. 'Oh dear,' she said dejectedly, 'Monica will be upset. And she was doing a lovely bit of sole. . . .'

I spent the evening writing up the lengthy invoices, as detailed as a solicitor's, with which PIs must provide clients, as they can never quite get their minds round the true cost of investigation work – especially Yorkshire folk. Norma would type them up in the morning; she was fretting about cash flow. I wondered if Vicky had managed to contact Denholm. Thinking of her made me think of Louise, and how much I'd like to hear her voice again; so I phoned her.

'I'd been hoping you'd ring,' she said. 'You must have sensed it.'

'I'd love to take you for a meal, Louise, but I'm locked in this really heavy case and working the clock round. But when it's over. . . .'

'Why not just come for a drink? Vicky told me about your workload. The penalties of success, I suppose.'

So I stuffed the wad of paper in my document-case and drove over to the little house above the woods. She looked as graceful as ever in another of her calf-length dresses, in white this time.

'Oh, John, it's so nice to see you again,' she said, kissing me on the lips in a way that wasn't remotely possessive, but gave a gratifying impression I could regard myself as part of her life now. We stood smiling at each other for a couple of seconds. I think we'd always sensed the similarities we shared, the pain that still throbbed from old wounds, which seemed to draw us to each other for comfort.

Later, over the drinks, I said, 'Vicky's doing fine, by the way. Between you and me, my PA and I are thinking seriously about offering her a job. I've certainly got more than I can tackle.'

'Oh, *John* . . . really?'

'She's certainly got ability. Talent, in fact.'

'I'd be so pleased to see her out of that awful Girl Talk.'

'Does she . . . have any idea about us?'

'No. When Clive left, I didn't want her confused or upset about other men – she missed him so much. I had one or two relationships. They didn't work.' She put a hand on mine. 'There aren't too many single men who are fun to be with and aren't searching for a clone of the woman they've left. Anyway, it was always their place, never mine, and the habit of discretion lingers on. On both sides, oddly enough; she never says much about her own boyfriends, as if she wants to keep a little corner where it's just me and her.'

We talked on, and though I didn't ask and she didn't invite, we both knew I'd stay the night again – because of the solace we found in each other's arms. I think we both knew that it would be a relationship of affection only, after the damage I'd sustained from Laura Marsh, and she from the husband who'd ditched her, but that the affection might become so strong we'd barely know the difference. I stroked her warm moist flesh in the darkness, heard her fluttering sigh in my ear, snd then her soft giggle.

'He was right, wasn't he, Henry Miller. . . ?'

I wondered if we'd finally found someone to settle down with, if we could see these occasional nights together leading to weekends, to even living together, able finally to watch the wreckage of our past lives floating off in calmer seas, as we pulled away in the lifeboat.

By midnight, Louise was asleep, but I was left with Durkin again, and the certainty that there was more to it than him being linked to a dead tom, a lot more. I wondered if I'd ever know. Suddenly, my mobile rang. I muted it, took it into the bathroom, closed the door.

'John,' Norma said quietly, 'I'm sorry to ring you so late, wherever you are. I couldn't get hold of Sukie, and I finally got through to Mr Greenwood in the other flat. He was very very guarded. I told him I was a family friend, would be in London tomorrow, and aiming to call on her, but she wouldn't answer her phone. I said I remembered his name from the last time I was there. I was going to tell you in the morning, but thought you might want to know as soon as possible. Someone got into her flat. Someone she knew; there were no signs of a break-in. She's dead . . . strangled. They only found the body yesterday morning – the police forced the door.'

ELEVEN

She opened the door wearing a red satin dressing-gown, her hair tousled, face slightly puffy. 'For God's *sake*, John, I was asleep. I was on the night shift or had you forgotten. . . .'

'Sorry, I wasn't thinking,' I said truthfully, not needing much sleep myself. I followed her into her flat.

'Anyway,' she said, in the same aggrieved tone, 'I got naff-all that would be any good.'

'You picked him up then.'

'No problem. You'd better have some coffee.'

The living-room was cheerful and basic. Hand-me-down furniture, cheapish curtains and carpets, framed Seurat prints, a portable telly, a portable CD player. But the windows gave good views over open country. I followed her into the kitchen, suddenly shivered; I'd followed her mother into her own kitchen an hour ago, and they looked so alike – the same graceful bodies and irregular features, the same gap in their top front teeth.

She glanced at me as she filled an electric jug, coloured slightly, as if she'd just realized how little she wore. Near-nakedness gave her a vulnerability she'd not want me to be aware of, not being spiky Vicky. For a second, there was a clouded look in her harebell eyes, impossible to analyse.

I suspected frustration, the same frustration I'd known lying sleepless at Louise's. Neither of us was getting anywhere. I had an urge to put an arm around her in commiseration. But I suddenly realized there was desire there too, as powerful as it was alarming, as if I was with a Louise of twenty years ago.

She gave me a beaker of instant. 'I'll get some clothes on,' she said hastily, 'and then I'll play the tape, for what it's worth.'

She was back in a few minutes in jeans and a shirt, holding a recorder little bigger than a credit card, and a microphone about as thick as a pencil and an inch and a half long, with a pen-type clip. 'I usually wear something with a scooped neckline,' she said, 'fasten the mike to that, and cover it with a chiffon scarf. It plays back through this....' She clipped the recorder into a speaker stand, pressed Play on the sounds of talk, laughter, piano music, the rattle of ice. 'Hello there,' Denholm's voice spoke. 'You looking for company? I'm Chris – let me buy you a drink.'

'Well ... thank you, Chris. I am a bit lonely.'

She fast-forwarded with a wry smile. 'I'll spare you the come-on scene. This is where he's got me in a room with him.'

'You know, Chris, I'm sure I've seen you before. Do you ever go to Maurice Durkin's place? It's called Maunan, has its own pool....'

'Maurice Durkin ... what do *you* know about Maurice Durkin?' The voice was slurred now, in the old familiar way.

'Oh, we used to be friendly once. How is he?'

'Oh, he's all right. Crap at playing the bloody market, but *he's* all right.'

'There's a rumour going around that he's left Crystal....'

'What's it to you?' He began to laugh unpleasantly. 'Fancy your chances? Well, you might bring him luck with the market, you never know. You feel like making out? Give me a kiss ...'

She stopped the tape. 'As you can tell, he was well pissed by then. I said I had to eat before anything else, and he finally had room service send up sandwiches. I couldn't get a sniff on Durkin's whereabouts. I could only risk bringing the name up once or twice more, and it just gets him banging on about this market stuff.' She spooled on the tape again.

'. . . Yeah, well, he could drop a bollock like everyone else, the great bleeding Maurice. . . .' Denholm's voice was now muffled as well as slurred, as if he was eating. 'He was . . . was all right . . . with . . . with der . . . derivatives and arbi . . . traging. It was currency . . . right.'

'I'm afraid you're losing me.'

'Example . . . the . . . peso's weakening, yes? So you . . . you borrow pesos short term, yes? And buy dollars with the pesos. The peso goes on weakening . . . against the dollar . . . say by five per cent. So you change the dollars . . . back to pesos . . . yes? Only . . . they buy five per . . . per cent more pesos than you . . . kicked off with . . . and . . . you can pay back peso loan . . . keep the change.'

She halted the tape. 'I brought Durkin's name up one last time,' she said, spooling a little further.

'Who did Maurice take up with after Crystal then, Chris?'

'Why all this interest in Durkin? Christ, we're . . . we're supposed to be . . . be having . . . a fun night.'

She stopped the tape for good. 'That was it. Pissed as he was, he was getting suspicious. Shortly after, he suddenly rushed to the loo to be violently sick. Must have been something he ate, poor love. I split. Can you make *anything* of the financial stuff?'

'Derivatives are a kind of future,' I said slowly, 'and arbitraging means you balance the risk between buying and selling. It's fiendishly complicated. What he was saying about currency was that you speculated between one currency and another and hoped to turn a profit.'

'It doesn't really help, does it?'

'I don't honestly think so, Vicky,' I said despondently. 'Durkin was retired, he spent his mornings on his investments. So he got a few wrong – he'd have got a lot more right. It just sounds like an accountant badmouthing a shrewd business brain that could run rings round his. You've done a good job. I'm sorry it didn't work out.'

'He wasn't so drunk he'd let anything slip.'

'I'm not really surprised, after Ferrara. Can I copy your tape on to mine?' I got out my own recorder, it seemed massive at the side of her MI5 special. 'I'll listen again later.'

As she synchronized the equipment, she said, 'You agreed we'd go back to the Lakes if this didn't work.'

I shrugged. 'All right. Give me a couple of days.'

She had the brooding look I knew so well, could see I was stalling. But it was clear to me it was all over. Another woman linked to Durkin was now dead, and inside twenty-four hours there was certain to be a full-scale police enquiry, making us both redundant.

'Something needs triggering,' she said flatly. 'I got those, to see if they'd help.' She pointed to some large-format books at the rear of the table. They were tourist guides to the Lakes, with pictures of fells and sheets of glittering water, alive with yachts and cruisers. 'I shall study them,' she said. 'See if anything rings a bell.'

I shivered, as before. When she wasn't reminding me of Louise, because of how she looked, she reminded me of me, because of the way she beat her brain around.

'Sukie Goddard,' I said. 'Durkin's London bimbo . . . she's bought it.'

He paused in dabbing eyes streaming from the smoke of his displacement cigar. I told him the story.

'What do you think?'

'Let's kick it around. Let's say someone, probably Challis, told Durkin Crystal had hired me. Maybe Durkin guessed I'd get to Sukie in the end. Only I got to her first, as Crystal had her phone number.'

'But she couldn't tell you much, as I remember.'

'Only that Durkin spent time at Ambleside when he was poor.'

'So why did Durkin see her off?'

'If it *was* Durkin who killed anyone.'

Fenlon shrugged, swung his head. He was anxious for a result. He'd had Durkin's name on the Tessa King file from the start.

'Look, Bruce, Durkin may be missing, but he's got six mates covering for him. Now it could be loyalty or it could be because they're in it *too*. Or it could be a mixture of both.'

'I can't buy that. It's *Durkin* who's legged it. It *could* have been coincidence with King, him just happening to be with her the same night someone did for her. But now his London totty suddenly kicks off. If *that's* coincidence it's the sort where you win the lottery twice in two weeks. Anyway,' he added heavily, 'let's *assume* Durkin saw to Sukie, then ask ourselves why.'

'He could have been genuinely uncertain *what* he'd let slip,' I reluctantly admitted. 'There could have been other things when he'd had a couple. It could have been a tidying-up operation, because he'd heard about me, and panicked. That's *if* we look at it in bog-standard police-force terms. Anyway you lot will be taking over now. . . .'

He glanced at me. 'You don't *want* to pack it in?'

'You know I don't. But with the increase in the body count. . . .'

'Sukie's a *London* murder.' He winked. 'She worked the scene. Living that life, anyone could have killed her.'

He ordered a second round. 'Give it two more days, John. The forensics are still tinkering with Tessa's body. You're in with Durkin's pals and you might still come up with something. If you don't I'm bloody sure we won't, not with the protection he's got. What were you saying about Lord Lucan? Did I tell you that that Challis guy plays golf with the chief constable, gives ten grand a year to police charities? I want to nail Durkin, if it's only to show those shits rich men get the same justice as poor, when they start wasting harmless young kids. . . .'

I sighed. I liked the vote of confidence, but there seemed nowhere else to go. If Durkin had been in London and seen off Sukie, could he also have been taking delivery of a false passport?

I kicked it around with Norma at the office. She'd often spotted things I'd missed. 'He comes across as too nice for murder, John.'

'My feelings. But he had been obsessive about Tessa. Both Vicky's snout and his manservant say the same. And Sukie, well, she told me that only Durkin had keys to her flat.'

'If he has killed he must be in a dreadful state. These friends, do you think they can possibly know any of it?'

'Only Challis, I think. After all, he acted as go-between for Durkin and Tessa. He's either protecting him because of what he owes to Durkin or because he might be damaged by the fall-out. The others may know where Durkin *is*, but not what he's done. Men like Denholm and Ackroyd couldn't countenance murder at any price. But they know damn fine it's not just Durkin running off with a woman.'

'All right,' she said slowly, 'let's say Challis has a total blind spot for Durkin, but why should the others go along with it, despite Ferrara? One of them could have tipped you off anonymously.'

'The thought had crossed my own mind. So what could they all be involved in that falls short of murder but is still against the law?' I gave her my pocket recorder. 'A copy of Vicky's tape. You might as well hear it before you put it on file.'

She played it. 'The financial stuff makes my head spin.'

'It seems to boil down to Durkin speculating on currency movements. Remember George Soros? All right, five per cent, say, isn't much, but on a million it's fifty grand.'

She looked sceptical. 'Do you think he'd really gamble so much? A million, half a million, whatever, when he could lose the lot?'

'He has a few million in the sock, and we know he was trying to increase his assets so he could leave Crystal with an unchanged lifestyle when he went into politics with Guinevere.'

She was still unconvinced. 'He'd made his money the hard way, John. Worked the clock round, extended his chain carefully. He sounds like a very astute businessman to me. Do you know what I'd do if I was wealthy – pause for shrieks of hysterical laughter – and I had wealthy pals? I'd invite them to chip in, like they do with insurance.'

The rush in the blood was like three glasses of Crystal's Krug. I leaned over and kissed her forehead. 'That's it! That's it!'

'What have I *done!*'

'He's not just pissed, on the tape, when he talks about Durkin and the market. He's *angry*. His voice changes. . . .'

She was already spooling back the tape until she isolated the sentence I directed her to. Denholm's voice said, 'Oh, he's all right. Crap at playing the market, but *he's* all right.'

She nodded. 'Agreed. For that one line he sounds as if he could throttle someone. I still don't know what I've done, but if you're so pleased it must be worth a rise.'

'I can't run to that, but play your cards right and I'll extend your contract another six months.'

My car seemed to fly up the zigzag roads to Maunan a foot off the ground. 'Ah, Brian, good afternoon. Madam about?'

'She is, sir, by the pool. I'll take you along. Any news of Mr Maurice. . . ?'

'I'm hopeful I have a new lead.'

He looked relieved, took me down to the patio, where Crystal, at her voluptuous best in a white sun-top and turquoise jeans, sat at an umbrella-table, feeding scraps to the be-ribboned draught-excluder.

'Johnny!'

It was impossible not to be touched by the intense pleasure she always seemed to be given by my unexpected appearances. 'Hello, Crystal, can you spare me half an hour?'

'I can spare you the rest of the day, chuck. Brian, get Neil to chill some champagne and tell Monica we'd like a nice meal about seven. Something summery.'

'Very good, Mrs D.'

'And look, Brian, this pool *still* isn't right. . . .' But Brian had vanished as suddenly as if he'd stepped into a magician's box.

'Crystal, I really can't stay long. I could be on to something.'

'Nonsense, you'll give yourself a heart attack rushing about in this hot sun. Have a couple of hours off on me. We'll not be able to see as much of each other, you know, when you get the bugger back.'

I smiled wryly. She thought when he returned she'd just give him a monumental bollocking and that would be that – it would be back to the parties and cruises with the old charismatic Maurice at her side. It would be secure again, the open marriage that suited them both; they'd been together since the market-stall days, after all.

I decided I'd not argue at this stage about how long I'd be staying. 'I need to look at Maurice's desk and safe, Crystal, if that's possible. Would you have keys?'

'I have, love. We had no secrets, not that I ever had a clue about his share-buying and so forth. There's not much in the locked bits, apart from bank accounts and certificates and the sale papers for the Crystalmarts. It was weird seeing them listed and this big sale price at the end; it gave me such a funny feeling. You can't *believe* how we scratted and scraped to buy the first one. Oh, well. . . .'

Her hazel eyes gazed unfocused over the gleaming pool, and I seemed to see the nostalgia I'd seen in the other wives for older, simpler days, when they'd been lively young women who worked hard and enjoyed a night out and travelled hopefully towards goals much more modest, and more easily coped with, than the splendid ones they'd achieved. 'Come on, pet,' she said, sighing, 'I'll take you up. . . .'

In Durkin's study, she unlocked his desk and wall-safe. I ignored the neat bundles of share certificates and VRDs and went for the bank statements, as Crystal stood looking out at her pool, a hand to her face. 'It looks *worse* from up here,' she said. 'If Cecily *Challis* was to see it. Wait till I get my hands on that fairy.'

There were four separate account-binders. There was a current account and a deposit account, both very healthy as Crystal had said, the one feeding the other. The third was closed, and seemed to have been opened specifically to cover the receipts and fees of the sale of the business. The final balance, presumably transferred into investments, had left Durkin with six million in his hand.

The fourth account was more interesting. It revealed monies being paid in and out in what seemed a pattern. Large sums would be credited, and seven equal shares of the sums paid out. The credited sums varied between £200,000 and £1 million, and entered the account about once a month. Occasionally, the reverse applied, with seven equal sums being paid in and the *total* of the sums paid out. But the statements for the last six months were missing.

'Crystal, have you any idea where the later statements for this account could be?' I said, after a fruitless search. 'And I can't find the paying-in book or the cheque books that go with it.'

'They'll be with Maurice, pet. Anything not there always went with him in his document-case.'

It figured. I said, 'The other night you mentioned a man at a merchant bank who kept ringing about Maurice's buying account.'

'Eynsford-Grey. He's still at it. I keep telling him Maurice'll sort it, but he says to open the letters and pass them on to the accountant. No chance, not till Maurice sees them. He'd go spare.'

The letters lay in a neat bundle at the back of the desk, marked STRICTLY PRIVATE AND CONFIDENTIAL. 'Would you have Eynsford-Grey's number? Mind if I rang him?'

'Oh, Johnny,' she said uneasily, 'I keep telling you what Maurice is like. . . .'

'I can say I'm police. After all, the police *are* involved. You see,' I lied, 'I'm positive Maurice *has* to be in touch with this guy soon about his portfolio. And he'll have to leave a number or a postal address. And then we'll have him.'

It didn't make too much sense, but it was enough to satisfy Crystal. 'Oh, all right, you stubborn young bugger,' she said, flicking open a telephone pad and reading out the number. I keyed it.

'Wendell, Street and Dummer. . . .'

'Mr Eynsford-Grey, please. This is Detective Sergeant Maddox of Beckford CID. It's in connection with a Mr Maurice Durkin.'

I was connected in seconds. 'DS Maddox, Mr Eynsford-Grey, of the Beckford police. I'm involved in Mr Durkin's disappearance.'

'*Disappearance!*' The word seemed to explode through the earpiece like shock wave. '*Disappearance!* But he was supposed to be on a business trip.'

'So Mrs Durkin believed, sir, and it seems he wasn't very good at keeping in touch. But he's been gone too long now without word.'

There was a very lengthy silence; it felt like the silence of a man in shock. 'You rang Mrs Durkin's residence several times, sir,' I gently prompted. 'Could you tell me why?'

'It's . . . it's completely confidential,' he said at last, in what was barely a hoarse whisper. 'Between Mr Durkin and ourselves.'

'Does he owe your company money, sir?' I persisted.

'I . . . can't divulge any details.'

'I understand, sir. I can apply for authority to examine Mr Durkin's finances, of course, but it would take time.'

Another lengthy pause. 'He . . . well, his last account is unsettled.'

'I see. Much involved?'

'Yes. I can say no more without an official request.'

'Thousands?'

It took him a long time to get the words out, in a strangled tone. 'You're talking tea money. . . .'

'Millions?'

Heavy breathing accompanied the silence this time. 'I'm not at liberty to say.'

'I see, sir. Then if Mr Durkin contacts you with an address or phone number would you please let Mrs Durkin know.'

There was a sound as if lifeless fingers had dropped the phone.

Crystal, still at the window, glanced over her shoulder. 'What was that about millions, Johnny? He's not saying that's what's *owed*?'

'God, no,' I said, thinking fast. 'The debt's only a few thousand.

The reason he's anxious to contact Maurice is that he'd had wind of a share flotation that could be worth millions if Maurice gets in on the ground floor.'

No point in worrying her now. It might all sort itself out. If not it would have to join the many other worries set to engulf her.

'Well, he wants to mind his manners,' she said. 'I'm going to tell Maurice what a prat he's been. Come on, pet, let's go for a swim. There are some trunks of Maurice's you can borrow. Brand new.'

There was no way of getting out of it this time without hurting her. She smiled at me, the sun catching her highlights. I thought, why not? It would be an enjoyable act of kindness with an attractive woman. It would lead nowhere and Louise would never know. And a swim, a glass of champagne, on such a fine day. . . . I could give her an hour or two and catch up later. I also smiled. 'All right, Crystal.'

We went down in the lift to the sunny pool-room; the water looked incredibly inviting. Then a phone rang. Crystal picked it up, sighed, handed it to me. 'Someone called Vicky for you.'

'I've got it, I've got it, *I've got it*! I know who *Veronica* is!'

TWELVE

My car seemed to be floating again as I raced into the valley and up the other side. She'd tell me nothing else over the phone; she needed to show me something.

'Give me twenty minutes,' I'd said. 'Sorry, Crystal, this is a red alert.' Her wail of anguish seemed to echo in my head as I tail-gated and lane-hopped.

'For Christ's *sake*, Johnny, don't say some other silly bloody cow's locked herself in the bog!'

'Crystal, things are breaking. I could find him by tomorrow.'

'Well, make it the day after and let's go for a *swim*.'

'Time's vital, in case he moves on. Trust me.'

'But Monica's made a start on her *salade* frigging *Niçoise*!'

The door opened before I'd rung the bell. She was flushed and her eyes shone. 'This is why I wanted to go back,' she said, her lips trembling. 'I just felt if we'd made the ferry crossing once more. . . .'

She grasped my hand and dragged me into the living-room, then picked up one of the tourist books about the Lakes. She had the page marked with an old envelope. 'Tara-a-a-a-a!'

The colour plate covered two pages. The title was *Springtime on Windermere*. It showed a lake as glassy as Crystal's pool, reflecting a clear blue sky. Various craft lay at anchor: yachts, motor-cruisers, a catamaran. The photograph had been taken with maximum depth of field and the detail was scalpel sharp, so sharp that the names of the craft could be read. The name on one of the cruisers was *Veronica*.

'It's *not* a woman,' she cried. 'It's a bloody *boat*!'

I couldn't stop myself putting my arms about her and swinging her round and round in the middle of the room. 'Well *done*! Bloody well done! It never crossed my mind, there were so many flesh-and-blood women in his life.'

'It was the crossing,' she said, her arms still round my shoulders. 'So many boats had women's *names*. My brain kept trying and trying to get it together. If I'd gone back perhaps. . . .'

I smiled ruefully. She'd had a hunch and I'd ignored it, when I worked on hunches myself all the time. 'Yes,' I said, 'we should have gone back. We'll rectify that. Are you free now?'

'You bet your sweet life.'

We took our arms from around each other rather self-consciously, as if we'd just realized our bodies were still pressed together. The scent of her breath, which had the clean sweetness of healthy youth, seemed to linger like the smell of carnations after rain.

We ran out to my car and drove north again, racing through the Dales at the full limit and beyond, gradually leaving sunlight behind for heavy cloud.

'What's the form, John? Drive round Windermere with the field-glasses?'

'Impractical, I'm afraid. There are long stretches where the road doesn't skirt the lake. And the clouds mean it could be misty. Our best bet's the boatyards. Durkin's people might own the *Veronica* or might have hired her. Either way, the boat people will have an idea where she is. The firms are in two main places: Bowness and Ambleside. We'll try Bowness first.' I touched her hand. 'You've done a tremendous job, Vicky. We could have searched the whole of Cumbria, but if he's lying low on a *boat*, with plenty of provisions. . . .'

We came on our first view of the lake, not blue and glittering this time, but shining darkly with reflected cloud, its islands seeming sombre and mysterious in the milky light. At Bowness, we drove a little way south along the shore until we came to Glebe Road. A track angled from it that ran behind the boat firm premises. I parked, and we began to pick our way through the yards, past sheds and piers, past open areas where boats were being repaired or serviced: boats on trolleys, on their sides, on blocks. It was late evening now, and the few men who still worked were preoccupied, not keen to make eye-contact. But we finally came upon a man who was relaxing over a mug of tea at the door of one of the cavernous sheds. He was young, tall, muscular, with lengthy fair hair and a tan, and he wore denims and a grandad shirt.

He smiled. 'Need any help?'

'Thanks. Do you know of a vessel called the *Veronica* and where she might be moored?'

'That's an easy one,' he said. He put down his mug. 'Follow me.'

I exchanged a puzzled glance with Vicky. We followed him a little further along the track until we came to a set of piers railed off on the shore side, open to the lake. Heavy, locked gates were set into the railings at the head of each pier. The gates were lettered PRIVATE BERTHING in gold, the piers alphabetically listed. He led us to B gate. Parked at right angles to the pier lay about six vessels on each side. The second vessel on the left-hand side, looking precisely like its photo, was the motor-cruiser *Veronica*.

It was one of the worst disappointments of my professional career. My own dismay was reflected in Vicky's complete absence of expression. Poor kid, she'd beaten her brain out on this, and we'd both been certain the boat would be moored in some quiet inlet, with Durkin playing the waiting game.

'Well, there you are, folks . . .' the young man said, his back to us and unaware of our bitter frustration.

'Is there . . . anyone on her?'

He glanced at me, shook his head. 'Hasn't been for weeks.'

'Who owns her?'

'Would you like to tell me why you want to know?'

'I want to hire her. My girlfriend's called Veronica, and we're getting married. I've seen the boat out on the lake and want to use her on a cruising honeymoon.'

'The firm I work for hires out cruisers.'

'He's set his heart on this,' Vicky said, fluttering her eyes with professional expertise. 'He's a bit sentimental, you know.'

He smiled. 'Sorry can't help. Wealthy people own these and they like their privacy. They don't need to hire.'

'Perhaps they would if the price was right.' I smiled back, and the ten-pound note that had somehow appeared in my hand flashed from mine to his like a spark passing between two electrodes.

'You could get me shot at dawn, you know. It's a chap called Ray Challis, from Beckford, Yorkshire. And forget you ever saw me. . . .'

I'd bought a Chinese on the outskirts of Beckford, after an almost silent drive down and we'd eaten it in her flat in a state of trance-like depression.

'It's a lever, Vicky,' I said at last. 'We know the boat's Challis's, we know Durkin was on her, and we know he's in big money trouble, quite apart from a dead tom and a dead girlfriend.'

'You said nothing would ever crack Challis,' she said despondently.

'Once. But we know too much now. I can pitch it to Challis that if he goes on making us find Durkin the hard way he'll end up facing an accusation of perverting the course of justice. I can tell him if he won't co-operate I'll lean on the others; he can't arrange to have them all put in hospital.'

'Why not bypass Challis and go straight to them?'

'Because he's a realist. He has a squeaky-clean reputation, plays golf with the bobbies. I believe he'd protect Durkin for good *if* he could be certain he'd never be found, but with what we know now he can't be sure of that any more. If I can convince him of it I think we can sort something out. He's a born fixer.'

She began to look less unhappy at last. 'Do you *really* think it made any difference, John, me finding out about the *Veronica*?'

I poured some more of the Bulgarian red I'd also bought. 'Look, Vicky, the *Veronica* and the stuff you got from Denholm will clinch this case, I'm positive. All right, we hoped to nail the bastard aboard ship, but it's hardly ever that easy in this game.' It was good to see her smiling properly for the first time since we'd seen the *Veronica*, berthed and uninhabited.

'Oh, well, it's been an awful lot of fun, however it turns out.'

'PI work's mostly humdrum, you know,' I told her, 'and yet the real toughies that only come along now and then, like Rainger and Marsh and Durkin, can make it all worthwhile.' I glanced at my watch, rose. 'Come on, I'll help wash up before I go.'

'Oh, John, for heaven's sake – two plates, two glasses, two coffee cups; I think I can cope.'

She got up, too, and we stood for a few seconds in the half-light of a small table-lamp. Her mobile face was still now, and there was a clouded look to her eyes I remembered from this morning. Our arms suddenly went round each other. It had been a day of surprises.

'Oh, John . . . I've wanted this for so long. . . .'

Her body trembled in my arms as I tried to cope with the shock. She'd attracted me this morning very much, tousled, wearing only a dressing-gown, but I'd never imagined it went both ways, in the marked absence of clear signals.

'You'll . . .' she whispered. 'Will you stay?'

'I . . . hardly know you.' It was true, virtually all our talk had been of Durkin.

'I . . . I . . . just know. Don't you?'

It was a lovemaking first for me. Not because of the expertise, as she had hardly any, it was the intensity of emotion I seemed to have aroused in her.

'Oh, John,' she whispered shakily, again and again, her hand almost clumsily stroking my face and hair, her body trembling so much it was barely possible to tell when the shudder of orgasm began. 'Oh God, John. . . .'

It was an experience as heady as it was unique. Because what she felt for me seemed the genuine article, and I'd never really known it before. I wasn't an easy man to love, due to old bitter hang-ups. There'd been Fernande Dumont, Laura Marsh, but even with them love had been an illusion. With Vicky there seemed no illusion and I didn't know how to handle it. But I knew I liked it, despite the sound of warning bells. I clasped her taut young body in the midnight silence, wondered how I'd cope with the responsibility.

'I'd . . . see you around town,' she whispered. 'After the Rainger case publicity. I couldn't get you off my mind. I'd get so *bitter* – feeling like that about someone who didn't even know I was *there*.'

It began to make sense of our once spiky relationship.

'I'm afraid I'm not very good . . . at this.'

I smiled. 'You soon will be, the way you master everything else. Anyway, it doesn't matter, it's the other things that count.' In my case the sheer volume of emotion cascading over me.

'It's your fault I've not been with many men,' she said, 'when the only bloody face I could ever see was yours.'

She began to kiss me, again and again, with an almost angry passion, as if to make up for the times I'd passed her on a city street and never known I was the focus of such an intense longing.

Later still, she said, 'Will you give me a job? I get on with Norma.'

'Think I'd let the opposition get near you?'

'I'm not possessive. I know the sort of life you live. We both like our space. But if we can work together, meet now and then at my place or yours, it's all I'd want.'

'It wouldn't be easy. I'm not bad out of the office, but I can be a difficult, moody bastard in it. Ask your chum, Norma.'

'We're professionals,' she said, with something of the old asperity. 'We can switch from one mode to the other.'

I was sure she could do that. She was Louise's daughter and shared some of her ability to be in effective control of her life.

Louise's daughter. My cheeks burned in the darkness. The day had been so crowded it simply hadn't struck me that within a handful of days I'd slept with both Vicky and her mother. And I liked Louise a lot, an awful lot, but I had to ask myself if I'd ever feel more for her than affectionate gratitude. It didn't begin to compare with how I felt about Vicky. I knew I'd have to devote a great deal of time and effort to ending with Louise as considerately as possible. I dreaded it, as I sensed that if I couldn't make a clean, decisive break all three of us would be caught up in a good deal of pain.

THIRTEEN

The servant called Charlie showed me into what seemed to be a breakfast-room. There was a circular table, and a sideboard was set with cereals, chafing dishes, preserves and fresh rolls. Seconds later, Challis strode in, dressed in denims, a check shirt and an old jerkin, a yellow hard-hat in his left hand.

'Ah, John,' he said with his usual indestructible affability, 'you catch me just off to a hard day's arse-kicking in South Yorkshire. I can only spare a minute.'

'That's all I need – at this stage.'

'Fire away,' he said, pouring coffee and handing me a cup.

'I'll not go into detail, but what it boils down to is that I know the *Veronica*'s a motor-cruiser, that she's yours, that she's at the Glebe Road landings, and that at some point Maurice was on her.'

Shrewd operator though he was, he let the silence go on too long. Face impassive behind the horn-rims, he said calmly, 'I never thought it wise to underestimate you, John, from the start.'

'I've also got it together on Maurice's futures buying and forex deals.' This time he couldn't control the rattle of cup on saucer. 'There's a merchant bank in London that's seriously pissed off about Maurice not getting in touch.'

He watched me in a lengthy silence. 'What are we saying here, John?'

'That if we can't sort this out between us I go and scare the entire shit out of the lawyer and the accountant. You'd have the police round here this afternoon.'

'What does that mean,' he said warily, 'about sorting this out between us?'

'I'm working for Crystal,' I said, equally wary, 'simply hired to find Maurice. I'm certain you know where he is. All I need is an address, so I can tell Crystal and get off everyone's back. Anything else about Maurice, like how much he might owe a bank, is outside my terms of reference.'

He went to the window, part of which stood open on his flawless lawn and his maples in perfect, painted leaf. He stood deep in thought as his driver warmed the engine of a Range Rover that stood in the yard. Finally, he turned back, his expression still benignly friendly, despite the wariness.

'You've thrown me a spinner, you bastard. I need to kick this around and get back to you.'

'I'll look forward to it. Don't leave it too long.'

Fenlon was there ahead of me, had abandoned the cigars, and was back to smoking cigarettes.

'Durkin,' I said. 'I've thrown a scare into Challis. He's chewing it over, but I'm pretty sure he'll come across. He's ringing me later. I think he's working on damage limitation.' I updated him on the *Veronica* and Durkin's multi-million pound debt.

'Why was he speculating so heavily?'

'He wanted to increase his assets so he could make a substantial divorce settlement on Crystal, marry Guinevere Denholm and throw himself into public life. He had flair, and I think the friends wanted a piece of the action – a share-out if they were ahead, a collection if he got it wrong. That would explain the Café Royal piss-ups. I think his last spec went disastrously wrong.'

'So they all lost?'

'I think they all lost *something*, but I reckon Durkin was in it for higher stakes than the others and lost his shirt. The others lost enough to make them bloody annoyed, going by Denholm's reaction on Vicky's tape, but no more. So they cover for their best pal. But what was making them so jumpy was that *their* debts were concealed by Durkin's disappearance. It's not that they *can't* settle their debts, it's simply that they can't settle with Durkin until he comes out in the open and settles with the bank – their own share-out was a gentleman's agreement. And Durkin can't settle with the bank because his share of the debt would break him.'

'Christ, it's like three-dimensional chess. And two dead girl-friends for good measure.'

'Stress perhaps. We've seen it before. His world falls apart and he tries to salvage some kind of life with a woman he was crazy about. She doesn't want to know, and it's the last straw. And poor bloody Sukie – perhaps he really did think she knew too much.'

'You think Challis knows about Tessa?'

'Highly probable. He doesn't know I know, of course.'

'Durkin's valet-guy: isn't he in Challis's pocket?'

'He won't talk. He's a decent type and I trust him.'

'So Challis just thinks you're on to the financial scam?'

'Just that. And he may genuinely believe Durkin isn't in the frame for the murder; his name's never been publicly linked to Tessa's in any way. He could be convinced now that Durkin's only real problem is the dealing account.'

'Even so, the sod's an accessory,' he said bitterly, 'and if he'd come to us the minute Durkin legged it we'd have Durkin in the slammer now and be playing nice detective, nasty detective.'

I shrugged. 'That's how he is about Durkin. I can't decide if it's simply loyalty or if he's worried about his own involvement in bringing Durkin and Tessa together getting out. But Durkin did once save both his life and his business – draw your own conclusions.'

He nodded. 'How will you play it?'

'By ear. I've told Challis if he doesn't tell me where Durkin is today I let the dogs loose . . . today.'

*

I spent the afternoon on routine work – a debt-collection trace, a lifestyle check, an interview with a prospective client. Driving around the city, I tried to work out the kindest way of telling Louise that I'd fallen for Vicky. I wondered if it would be the slightest comfort that the daughter she was so protective about would now be given a great deal more protection by someone she could trust.

Louise's face merged into Vicky's, and I wondered if this was the point where it really would change, my loner's life of brief affairs that had left me only too vulnerable to the disastrous involvements with Fernande, with Laura Marsh.

The car-phone rang. 'Challis, John. Could you make it to Valley View again?'

'Give me half an hour.'

I rang Norma, told her where I'd be. 'Vicky's in your office, helping to process client accounts. Seems as happy as Larry, I can't *imagine* why.'

'We may have news for you, as if you didn't know. The dilemma is could I inflict you on anyone, let alone Vicky. Give her my . . .' – I stopped myself in the nick of time – 'regards.'

Charlie was waiting at the door of the Challis mansion, and took me up to his office. 'Sit yourself down, John,' Challis said, from the other side of his big desk. 'Drink?'

'I try not to when I'm working, thanks.'

'Me too. And never when there's a deal to be cut.'

'Does that mean there's some kind of a deal to be cut here?'

'I've done some hard thinking, John. In fact I abandoned my trip to South Yorkshire. You've got police contacts, I'm sure.'

'Agreed.'

'Maybe we can come to an arrangement. You wouldn't be wearing a body-mike, by any chance?'

'You're welcome to give me a brushdown.'

'I believe you. Look, let's say this pal of mine does find himself in a spot of money trouble. And let's say he *might* be talked into coming back if someone with clout in the Beckford force could ask this merchant bank that's owed the money to go easy on the debt. Settle say for half and give him time to pay. A long time.'

'I doubt the police would want to know, Ray,' I said cautiously. 'I'd say we're talking the SFO here – the bank might already have alerted them. It would be between the bank, the SFO and your friend.'

'Come on, John,' he said gently, with his benign smile. 'No bank wants that kind of publicity. Get one punter losing you money and the rest are going to think you couldn't run a chip shop.'

'On the other hand, they might want to throw the book at him as a warning to others tempted to take risks they can't cover.'

'If my friend made a comeback the bank would get *something*; if he doesn't they get sod-all. The bottom line being that if they'll not deal he'll not return. Ever.'

I hesitated. 'I can't give you an answer at this stage. I'd have to speak to my contacts and get back to you.'

He watched me in a lengthy silence. 'Look, John, I'll level with you. I trust you and we're talking good faith here. Frankly, I don't know if I can convince my friend to even *consider* a comeback. We're almost too closely involved with each other, well, you know the story. But if you and me were to see the guy together, and you explained his options as the honest broker, it might swing it.'

It took me by surprise, and for all my experience I couldn't conceal it. He added softly, 'The deal would be, of course, that if he didn't agree to you sounding out the bank, etcetera, for a possible comeback you'd forget you'd seen him. Think about it.'

I didn't need to think about it for long. It was an unexpected move, but I suspected a strong reason for making it was that if Durkin *could* be talked into considering a comeback, Challis and Co would be able to settle their markers with him and sleep easily at night. It was clear he believed I didn't know about Tessa King.

Danger? I couldn't really see any, despite the veiled threats I'd had earlier, despite Ferrara's beating – I knew now anyway what they'd closed his mouth about. And, as we'd agreed, I had connections. 'I've thought about it,' I said, 'and I'm willing.'

'Good man. Can we go now and get this thing settled?'

I nodded, and we went rapidly downstairs and out into the yard, where a black BMW, keys in the ignition, had now replaced the Range Rover. As we got in, I said, 'Do you blindfold me?'

He smiled faintly, shook his head. 'I said I trusted you and you've agreed the terms.'

It put me in a moral dilemma. I always had to bear in mind that Challis, tough and devious as he was, might be protecting Durkin simply because of their powerful bonds. And I was going to tell Fenlon where Durkin was, despite agreeing Challis's terms. Challis was going to feel badly let down. I could understand it in a man whose love for Durkin possibly knew no reasonable bounds, even perhaps going as far as helping him cover up a murder. I'd have to keep reminding myself I was doing it for two harmless kids now dead.

'I'm looking forward to meeting this . . . friend of yours,' I said, as Challis began to drive along that route I knew so well. 'He must be quite a guy.'

'You'd have to know him, John,' he spoke sadly the words of the old refrain, 'to begin to understand why we all. . .' He didn't finish the sentence, it wasn't necessary.

Once on the bypass, he gave the car full throttle, with the sure touch of a man who'd driven many thousands of miles in his time. 'I couldn't be certain he was still up here,' I said. 'I was always worried he might be in South America by now.'

'We have the contingencies almost in place,' he said, with the heaviness of the earlier sadness, 'but yes, he's still up here.'

He didn't speak again until we sighted Windermere, its oppressive mood of yesterday unchanged, clouds still grazing the fells, islands still with a dark, forbidding look against white, shining water.

'Me and . . . my friend, in the old days, we'd drive up in some clapped-out banger we'd bought for a hundred quid, and we'd walk the fells. The others were more for Blackpool, but it pulled us.' He seemed almost in a state of clinical depression. It did nothing to relieve my guilt at the trust I was going to break.

In Bowness, he made for the Glebe Road landings, then parked. I wondered if this meant Durkin had a key to the berth gate, and was back on the *Veronica*. As we moved out of sight of the main road, several men suddenly emerged from the side of a shed and began to follow us. They were men I'd got to know well: Doherty, Speight, Ackroyd and Denholm. Only Ferrara was missing, and Ferrara was half-dead. They wore old casual clothes, like Challis. None of them spoke, they simply gathered behind us, walking at the same steady pace.

'The friends, John,' Challis said quietly. 'They know the situation and we need their input.'

FOURTEEN

My hands began to tremble with a fear my mind couldn't entirely rationalize, but I was certain all of them showing up had to be bad news. I couldn't see why he'd not told me they'd all be there. I'd gone to him because I knew a leader of men when I fell over one, and he'd given no indication it would be any other than just the two of us and Durkin, with him speaking for the rest, as usual.

I glanced over my shoulder, but they all plodded on, looking almost stonily past my face. Perhaps Challis had decided he could pitch a deal more forcefully to Durkin if the rest were there to back him, after all most of them must have been there at the original meeting on the *Veronica*, when they'd have been given the full story of the financial mess Durkin was in. When they'd agreed to conceal him.

I didn't know, and I couldn't control the fear. Nor did the fact that none of them smiled or spoke help to dispel the air of menace they seemed to give off. It could be that they found it difficult even to pretend friendliness towards someone who'd brought them such anxiety and stress. Perhaps they simply wanted to get it across to me that if I ever thought of opening my mouth in the wrong way about what I was now going to learn I'd get what Ferrara got.

I glanced at Challis. As if sensing my need for reassurance, he smiled faintly and touched my arm. It helped. I'd not been blind to the possible risk involved in coming up here, but I still felt I could trust him. Hard case that I knew him to be under the benign mask,

I'd always been convinced he was a realist, never keen to handle a well-placed man like me the Ferrara way, and anxious now to sort out a compromise. But Challis was one man among five, and though he was the natural leader it could be, with men as wealthy and powerful as himself, that he was only just in control – of a bunch of loose cannon.

I looked round anxiously as we passed through the open areas where boats were being serviced and repaired, but it was evening again and there was the same air of preoccupation among workmen not keen on distractions during the busiest time of the year. I wanted someone to notice I was being taken towards the *Veronica*, but no one did, I was merely an unremarkable member of another group of anonymous tourists.

Challis unlocked the gate of Pier B, and when we'd filed through, relocked it behind him. He caught my eye and said, 'We rendezvous. . . .'

'He comes out in a separate boat?'

He didn't reply, and we all stepped from the pier through an opening in the guard-rail to the cruiser's cockpit area. Challis slid back teak doors that opened on to steps. Doherty now leading, we went down the steps and forward through a narrow section that opened into a roomy, carpeted saloon. The saloon had a long table that ran between upholstered banquettes that would convert to berths. Another set of sliding doors further forward would lead, I supposed, to the other cabins; the cruiser looked as if it would sleep five or six comfortably.

'There's Scotch, Sean,' Challis called from the cockpit. 'You know where.'

Doherty returned to the narrow section between saloon and cockpit and opened a door – I supposed that would be the galley. He came back with a bottle of whisky in one hand, a soda syphon in the other and a roll of glasses under an arm.

'You want a drink?' he asked me grudgingly.

'Just soda.'

'You want a drink up there, Ray?'

'I'll have one when we get there. You go ahead.'

But he'd not be drinking until all this was over, and neither would I, and I wished he'd not offered the others alcohol. But if he hadn't I supposed they'd simply have pulled out their own hip-flasks, hard drinkers that they were.

We heard what sounded like twin engines roaring into life, and after a couple of minutes, during which Challis warmed them up and Doherty poured lavish measures of Scotch, the cruiser jerked into slow movement. Challis manoeuvred carefully past the other vessels, then gathered speed as he steered toward the centre of the lake.

From where I sat, next to Doherty and facing Denholm, Ackroyd and Speight, I could see between the heads of the men opposite the landing stages, flowerbeds and hotels of Bowness rapidly receding as Challis took us on a curve round Belle Isle and up the lake's western reaches. I could then see the distant, tree-lined eastern shore, with its open stretches where the main road skirted the water and moving cars were in clear view, their colours dull in the misty light. I pinned down what I decided must be the Langdale Chase Hotel, with its prime lakeside position, and then a second hotel, lengthy and white-painted, whose name I couldn't remember, but which provided a landmark.

The men maintained their dogged silence, sipping steadily from their glasses, deliberately not making eye contact with me. Doherty, at my side, seemed to give off an air of hostility I could almost feel, like body heat. My unease deepened, and I wished Challis would get to where he was going and rejoin us.

In fact, shortly after that, and somewhere at a guess between Bowness and Ambleside, Challis cut the engines. It became eerily quiet then, so quiet we could hear the slap of water against the sides of the gently swaying vessel.

He then padded down from the cockpit, bringing with him a folding canvas chair, which he opened and sat himself on at the head of the table, clearly inferring that he was taking the dominant role. I breathed a little more easily. He was in charge, even if only a first among unpredictable equals. Doherty poured Scotch for him and pushed it along the table with the siphon. Challis accepted it, but didn't drink. 'Well, here we are, John,' he said, smiling faintly. 'Rendezvous. . . .'

'What time does your . . . friend get here?'

He didn't speak for some time. 'John,' he said at last, shaking his head slowly, 'you didn't *really* think you'd be meeting Maurice. . . .' He smiled again then, but ruefully, as if he was the reluctant winner of some game he'd not wanted to see ended. 'Sean, would you kindly check out our young friend here for mobile phones and body mikes.'

I'd had it before, the impression that iced water was running across the stomach. I'd had the sudden dry mouth too, and the single bead of sweat that slowly trickled down the spine. But fear was the only emotion that never got easier to control with repetition, it seemed if anything to gather strength, like a virus whose repeated attacks gradually weakened the immune system. I'd walked into this. I'd been certain I could read him and I'd trusted him. My monumental error had been to trust anyone who felt about Durkin the way he seemed to.

'You . . . were right, Ray,' I said, struggling to control the trembling of my lips. 'It looks as if I'd have to have known him to understand. . . .'

He shrugged, still smiling the wry smile that seemed to indicate his disappointment at the complete success he'd made of tricking me on to the *Veronica*.

'Stand up, Goss,' Doherty said, 'and keep very still.'

'I told you I was clean, Ray,' I said bitterly.

'And I believed you, John. Except when you get to my age you check it out just the same.'

Doherty ran his big hands expertly over my body, making absolutely certain no limb could possibly have anything attached to it. He finally nodded at Challis. 'You can sit down now, Goss.'

Silence fell again in the saloon, but not this time the profound silence that had seemed to follow the switching off of the engines. The small sounds of the lake were evident now – the buzz of motor boats, the faint music and laughter of one of the big passenger vessels on a wine and dine cruise, together with those other faint and nameless noises that always seemed to echo off-shore across sheets of calm water.

'If Durkin's not coming,' I said bluntly, 'why am I here?'

'Because, John,' Challis said softly, 'we couldn't get you to drop the Durkin case however hard we tried. And we did try, very hard.'

'You're a bloody young fool, Goss, so you are,' Doherty growled. 'For the love of God, man, you could have come *in* with us. Five years out and you'd be pulling down our kind of money, the work we could throw your way.'

'You ... still haven't explained why I'm here. You could have told me what a bloody fool I am in one of your houses.'

'We felt we needed your undivided attention,' Challis said. 'No distractions, no phones, no wives charging about; none of those bugging devices you must have used to have found out so much about Maurice's little spot of bother with the merchant bank.' He gave the others a sudden hard look. 'I said we'd underestimate a clever young guy like you at our peril. Many times.'

The men opposite sheepishly dropped their eyes. Denholm flushed slightly. I wondered if he was thinking of the young pick-up who'd been so inquisitive about Durkin a couple of nights ago.

'This little spot of bother Maurice is in at the bank,' I said harshly, 'there's a man called Eynsford-Grey who sounds as if he's on the verge of attaching a hose-pipe to his exhaust.'

Challis shrugged again. 'These things happen. They'll just have to write it off and declare a smaller profit. Currency, derivatives . . . it's a risky game.'

'I don't think it's meant to be risky for the bank. It's supposed to be the punters who take the risk.'

'They made an awful lot of brokerage out of Maurice over the years, John.'

'And that's why they trusted him when he went for the big one. As long as he'd covered his margins . . . yes?'

'For Christ's *sake*, will you cut the blather!' Doherty broke out, correctly guessing why I was trying to work up a dialogue. 'It makes me head spin, so it does. Tell the stupid sod what's what, Ray, and let's get away off home.'

Challis watched me in another lengthy silence, his lips compressed, the earlier ruefulness still tempering the shrewdness of his horn-rimmed eyes. He slowly slid the glass of whisky Doherty had given him down towards me. 'It might be better if you took a drink, John.'

I felt my heart dilate, the short hairs rise in my neck. My entire stomach felt like a bag of crushed ice. I'd not known such fear since I'd stood side by side with Rainger in a barn in North Yorkshire awaiting what seemed like certain execution. I was strong and in good shape, I could tackle anyone my size and weight, but there were five of them, and three of them looked as tough as me.

Challis said, 'We decided, with the greatest reluctance, that there was only one way to handle this thing. You see, we're simply not prepared to see Maurice brought down, bankrupted, humiliated. We tried threats and we tried substantial bribes. Apart from anything else, you seem incorruptible. So I'm afraid it has to be a little of what poor Tony Ferrara got. Now don't worry, we'll not damage your head or your cobblers, not seriously anyway, but we have to feel certain you'll drop the case. For good.'

'Don't go worrying yourself about hospital treatment, John,' Doherty said. 'We'll get you to a Casualty department fast, so we will. We can tell them you fell down the cockpit steps.'

Incredible as it seemed, he spoke in a warm and kindly manner, like a specialist explaining that surgery was vital to my condition, and that there might be a little pain involved, but I'd get the very best after-care. It gave the words a banal, skin-crawling, dreadfulness.

Silence fell again. The sounds on the lake were now dominated by that of a single motor boat. It was the sound of freedom; there'd be a couple fresh from the city on board, spinning across the lake and laughing happily, while a few hundred yards away wealthy men calmly explained why I required to be beaten senseless.

'I'd have that drink, John,' Challis said. 'They say it really does help in situations like this.'

But I knew then it wasn't to be just a beating. Not with men like Challis and Doherty. How could they give me a beating and let me return to Beckford? I wasn't some cowardly pretty-boy like Ferrara, I was John Goss and I had a track record in difficult cases. They would know a beating wouldn't solve anything. It might start off as a beating, but Doherty would somehow contrive to get in the blow that would turn me into a human vegetable, which he would swear on all the saints in Ireland was accidental.

Because he and Challis considered my life worth a lot less than Durkin's freedom.

'Drink, John . . .' Challis said, in the same kindly, nurse-like tone of Doherty. Desperation gripped me like paralysis, I seemed scarcely able to move or think. A savage beating that could even end in death. They'd deny everything. They'd say I'd been at Challis's and gone home; my car would be secreted to my own driveway on Bentham Terrace. And I knew only too well that the workmen on the landings would have seen nothing they could remember. The friends of Durkin would have a cast-iron story and I'd be at the bottom of a lake.

I sipped a little of the Scotch to give myself time. Presumably they'd let me drink it all, but would expect it done quickly. I breathed in slowly and deeply, tried to think, to suspend my imagination from the thought of pain and death in a place from which there seemed as little escape as a dungeon. My mind seemed to clear a little, enough to tell me that if they were going to kill me the beating was pointless, but had to be gone through for the benefit of the men sitting opposite. Because two of them at least wouldn't buy a killing, would only be forced into accepting it if it appeared to be completely accidental.

I sipped another drop of the whisky, studied the three men across the table. They were each flushed and perspiring, and were profoundly uneasy. Denholm and Ackroyd kept darting troubled glances at each other. I wondered if the proposed beating came as much of a surprise to them as to me, wondered if they'd thought only in terms of killing my reputation and closing my agency, which would certainly be in the power of wealthy, connected citizens acting together. I looked at Speight. His large features had the same aggressive look they'd had in his warehouse, as if his face could no longer form any other expression, but his pale-blue eyes seemed to have a haunted lack of focus. Perhaps he could go along with the rough stuff, but I was positive the professional men would find it totally abhorrent, not because of me, but because of the ethical standards that governed their working lives.

'Get it down, John,' Challis said. 'It only makes it worse, putting it off.'

'What if I say I don't *need* a kicking, that I'll give my word I'll drop the case anyway. . . ?'

'I don't think we'd be able to believe you. You see, you're a bit of an obsessive, you only have to read about the Rainger case and the Marsh case for that to come across. Once back in the city, with your chum Fenlon. . . .'

I wondered how he'd ferreted out the name of my closest police contact. 'You're all in agreement on the kicking then?' I said. 'Including the lawyer and the accountant? They don't, frankly, look madly keen.'

They both gazed anxiously at their whisky glasses, Denholm's lips twitching. I felt that if I had the remotest chance of survival it would be through them, my original soft targets. 'You could get struck off, Bill,' I said evenly, 'if it ever came to light, behaving like some dirt-bag from Bethnal Green. And what would the Institute have to say about an accountant who duffed people up, Chris?'

'Stop this pack o' nonsense right now, Goss,' Doherty said, in a low voice. 'All you had to do was walk through this bloody case and give Crystal the humping she was paying you for.'

'Ray,' Ackroyd said hesitantly, 'I've got to admit I thought we were here to give Goss a clear and final warning. Talk to him, hard. You know our feelings about physical violence, mine and Chris's.'

'That's right,' I said, in a helpful tone. 'And you're already involved in putting what's left of Ferrara in hospital, even if Sean did get some tame crackheads to actually put the boot in.'

'We weren't asked about that,' Denholm said quickly, and almost certainly involuntarily. 'We had no part in that.'

'For the love of *God*, will you just listen to your man!' Doherty cried. 'When we all *knew* the sodding Eytie couldn't hold his pee, let alone his tongue. You didn't *complain* about it, dickhead, did you? You and the brief just like to keep your soft hands nice and clean, don't you, except when there's a poke of money to be made.'

Challis began to rap on the table with a metal spectacle-case. As usual, his emotions were completely under control; there was only the slightest flush in his cheeks to hint at how unsettled the turn of events had left him.

'Sean,' he said easily, 'Bill, Chris ... there's no *point* in arguing among ourselves. Can't you see, that's exactly what Goss *wants*. What's done is done. We're all agreed about Maurice's situation, and if Crystal had hired anyone but Goss there'd have been no problems. But Goss is in it now and knows too much, and if we don't do something he'll find out where Maurice is living. So he has to be dissuaded, just like Tony. It's the only thing that'll work. Christ, if the bastard could be bought I'd have had him wrapped and paid for a week ago.'

Silence fell again, broken only by the sound of the motor boat that still distantly circled. Challis got up and switched on an overhead light against a dusk that was falling early because of the ceiling of heavy cloud. A few minutes ago, distracted as I was, I'd seen the big passenger-cruiser, its lamps lit, floating serenely down the eastern side of the lake on what was probably its final circuit, and it had somehow increased my sense of isolation and fear. I looked across at Denholm and Ackroyd, willing them to meet my eyes, but they wouldn't raise their own from the table. I thought of them as soft targets, but the trouble with weak men was that they could be pulled just as easily in one direction as another. Speight continued to stare miserably into space, as if he was prepared to go along with anything, but didn't want to be directly involved.

'Get the Scotch down, John,' Challis said, in a voice that was now giving an order rather than making a kindly request.

I drank a little more. Challis still hadn't got the wholehearted backing of the two professional men, I could sense a definite resentment. I had to remind myself again that these people were all very rich, all used to power – they were like directors in a boardroom past whom the chief executive was trying to slip a minority decision from a secret agenda agreed elsewhere. I was quite certain that that lack of total agreement, slight as it was, was all I'd got, the single fissure in the sheer cliff wall into which I might be able to drive a crampon.

'Is this . . . what Maurice would want?' I said slowly.

'Oh, for God's sake. . . !'

'But look, Sean,' I said, in a reasonable tone, 'I came up here in good faith, supposedly to help Ray talk Maurice into coming back to the city and sorting out his affairs.'

'John.' Challis's voice held at last a note of the hardness I'd never heard before, but which I'd always known was there. 'Either get the Scotch down or take what's coming cold sober.'

'But it doesn't make sense,' I persisted, in the calmest tone I could muster. 'Maurice owes the bank a bunch of money, and everyone keeps telling me how much you care about him for all the help he gave you to get yourselves going. Aren't we agreed, Ray, you'd have gone under if Maurice hadn't stepped in? What I can't get together is why you don't help him to make a comeback. You're all rich, all skilled negotiators, surely between you you can offer the bank some kind of a deal. And then Maurice would be able to *rebuild* his life. You're not going to tell me he wants to spend the rest of his life in Mexico City.'

'Shut it, John,' Challis said curtly, 'you don't know what you're on about here.'

But my words weren't for him, they were aimed at the three opposite, the worried professionals and the man who'd once been a decent type with a nice going-on at the Co-op, before Durkin had catapulted him to blood pressure, wealth and stress. They'd still not meet my eyes, sat gazing straight ahead, their expressions uncannily similar, expressions I seemed to have seen before, many times, on the faces of young salesmen and accounts clerks who'd trapped their hands in the till, but wouldn't admit it, even though their mottled and guilty expressions said it like tabloid headlines.

And that was the trigger. In that second I knew the truth. It was yet another aspect of that lateral thinking I'd neglected in concentrating totally on pinning Durkin down. But it was more than that, it was the powerful waves of genuine emotion Durkin seemed to have aroused in everyone who knew him. He'd gone under, and even I had come close to reluctantly accepting that they'd covered for him because he was so special, because they owed him their prosperity, because they loved him like a brother.

'It's not just Maurice, is it?' I said, almost wonderingly. 'I thought he'd put his shirt on futures and currencies, and you'd had a few modest side-bets. But you're *all* in it, aren't you? Equally. I've seen the statements: the share-outs when Maurice got it right, the cheques you paid in when Maurice got it wrong. But the statements for the last six months were with Maurice, when you were shooting for bigger and bigger returns. And that's what it comes to, isn't it, if Maurice resurfaces you *all* go to the wall. . . ?'

*

The moment the words were out, I realized my mistake. It was as if I'd been thinking aloud, disorientated for a few seconds by the shock of pinning down the stark truth behind all those protestations of brotherly love.

There was no word of denial from any one of them. The darkening lake now seemed completely silent at last, even the motor boat appeared to have made its last exultant circuit. The absence of disturbance on the lake meant that even the water no longer lapped against the cruiser's side. Challis rose. He must have had a baseball bat at his feet; he now held it in his hand. 'You see how he ferrets things out,' he said, in a quietly victorious voice, 'and how essential it is he's made to keep it to himself? Sean . . . Joe. . . .'

Doherty got to his feet, but not Speight. I felt the sweat my body had been steadily pumping out suddenly chill. It was still two to one, and it was the burliest two. I could struggle, and would, but one of them would hold me in a bear-hug while the other swung the bat. The 'accidental' blow to the head would come when I could no longer stand or move my arms, and the others would have to accept yet another cover-up or face a murder charge.

Murder! I could see Challis and Doherty exchanging glances in the co-ordination of their attack. I had one card left and a couple of seconds to play it. 'You're not just covering for Maurice's debts, you fools!' I shouted at the three across the table. 'You're covering for a killing as well. Ask Ray; he knows all about it.'

For the first time since I'd known him Challis wasn't in control of his features. His face slackened with shock, his mouth fell slightly open. But he'd had plenty of shocks too in his hard-driving life, and it only threw him for a couple of seconds. 'Take him, Sean, take the lying bastard!'

'Hey!' Speight suddenly shouted. 'Hold off, Sean, I want to know what this is all about.'

'It's about the bastard trying to think of anything, anything at all, that ''ll put off what he's got to have,' Challis said, breathing hard and talking quickly. 'We're in cloud-cuckoo land now.'

'Tessa King!' I cried. 'Try that for starters – a tom Maurice was with at Seven Arches the night before he went on the run. And she never left Seven Arches, do you know why? Because someone hit her over the head with a brick. Ask Ray about it, it was him arranged for Maurice's valet to ship her out to meet up with Maurice.'

'Rubbish!' Challis seemed to spit out the word. 'Total bloody *rubbish*!'

'It was in the *Standard*. Woman's body at beauty spot. The police haven't named her, and they're taking no action yet, but they will, you watch.'

'For Christ's *sake*!'

'There was something in the paper, Ray,' Speight said, in a low voice. 'Dora read it out ... we sometimes take a walk on the towpath.'

'Joe, it's nothing to do with *Maurice*.' Challis had rapidly re-adopted the even, patient voice he knew from lengthy experience carried the most conviction; he was back in control of himself. 'He's taking a true incident and linking it to Maurice to keep us all arguing. How many more times do I have to tell you what a devious prat he is?'

My shouting had delivered the initial shock, I now followed Challis's lead in reverting to the tones of calm reason. 'Have I got anything wrong in this mess?' I asked Speight directly. 'I found out about the house at Esthwaite Water, the conference on here about Maurice's multi-million pound debt, your joint decision to conceal him. Well, I also found out that the last time Tessa King was seen by *anyone* was getting into Maurice's Rolls and the wench is now dead. And if you're trying to cover up for that as well you'll be up a shit creek so deep it'll make Windermere seem like a paddling pool.'

Denholm looked so ill his features were taking on the slightly greenish tinge I remembered from Doherty's party. There was so much sweat dripping across Ackroyd's forehead his granny glasses had slid down his nose, giving him a magisterial look that was wildly inappropriate. Speight, his face brightly flushed with his dangerous blood pressure, was looking at me, but through me, as if trying to cope with this frightful new spectre, not just going broke and the humiliation that would go with it, but being named as an accessory to a squalid murder.

'Sean!' Challis suddenly barked, raising the baseball bat. 'Let's put an end to this nonsense right now.'

'Do you honestly believe this will be just a duffing up?' I leant across the narrow table till my lips were inches from Ackroyd's streaming face. 'With what *I* know? They'll kill me, drop me over the side. And then you'll be covering for *another* murder, won't you? Only my best friend is a DS called Bruce Fenlon, and if I disappear he'll not stop searching for the truth till the day he retires. It's the kind of thing you all have with Maurice. And then it'll be *three* murders and a bank fraud you're in it for.'

Denholm suddenly sprang to his feet and almost climbed over the legs of the others to rush to one of the doors that led off the passage to the saloon. A second later we could hear the sound of vomiting through the thin bulkheads, a hell-raiser who'd failed the practicals.

'*Three* murders?' Doherty muttered in a puzzled voice, still standing motionless at my side.

'Ah,' I said, 'perhaps I forgot to mention that Sukie Goddard seems to have bought it as well. Maurice's London crumpet . . . yes? I think it must have been in the nature of a tidying-up operation in case I got round to seeing her and she said too much. Trouble is, I saw her on the first day of the case, and she did say too much, poor bitch.'

More silence. Denholm came back, stooped, his face moist and waxy. He poured whisky again, the bottle rattling against the edge of the glass like a drummer's rim-shots, but then, unable to face it, he pushed it distractedly away.

'I can't believe it,' Speight almost whispered. 'Not Maurice. He'd not harm a fly. He'd scarcely even raise his voice. He never lifted a finger to that son of his, never chastised him – the rest of us would have slaughtered the little sod.'

'These things can happen with the nicest men when the roof falls in,' I said. 'Believe me, I know. He was crazy about Tessa King. You all *knew* that, you all knew about one another's girlfriends. And Tessa King wasn't interested. It seems incredible a tom would want to turn down a man like Maurice Durkin, but she was an odd kind of a girl. It must have been the only time in his life he couldn't get a woman he'd set his mind on.'

'Faith, it's just not Maurice's *style*,' Doherty muttered. 'Me, Ray, even Joe, we've had to sort a few things out the hard way in our time, but Maurice *Durkin*. . . ?'

'Exactly.' Challis came in with perfect, deadly timing. 'We all *know* Maurice. No one knows Maurice the way we do. We've known him since we were twelve. He hasn't got a violent bone in his body. Can you see him topping a pair of hookers? *Maurice*! For God's sake, the Seven Arches, anything could happen along there with some of the men the women take down.'

'But his valet took Tessa King out there to meet Maurice on the last night anyone can remember seeing her,' I said quietly. 'On your instructions.'

'He was *lying*. We all know that fruit's game. He did it all the time, when Maurice didn't need him – took girls out to meet punters, because high-level punters don't want to be seen inside a *mile* of Dresden. Brian got a cut from both ends and Maurice turned a blind eye because he was soft with his servants too. Well, am I right, Sean . . . Joe?'

A second or two later Speight slowly nodded, and I began to feel a rising of the nausea that had sent Denholm scurrying to the toilet. I could have shaken Brian till his teeth rattled for not admitting to his regular pimping activities. It had seriously weakened my case, coming on top of the certainty of everyone here that Durkin couldn't harm anything that moved.

'Sukie Goddard . . .' I ground out doggedly, between clenched teeth.'

'*Another* harlot,' Challis said to the others, as if he were the chair through which every statement had to be filtered. 'In *London*. Looking after those weird Arabs and Americans and Japs, all so high up the tree they'd have diplomatic immunity for just about every damned thing. So one of them goes back to her place and the service he wants is too special even for her, and she won't come across. So he wrings her neck and gets back in his Merc, and his chauffeur takes him back to the embassy, and that's the end of that. Christ, we all *met* Sukie . . . you had to be sitting on a million before she'd even show you her melons, but she was still a slapper. A slapper who went for the high stakes, and high stakes carry high risks.'

That earlier sense of desperation and fear, which had been lulled slightly by the breathing space I'd seemed to be winning, was slowly creeping through my blood and tissues again. I was losing the battle of the boardroom. Whatever I might be able to prove when I was back in the city meant nothing because Challis was determined I'd not get back to the city. The three men opposite, whom I'd finally forced to meet my eyes, now looked down at their restless hands again, almost apathetically, as if prepared to let the dominant personalities have it their own way, as they probably always did. Challis still grasped his baseball bat and watched me unflinchingly. When I glanced sideways at Doherty I seemed to see nothing but contempt in his broad Irish face, and it could only be because I'd been crazy enough to try and win time by accusing Durkin of unbelievable acts.

And in that second the rest slid into place. It was as if fear and adrenalin had forced open a part of the brain rational thought had been unable to reach. Elation now mixed with the fear, the sort of elation Vicky had felt when she'd turned a page and seen a cruiser called *Veronica*. I began to tremble again, because I knew that what I'd just picked up gave me two chances: it either made my position impregnable or it put me beyond hope. There was no middle way. I took a large sip of the Scotch. I needed it to play this particular hand. I couldn't believe the mistakes I'd made in the case, the conclusions I'd let myself be drawn to because of the circumstantial evidence, because of the magic Durkin had spread around himself that in the end had made him seem too good to be true.

'Get the rest down, Goss,' Challis said curtly, as if positive there was nowhere else for me to go, as if convinced now of the backing he received from the others, however half-hearted in the men opposite, because my allegations about Durkin had ruined whatever chance I had.

'Where *is* Maurice, Ray?' I said, trying to force the calmness into my tone that went with putting my entire roll on the one card. Because the stakes didn't come much higher than getting to go on living.

'Sean . . .' Challis spoke past me to Doherty.

'Why not tell me? What does it matter, if you're going to see me off? He is going to see me off, you know,' I told the others. 'Don't kid yourselves he'll just break a few ribs, like Ferrara. He couldn't let me go back now. But I think you should know that when Sean and Ray have finished with the baseball bat it'll then be *four* murders and a bank fraud. Sounds like a film title, doesn't it?'

'God almighty, doesn't it just *show* what a blather the man is,' Doherty said irritably. 'He can't even remember how many murders we're supposed to be covering for.'

'Oh,' I said, in a tone of apology, 'didn't I mention the fourth? Silly of me, because that's the main one, really. The big one. To be absolutely honest, it only occurred to me in the last few minutes. You see, in order to make the job a good one, old Ray here, good old tough, fair, straight-talking Ray had to kill Maurice as well as Tessa and Sukie. . . .'

*

The sounds of exhaled breath were like air being released from car tyres. Challis, his face seeming set in stone with cold rage, suddenly took the bat back in an arc and swung it towards my head. But it was clutched in mid-air by Speight. 'Now just take it easy, Ray, I want to hear what the guy's banging on about. We all do.'

Challis tried to wrench the bat from him, without success.

'Look, Joe,' he shouted, 'that shithead's calling me a murderer on top of all the other claptrap, and I'm not having it! Christ, it's the same bloody game he's been playing all along, trying to get us fighting among ourselves.'

'I know that, Ray. I wanted to kick the sod's face in when he came to my place, but the guy's connected and he's got a reputation, you said so yourself. And I want to know why he thinks you topped Maurice.'

'Joe, you can't *believe* . . . for God's *sake*, man.'

'I didn't say I believed him, Ray, I just want to know why he said it.'

There was a sudden quiet authority about Speight I'd not seen before, as if below the bluster that seemed to have developed with power and wealth that other man still lived, who'd been liked and respected by all when he'd been on the Co-op fast track.

'I'm saying it,' I said, instinctively raising my voice as if to pierce the deadening atmosphere of shock, 'because Ray can't produce Maurice. Stop me if I'm wrong, but I think it happened this way: after you'd met with Maurice on this boat, Ray then dropped you all at the Glebe Road landings, and cast off again with just himself and Maurice on board. Right?'

After a silence that must have stretched to ten seconds, Speight finally gave an infinitesimal nod of his large head.

'That was the *agreement*,' Challis said. 'We'd both stay on here overnight, then I'd fix him another billet, and then I'd arrange to get him a new passport and ship him abroad.'

He'd let the mask slip once or twice, and no one grasped better than he did how undermining that could be. His lengthy experience now paid off, of facing down workmen and creditors and men who sold land. He was at his benign, almost fatherly best, his eyes steady behind the horn-rims, his body language again impossible to translate.

'But . . . you never actually told us where you had him hidden, Ray,' Doherty said, in a tone in which I could detect a faint but definite note of embarrassment.

'That was part of the agreement too, that the fewer people who knew the exact location the less chance there'd be of it getting out. Don't forget, we had blabbermouth Ferrara in on the deal.'

'People don't come much fewer than that,' I said. 'Just you. . . .'

'Look, Ray,' – Doherty still sounded uncomfortable – 'maybe you'd better tell us where he is, just for the record. Ferrara's not involved now.'

'Raven Cottage,' Challis said promptly. 'Just beyond Watermillock at Ullswater.' He sighed. 'And you do realize he'll have to be moved again, now that this prick's heard it.'

'Is there a phone on the *Veronica*?' I said. 'Does anyone have a mobile?'

'It . . . might be an idea to speak to him, Ray,' Speight said. 'If only to shut Goss up.'

'I'm sorry, Joe, it's a fairly primitive sort of place and there's no phone. We chose it because of the isolation.'

'Strange,' I said. 'It's impossible to imagine a man like Maurice trying to cope without a phone. How can he order his groceries if he doesn't go out? How can you keep in touch?'

'He has a mobile, but the sound keeps breaking up. Something to do with the fells. I go and see him every few days.'

It was difficult for me to decide if the silence that followed was a sceptical one. 'Look, Ray,' Doherty said at last, 'I think we'd better drive up there and see him. Like tonight. Just to show we've not forgotten the poor guy, apart from anything else.'

'Well, you've put your finger right on it, haven't you, Sean?'
Challis said quietly. 'None of you really wanted to know *where* he
was, because of all the trouble he'd dumped on us, best friend or
not. Admit it, not one of you has asked me where he was or how
he was getting along, from the night we all met on here till today.'

There were looks of reluctant and guilty agreement on the moist
faces in the soft saloon light, and I now understood Doherty's
embarrassment. 'Convenient, that,' I said bluntly, 'nobody really
wanting to know how he was making out, this man you all love like
a brother.'

'Shut it, prat.'

'Is that what the poor sod *really* wanted,' I said, 'being bundled
away in a glorified cowshed till you can ship him out to South
America? Because I don't think it was. And what's more, I think
Maurice was in a position to *pay* his end of the bank debt. I think
he was too intelligent to lay his entire stack on a single deal. Only
he couldn't pay your debts as well, and everything had been
bought in his name.' I glanced round with a look of contempt I
couldn't control. 'A *gentlemen's* agreement, right? Except that
there was only one gentleman involved, and that was Maurice.
And the rest of you had got so greedy you knew your debts
would wipe you out. And Maurice, being the gent he was, agreed
to lie low till you'd got your act together and found the bottle to
sell up and face the music. Only you couldn't face the music, not
one note of it. And that's why you never asked Challis *anything*,
because you were hoping Challis had persuaded Maurice to go
abroad. And there was no way Maurice would – why should he?
– so Challis got out his baseball bat and then gave him the heave
ho.'

Challis was smiling contemptuously, in almost daunting control
of his box of facial tricks. 'Ask Goss about the Rainger case,' he
said to them, 'and how he got carried away with himself. He's a
clever guy, but once he's got an idea in his head he'll do any mortal
thing to make everything else fit. Does any one of you honestly

believe I could harm a hair of Maurice's head? The man who saved my life, my business. . . .'

'It still leaves two dead hookers,' I said, 'whether you killed him or not.'

'What point would there be in *me* topping hookers?' he said, again past me to the others. 'They were nothing to do with me, and if they're dead it's because they lived dangerously. It's just coincidence they both knew Maurice, what else?'

'The point, Challis,' I said, 'is that you got Brian to go for Tessa King in that shiny great Rolls so it was going to seem obvious to the police Maurice was involved in her murder, and that's why he'd made a run for it. And if the police were looking for him for a murder it would deflect their minds from what he was really on the run for: your sodding great debt. And if Maurice couldn't be found there'd be a good chance the bank would sue for what assets of his they could lay their hands on and call that it. And even if it came to light you were all involved, it would take years for them to make a case of it, and in the end they'd probably decide it wasn't worth the hassle, good money after bad. Right, lawyer?' I said to Ackroyd's damp, bowed head. 'You know the ways of the City.'

'Ray, I think we'd better go up to this Raven Cottage,' Doherty said again. 'I can't stand any more of this bugger's rattle.'

'Now, come on, Sean, this shit's dragging me through the mud. He's making it up as he goes along now, and I insist we settle this thing before we do anything else. I mean, you're my *friends*; are you really trying to tell me you put any credence in these wild accusations?'

'They don't look wild from where I'm sitting,' I said. 'It all seems to hang together, if you think about it. You saw to Tessa to draw the police off the scent, you did the same for Sukie because you didn't know how much Maurice had told her, and what she might tell me.'

'I can't believe I'm hearing this,' he said sadly to the three across the table, in his best chairman manner. 'If you'd let me and Sean teach him a lesson it would all be over. They'd be getting him ready for a month in hospital, and we could all go to Raven Cottage to sort things out with Maurice, if that's what you want.'

I said, 'They didn't know they did want till I suggested it.'

'Goss, would you keep your trap shut for two minutes?'

'Perhaps you'd like to tell them how you know Sukie Goddard was strangled, Challis.'

'What?' He looked genuinely puzzled. 'What on God's earth are you blathering about now?'

'*I* didn't say she was strangled.'

'Well, neither did *I*.'

'You said some diplomat had probably gone back to her place with her and wrung her neck. *I* didn't say how she'd been killed, or where, but it was in fact exactly as you said – someone wringing her neck, someone she knew well enough to let into her flat.'

However well people could control their features, and Challis was master class, it was virtually impossible to control skin colour, and Challis's face, beneath his light, permanent tan, slowly reddened. But he knew he was flushing, and I was certain the slight lack of control he now allowed himself was to cover for it. 'Well, so *what*!' he cried. 'So bloody *what*! I said the first thing that entered my head. I could have said he'd stabbed her or suffocated her.'

'Or poisoned her, or shot her, or thrown a hair-dryer in the bath. And it could have happened anywhere – on Primrose Hill, or up a back street, or in a multi-storey car-park. Except that it happened exactly the way you said and in exactly the place.'

'Ray . . .' Doherty said, in a low urgent voice, 'we've got to go back to the landings and drive up to Ullswater. Dear God, we're getting all this twaddle from the pair of you, and it's too much. We've got to see Maurice, talk it all through with him.'

'Sean's right,' Speight said uneasily, but in the same authoritative tone as before. 'Goss has opened a can of worms here, and it may be to get us all in disarray, but we must talk it over with Maurice, God knows, we *have* pushed him to the back of our minds.'

Ackroyd and Denholm seemed to be falling apart before my eyes. They had the look of men too shocked to continue thinking coherently, a look I knew only too well. Between them they'd know better than anyone at this table the penalties involved in defrauding a merchant bank, in concealing the possible killer of three people. It was the reason they'd stopped thinking.

Challis's flush had faded, and his eyes passed slowly from my face to Doherty's, and then to Speight's and the blank, crumpled faces of the professional men. It was a long slow perusal in what seemed the lengthiest silence yet, and it gave an impression he was trying to reach some impossibly difficult, even agonizing decision.

'All right,' he said at last, sighing heavily. 'I do know how Sukie was killed. I know because Maurice told me. You can't think what it means to me to have to admit it, but Goss had it right the first time. Tessa wouldn't go abroad with him, and he lost his cool. Don't ask me why he couldn't stop getting his rocks off with that bloody stick insect. And then. . . .' He looked down dispiritedly at his square fingernails. 'Well, he was out of his head by then. He couldn't stop himself telling Sukie what he'd done to Tessa, wanted her to take him in till he could skip. She didn't want to know. She wouldn't take him in. She said if he didn't tell the police she would have to. And . . . well . . . he panicked and he . . . and he . . . .' His eyes were glinting with tears; he couldn't go on.

'But the trouble is, you see, Challis,' I said patiently, 'we've all reached a very firm conclusion, and you yourself were the most adamant, that Maurice was too softhearted to kick a dog if it was biting his hand off.'

FIFTEEN

'Dear God,' Doherty whispered. 'Dear sweet Mother of God. . . .'

It didn't sound like casual blasphemy this time, it sounded as if he were at half-past nine mass praying for guidance. Speight groaned softly and buried his head in his hands. Only Denholm and Ackroyd were unaffected, but they were like boxers who'd already received the knock-out blow, there was no further pain or shock to feel.

Challis looked round again, his glance a mixture of fury and surprise, which this time he was powerless to control. The tears now looked as if they'd been touched in by a make-up artist. 'I'm giving you the *truth*!' he cried. 'Tessa King, Sukie Goddard – they were *his* women, not mine. He was the one on the run; he was the one who couldn't face it – the shame, losing Maunan, all his money. I wish you could have seen him. He was *crying*. Maurice *crying*. Like a baby. And I promised him on my mother's grave we'd always make sure he stayed free, that we'd always wire money out, whatever it took. How could I see him banged up? How could any of us?'

He could have been talking to himself for all the effect it had on the others. The only sounds in the following silence were those of Speight softly groaning and Doherty endlessly whispering his mantra.

'Well, it's the *truth*!' he cried again. 'Sean . . . Joe . . . you've known me since we were twelve. Have I ever bullshitted you?

Ever? You can't be going to take this tosser's word against mine.'

But, for the very first time, there was a slight hysterical crack in his voice, like a single wrong note played on a cor anglais by a musician whose mastery had always been faultless.

'We'll go then! We'll go to Raven Cottage. We'll have it out with poor Maurice, and you can all carry the can with me; you were only too bloody keen to let me carry it on my own.'

'Oh, Ray,' Doherty muttered, in an anguished voice, 'drop it, for pity's sake. Maurice isn't *there*, you know he's not there. Wherever he is, I hope the dear Lord gives the poor sod the peace and happiness he deserves to make up for what we've done to him.'

I had never seen men so still. They sat about the table like waxworks, even appearing to have that minor but unmistakable inaccuracy of feature that waxworks bear to the living person, because their faces were so totally devoid of the endless flickerings of expression normal ones had.

Challis suddenly smashed the baseball bat down on the table with all his force. Glasses fell over, whisky splashed across the polished surface. Shock threw us all back on the banquettes like the impact of massively displaced air. 'You left it all to *me*!' he shouted. 'You left it all to *me*! You didn't want to *know*! As long as he was out of sight so you could get on with your lives. Do you know what he said when you'd all pissed off – he'd give us one more week to get our act together, and then he was coming home. A *week*! A week and we'd all be bankrupt. A week and you'd not have a penny to scratch your backsides with. We'd have nothing . . . *nothing*! NOTHING!'

He smashed the bat on the table again. A section of the beading that edged it flew off at an angle. It was one of the most disturbing sights I'd ever seen. His entire body was shaking as if in fever, and his eyes continually flicked from one side of the table to the other like those of a dangerous animal finally cornered.

'Oh, Ray . . . Ray.' Doherty's voice was barely more than a croak. 'All right, man, we buried our heads in the sand, but we knew we'd have to sort it out in the end. You swore you'd talked him into going abroad . . . we'd club together and make sure he had a good life. For the love of God, this was Maurice. This was Maurice *Durkin*.'

'He'd have wiped us *out!*' the other shrieked. 'Because of a bloody stupid currency spec. He knew we were getting in too deep, knew we were pledging too much. He should have talked us out of it; he knew what would happen if he got it wrong.'

Drops of saliva specked the table's battered surface. It was like witnessing the barely imaginable, like seeing the prime minister go berserk at the dispatch-box under hostile questioning. Few men I'd ever known had been so completely in control of themselves, or earned quite so much of my respect for what I'd considered to be his qualities of tough, capable, common sense. I remembered how I'd once envied Durkin the intense, indestructible loyalty that, cynic though I was, I'd felt I sensed in his closest friend.

'It was our greed,' Speight said flatly. 'Maurice warned us a dozen times not to put on more than we could afford to lose. But he got it right so many times we got blasé. We thought we'd not just be millionaires, but millionaires with two or three million, like Maurice, and we went over the top.' He held a long, expensive cigar in his hands that he must have had in his jerkin pocket. He suddenly broke it in two and tossed the pieces into the puddles of Scotch among the debris of glasses. It was a powerfully symbolic gesture. 'But Maurice didn't go over the top. He never went over the top. He was a high roller, but he could always cover his end.' He looked across the table at me, dull-eyed. 'You were right, Goss . . . you got it all right, damn you.'

'He should never have let us put that kind of loot on. He could see we were over-extending, even if he did warn us.'

'He didn't *want* to put the bloody money on,' Doherty said bitterly. 'So you said we'd form our own syndicate and go it alone. And the poor bastard knew that would be worse still – we know as much about forex deals as we do about brain surgery.'

'Oh, *shut* up, you stupid Irish sod!'

There was an ugly look on Doherty's face I'd once glimpsed when he'd caught me pressuring Denholm and Ackroyd in his dining annexe. 'Don't you tell me to shut up, you murdering swine. And don't try and tell me it was Maurice's fault you had to see to him. He was your best friend in the world and I hope you rot in Hell.'

Challis smashed the table a third time. 'He was no friend of mine!' he screamed. 'I needed friends like Durkin like I needed leprosy!'

'He saved your life, you crazy bastard!'

'So he could go on *humiliating* me . . . so he could go on rubbing my nose in it. Whatever I did, whatever I had, he had to go one better. He couldn't just let me struggle to the riverbank or frigging drown, could he, not the great sodding Maurice, he had to fish me out with all the other kids looking on . . . *sneering*. And he could have had any woman in the world he wanted, couldn't he, but he had to have my woman. You didn't know that, did you? *I* was going out with Crystal Potter before him. God, I loved that woman, I worshipped the ground she walked on, I'd have gone through fire and water for her. I still can't get her out of my head. And Durkin *knew* that, so he had to have her himself. He gets Crystal and all I get is Cecily, Durkin's bloody cast-offs. And then, when I have trouble with the business, he's there waving a cheque for a hundred frigging grand at me, because that's all he lives for, to humiliate me. And then he builds Maunan, and it makes my place look like a dog-kennel, and if I get three cars he gets six, and if I get a housekeeper and a manservant he gets a housekeeper, a manservant, an assistant sodding manservant and a cordon bleu cook. And if I say I'm thinking of local government he says he's thinking of Parliament and a place in St John's Wood. And he has women *everywhere*, and he's still got my Crystal – the only woman he knew I ever wanted. He's got Crystal and the biggest house in the Aire Valley, and he doesn't even need to work, so he can go and fart about in Parliament and have the time of his bloody life, like he *always bloody has*. And he's screwed my life up and I hated the bastard, I hated the bastard. I hated and despised and *loathed* the bastard.'

We all looked on in trance-like silence, as if in a theatre watching some towering actor give the frothing, screaming performance of his career. I realized then what a desperately hard battle he must have had to achieve his normal relaxed manner, that impression of always being in complete control. He'd laboriously built them up, those qualities of calmness and discipline, until they were like the massive, pre-stressed concrete blocks that buttressed a vulnerable sea wall, to hold in check the colossal tides of emotion that seemed never to have ceased their battering onslaught.

'Yes, well . . .' Doherty muttered at last, 'he'll never get up your nose again now, will he? Oh, Ray . . . Ray, he wasn't *like* that, he just liked to compete, that's why he helped us . . . so we'd all be players in the game . . . like the old five-a-side days. . . .' His voice trailed off. He'd never been a man I'd considered to have much of a feel for aspects of behaviour, however extreme, but even he seemed to realize what raging paranoia was when it hit him like a ten-ton truck.

Speight said dourly, 'Before he starts raving and ranting again, will someone please tell me where we go from here?'

Challis was visibly calming himself down now, as if the strait-jacket of self-control, so rigorously imposed over the long years, could even cope with near-insanity. His gaze passed slowly from one to the other of us with that panning motion I remembered so well from the first pool party, when the friends, their faces stained by the colours of the overhead lanterns, had sat round the circular table, nervous and fidgeting.

'We don't go anywhere,' he said, in a startlingly even tone, 'if we don't see to Goss. Because if any of this were to come out I'd say you were all in it – and that means in everything – from day one.'

It was as bad a moment as any since I'd stepped on the *Veronica*.

It was as if everything that had happened in the saloon had taken place in a time warp. They all looked towards me, their faces impossible to read. They now knew everything, knew that Tessa, Sukie and Durkin were all dead by Challis's hand, all dispatched with incredible efficiency by this controlled maniac. And they knew that if I lived, and he carried out his threat, they'd be inside until their middle years were behind them and they'd be husks of the men they'd once been. I wondered if it crossed their minds that if I *did* live I'd be a valuable witness for their defence, could help clear them of the killings, if nothing else. I wondered if they'd care, even if it did cross their minds. They'd still be up for the bank fraud, would still lose their money and their possessions and their status. What they really needed was time, time to plan, to think things through, and they'd not have that if they didn't get rid of me.

I didn't know, but I didn't like it, their silent scrutiny. Perhaps a little of Challis's paranoia had rubbed off on to me, because all I seemed to see in their eyes was the earlier hostility.

'Excuse me! Hello! Hello! Could someone please help me? My engine's cut out and I can't restart it. . . .'

It was a woman's voice, carrying faintly down through the open cockpit doors.

'Ah, the hell with it,' Doherty growled. 'God, we've got enough on down here. There'll be someone else by soon – the lake's crammed with boats.'

'We can't do that, Sean,' Challis said, with the old authority. 'It's the unwritten rule of the lake that you help people in difficulty. In any case, if other boats gather round it'll draw too much attention to the *Veronica*. I'll have to take a look. You'd better come too, we'll probaby need the dinghy.'

'Oh, shit!' Doherty said irritably, but got up. 'Let me through, Goss.'

He went after Challis up to the cockpit, followed a few seconds later by Speight, who looked as if he welcomed anything that would distract him from the mess they were in, now that Challis's floor show was over. Ackroyd, Denholm and I were left alone together. It was as if reactions were returning to brains that had seemed in a state of near coma in the two men, and they seemed now to watch each other speculatively, as if each were trying to judge which way the other's mind was working.

'I need to use the toilet,' I told them curtly. They barely glanced up, but began speaking as I moved away, in words too low for me to catch. I opened the door I'd seen Denholm claw at when he'd been dashing to be sick. Once opened, the door almost obscured the view of the steps from the saloon, and by keeping to one side I was able to climb swiftly up them without being seen.

The three men on deck, their bodies like shadows in the darkness, stood together on the cruiser's starboard side. 'Is she completely dead, dear?' I heard Challis say, in a pleasant, fatherly way.

'Dead as a door-nail. I've tried everything.'

I slipped over the port-side guard-rail and slid myself into the water as silently as possible. It was so cold after the sweating heat of the saloon I felt as if my heart was going to stop.

'We've got an inflatable. I'd better come and have a look. . . .'

'Oh, would you . . . I feel so helpless.'

'We'll sort it out one way or the other, don't worry.'

I swam quickly to the cruiser's bow, got a fix on where the motor boat lay, about ten yards from the *Veronica*, and began to swim underwater towards it. Its outline showed darker than the darkening sky, and I came up on its starboard side, the side away from the *Veronica*.

'Right, Vicky,' I gasped, 'get the bloody thing going, unless it really is knackered. And throw your weight the other way for a couple of ticks.'

But there was nothing wrong with the engine, and it burst into life as I pulled myself into the boat. Seconds later, followed by the shouts of the men on the cruiser, we were weaving south, as rapidly as we could among the motionless craft that dotted the lake's surface in the darkness.

'I don't know how you did it,' I said, 'but did I ever need the cavalry. . . .'

She turned and gave me a brief smile, then concentrated on steering the boat. The controls were basic – a car-type wheel, a key and button ignition and a lever like a gear-stick, which I assumed linked with transmission to the propellers. It had the utility appearance of the type of boat hired by tourists, which would mean its throttle had been adjusted so as not to exceed a certain modest speed. It would probably be enough for us. I glanced back at the cruiser. A cockpit lamp had ignited, and the vessel seemed to be slowly turning.

'Go east,' I said. 'Sorry, I mean make for the opposite shore. We'll keep as close to it as possible. There are a lot of boats moored along there; that'll stop them trying anything on the lake itself. How on *earth* did you pull this off?'

She steered the boat in a wide chugging curve towards the eastern shoreline. 'It was Norma's Community Centre night,' she said, speaking rapidly. 'I offered to lock up and drop the post off. I was just going when DS Fenlon rang. He sounded very worried, wanted to speak to you urgently. He wouldn't tell me anything at first, but I made him. I said I knew everything about the case and I had to know. I said I knew about him being your police contact, and I was just as worried as he was. In the end he told me the tom called Cheyenne had found out that one of the Dresden girls had been at Seven Arches the night Durkin's servant brought Tessa there. She was with a punter on a car-rug in the undergrowth. They were only a few yards from where the car stopped that was supposed to have Durkin inside. Only Durkin wasn't inside, it was Challis.'

'How did the tom know that?'

'She didn't, the punter did. And he got her out fast, because the punter didn't want Challis to bring *his* woman into the undergrowth and recognize him.' She smiled sourly. 'Seeing as he was going to be next year's lord mayor or president of the chamber of commerce, or whatever.'

I nodded sadly, my plastered hair and sodden clothing forgotten in my concentration on her words. 'And if he'd stayed, Tessa might still be alive. He's seen them all off, Vicky, Challis: Tessa King, Sukie Goddard, even Maurice Durkin himself. Can you believe it? It all came out on the *Veronica*. There's no question it's the truth.'

Her hands shook on the wheel and the boat veered slightly before she could bring it under control. We were perhaps twenty yards from the shoreline and moving steadily south to Bowness. The cruiser was now following us in the distance, but throttled well back. A collision would be the last thing Challis would want at this stage.

'I told Fenlon I'd try and find out where you were and get back to him as soon as I could. I knew you were in danger. I rang Challis's house and his PA said he'd gone off with you somewhere, but she had no details. So then I looked in your case-notes and rang the other men to see if you and Challis were at one of their houses. They'd *all* gone off somewhere, hadn't said where, and hadn't said when they'd be back.'

'How did you know to come up here?'

She shrugged, weaving her way carefully in between a group of yachts, their sails furled, their lights cosily lit, people below eating and drinking, or entertaining themselves with radios and board games. The *Veronica* glided steadily behind us, and at about the same cautious speed. 'Everything seemed to be happening up here, didn't it? I took a chance. I knew where the *Veronica* should be, and when it wasn't there I hired this.'

'So late. . . ?'

'I talked Paul into it – the hunk with the tan and the long hair. I said I'd booked a meal at the Langdale Chase and I wanted to take you by boat, as a surprise. It kind of went with wanting to have our honeymoon on the *Veronica*. He said I'd get him hung, drawn and quartered, but another tenner worked like a charm. Then I started searching.'

I smiled faintly. 'I heard you, now I come to think about it.'

'When I found her I cut the engine and just waited. I hoped you might come on deck or something. If nothing happened I was going to tie up at the Langdale and ring Fenlon. And then I heard that frightful banging and shouting. I was dreadfully worried. That's when . . . well, you know the rest.'

'I'm speechless with admiration,' I said, running a hand over her hair.

'You'd better not be, I need talking through the rest of it. What do we do now?'

I glanced backwards at the cruiser again, its saloon lamps and its graceful white lines giving it an incredibly romantic appearance as it glided over the dark, still water, past the little hamlets of moored vessels.

'They'll know we're heading back to Bowness, and they'll probably have narrowed it down to the Glebe Road landings, seeing as that's the main spot for hiring boats for longer than an hour. So what if, when we get to Bowness Bay, we creep in among the boats tied up on the public piers, leave this there, and melt into the local nightlife? I know where their cars are, but they don't know what your car is or where it'll be. We hang about out of sight until we see five expensive motors hit the road. There'll not be much other traffic by now. Then we go to the landings and get yours.'

'John, I thought about that. I decided to park well away from the landings. It's on a side street just off the bottom of the Windermere–Bowness Road.'

I smiled again. 'I thought you were asking *me* what we should do.'

'I tried to think it out the way I thought you would, assuming we might want to keep our heads down.'

Just then it sounded like one of the nicest things a woman had ever said to me. 'Right,' I said, 'Bowness isn't far away now. My plan? We tie up at a public pier and leg it to your car.'

'What if Challis makes for a public pier too?'

'No, the cruiser's too big. He'll have to go back to his private berth.'

'What if he drops some of them *off* at a public pier?'

'If we're lucky he'll never know we've made it to one. We'll be into the area ahead of him, and there'll be so many small craft we'll just blend in. No, hopefully he'll keep straight on to the landings.'

'What are we going to *do*, John?' The words came shakily from trembling lips.

'I don't know. I really don't know. They were all in total shock when I screwed it out of Challis he was down for three killings. That's when you heard all the banging and shouting. He's crazy, but control-freak crazy, like so many killers are. The others have lost everything, by the way, on the currency spec. I'll fill you in later, but they're all ruined, unless they can keep my mouth shut. When you shouted, I was trying to figure out where I stood. We could be talking lynch mob, I'm afraid. Separated, they could probably be reasoned with, apart from Challis, together, they might be a loaded gun.'

She looked very frightened, in the peculiar whiteish darkness of a midsummer night beneath low cloud, but she had to know the worst-case scenario, had to be geared and ready. I wondered if I owed my life to this fast-thinking, resourceful woman, wondered if it would be a debt I could ever repay.

We were into the great sweeping curve of Bowness Bay then, with its hotels and shops and modest activity. A single, deserted passenger cruiser towered in front of the little ticket office, and lines of small boats nosed against the many piers. Vicky swung hard to port, and made for the nearest one. We'd almost reached it when the *Veronica* came into sight. The cruiser didn't stop but continued south towards the private berths.

'Get down,' I said urgently. 'Fast. . . .'

The *Veronica* had a movable headlamp, which now raked its

beam over the piers as she swept gracefully past. The finger of light crossed over our heads.

'Do you think they saw us?'

'Impossible to tell. Let's hope not.'

I leapt on to the pier, and held the boat while she stepped out, then looped the painter over a pillar. I wanted to run, but had to walk, slowly and cautiously, because I'd ditched my shoes in the lake and now had to be careful not to cut or injure my feet. Strollers looked on with faint smiles at my flattened hair and sodden clothing in the light of streetlamps, but there was nothing I could do to conceal my condition. We walked steadily along the front, round the bend, and up into the High Street that became the Windermere–Bowness road. Vicky's car was parked inconspicuously among other cars on a quiet street than ran off left to a caravan park. My spirits sank when I saw it. It was a small Volvo saloon.

My disappointment must have shown because she said defensively, 'It's Mother's. It was either this or my Fiat Uno. It's OK when you get it into fifth – really.'

'Take no notice,' I said, putting an arm round her. 'The fantastic job you've done I couldn't expect a Lamborghini on top, could I?'

She handed me the keys, as if only too relieved to let me now get behind a wheel. She'd turned the car before parking, and we had a clear view of the main road and any group of expensive motors that might go by.

'What if they go right at the landings? Doesn't Glebe Road also link up with the 591?'

'It's difficult to know how their minds will work,' I said slowly. 'The fact that they were shining their lamp around could mean they'd got an idea we'd land at Bowness Bay. Challis is one cunning bastard, but he can't know if we're aiming to drive north or south, because we don't know ourselves yet. But he will know that if we go up to Windermere town we have two chances and can make our decision at the junction. My money's on them thinking they might catch us up before we reach the junction. If they don't catch us up, the logical thing would be for them to split, some to go north, some south. If I'm right, they'll come belting past the end of this street any minute now. If and when they do, we make for Glebe Road which, as you say, also links to the 591, and head south. If we can make it to Kendal safely we can go east for a few miles and pick up the M6. That'll give us a lot more anonymity.'

I suddenly began to shiver, and the state I was in seemed to make its full impact for the first time. I was wet through, shoeless and chilled, it seemed, to the bone.

'You need dry clothes, John.'

'We'll worry about that later.'

'You must put on the heater, full blast, when we set off.'

'Shoes are the real problem. I never realized how helpless you feel without them.'

As we waited for the cars, I told her briefly the full story of the *Veronica*. But the waiting lasted too long. 'They *could* be thinking we've got to go back and get *my* car,' she said. 'They might assume I'd park on Glebe Road too.'

'Good point. They don't know who you are, but they'll assume you had to get to the landings in a motor. They'll have worked out that we couldn't get to Glebe Road from the public piers on foot before Challis had berthed the *Veronica*.'

'But what are they going to do, John? I mean, if they do catch up with us.'

'I simply can't decide. If they were villains with form I'd know, but they're not, they're simply hard-nosed businessmen. Believe me, it blew their minds when they found out what Challis had done. But if he goes down he's threatened to take them with him, and I don't know if they can handle that. The lawyer and the accountant, I don't think they'd want any part of it, whatever the consequences, but Doherty's a wild card, and so is Speight, and they're the dominant personalities.'

'We could go to the police.'

I nodded. 'And might have to in the end, but it's complicated. I know too much about Durkin and Challis from a lead that came from Bruce Fenlon, acting well out of line. I'm anxious for Bruce to be able to nail Challis without anyone knowing he cut a few corners. That wouldn't be easy if I had to involve the local Plod.'

She didn't speak, but I could sense her uneasiness. 'I think we'll take a chance,' I said. 'Assume they're still waiting at Glebe Road. We'll go up to Windermere town and head south from there.' I turned the key in the Volvo's ignition, thankfully switched on the heater fan.

'The lever's stiff in the lower gears. . . .'

'I never knew a Volvo that wasn't,' I said, forcing the stick into first with an effort.

It was very odd, in an unpleasant way, driving in stockinged feet. The car moved off like an articulated lorry with all the safety cladding that was one of its main features, but the wheel was surprisingly light and responsive, and once in the higher gears it could be encouraged into a decent turn of speed. It was just as well, because we'd not gone a quarter of a mile towards Windermere town before I saw a set of headlamps behind me, and, intermittently, another set behind those. I could tell by the shape of the first car's lamps that they were of the type that can be retracted into the bonnet to reduce drag, which meant it was almost certainly an expensive car that would move very fast.

SIXTEEN

I glanced at Vicky's profile, decided to say nothing at this stage; they could simply be the cars of wealthy tourists. 'I know, John,' she said quietly, in a voice that wavered slightly. 'I've seen them.'

The Volvo had door mirrors adjustable from within on both sides of the car – she was watching hers intently.

'They must have split up. Lain in wait in different spots. Asked passers-by if they'd seen anyone walking around looking like a drowned rat.'

'Oh, John. . . .'

We filtered through the one-way system just below the junction, and when we came to the A591 I turned left and north and put my stockinged foot down. The car, as she had said, wasn't bad when you'd cranked it up to fifth, and these weren't in any case the kinds of roads that any car could give full throttle to. I knew this stretch of the A591 backwards from the days of the family holidays, and this was a distinct advantage, as the drivers behind – who had to be tailing us – clearly didn't. It was a road that widened, narrowed and curved again and again, and knowing where the fast and slow sections were I could get far enough ahead of them to be occasionally out of sight. I had a stroke of luck when we passed through a village that had a set of traffic lights; I scraped through on green turning to yellow, they were held on red.

'They might catch us up when we get past Ambleside,' she said nervously.

'There's absolutely no doubt of it, Vicky; there's several miles of dual carriageway just beyond Grasmere.' I smiled faintly. 'Only we're not going through Ambleside. . . .'

I suddenly swerved right, on to a minor Troutbeck road, and flicked off the headlamps. 'With any luck,' I said, glancing every couple of seconds through the rear-view mirror, 'they should keep straight on.'

The two cars came into view below us and swept forward on the main road. Even in the darkness I could tell they were low, streamlined and tuned to the hilt. 'Good,' I murmured.

'Where does this road take us?'

'Either north via the Kirkstone Pass, or in a loop back to Windermere town.' At a point where the road curved and widened I began a three-point turn.

'Why not stay on it then and go back to Windermere?'

'Because it's not where I want to be. This road is too quiet and lonely. They'll soon realize we must have turned off and they'll be back. The Langdale Chase is just along the main road. If we can make it there we can park up in their grounds till those two have come back and gone up this road, which is the only obvious turn-off we could have taken. They'll assume we'll not put ourselves in a blind alley like the Langdale. Once we're certain they've gone up here we can go on to Ambleside and get right off the 591, which is too exposed.'

She shook her head. 'How do you think all this out while you're driving like crazy?'

'I learnt to think on the run when I made a dash over the Goathland Moors with Miles Rainger. Now he *was* a strategist.'

But it was no good. Intricate planning depended on people behaving as you'd hoped they would, and in this case they didn't. My spirits sank; the men in the cars had realized far too rapidly they were chasing fresh air. They must have been turning the moment I also turned. As I coasted down the incline, my lights still off, I saw the two cars being positioned at the junction so that they faced each other and blocked off our passage back to the main road. As I watched, they too switched off their lamps.

'Shit.'

'We'd better go back.'

'They'll probably have turned off their engines as well. They'll hear me low gearing in another three-point turn. They'll have us.'

'We might make it back to Windermere.'

'They'll be in touch with one another, Vicky. They'll have carphones, mobiles. There'd be a reception committee.'

'Look, John, perhaps they simply want to *talk*, sort it all out. If there's a lawyer among them he'll want to put the best spin on it, even if they've decided to give themselves up.'

'I'd give anything to believe that. I can't take the chance. It's something else I learnt from Rainger.'

'We'll *have* to stop, there's nothing else we can do.'

Fear had now replaced anxiety in her voice, the same sort of fear that seemed to have dogged me ever since I'd first stepped on the *Veronica*.

'Hold very tight. . . .'

'Oh, John, you *can't*! You can't *possibly*. They're almost nose to nose!'

'They won't be.'

I was suddenly grateful for the Sherman-like qualities of the Volvo then. We sat in a reinforced metal box that had a tough bumper which jutted out at least five inches, like a sore lip. It was designed to take an incredible amount of impact, well, you've seen the adverts. The two cars below, on the other hand, were built like greyhounds, each component constructed of the lightest possible materials, to give them the very finest nano-second zero-to-sixty money could buy.

I engaged gear, and with engine roaring began to move towards the cars. I drove at a speed that left absolutely no doubt I wasn't going to stop, but gave them just enough time, if they responded with total frenzy, to restart their engines and back away from each other. They did exactly that, but the Volvo, with a frightful grinding collision clipped both cars before they were fully apart, without doing itself much obvious damage. I swung on to the deserted A591 and drove with everything the car had towards Ambleside.

'With any luck I'll have knocked them a wheel each out of track,' I muttered. 'Whatever damage I've done to your mother's mobile car-crusher I'll pay for.'

Vicky sat almost rigid with shock, and I couldn't help recalling, with a wry smile, that she was supposed to be coming into private investigation because decoy work was considered too dangerous.

At the Ambleside tip of Lake Windermere, I took a left on to the Coniston road. The first house we came to that had that deserted, soon-to-be-rented look I drove into its drive.

'What are we doing now?'

'If they've managed to get themselves mobile they've probably assumed we've driven towards Keswick. Again, they'll soon realize we must have turned off. The only road that's really going anywhere is this one. We wait. If they come along here they'll not be looking into the drives of private houses. If they do go past we give them fifteen minutes and then we set off ourselves.'

'To. . . ?'

'I really could do with dry clothes, and I *must* have shoes. Above all, we need to contact Fenlon direct. He'll know the best thing for us to do. That house at Esthwaite Water where Durkin was living . . . it was booked to him until the end of the month. Well, he left clothes and track-shoes. He was about my build. The house will probably still be as it was. The next turning to the left will take us to it.'

She gave a sigh of relief and closed her eyes. I felt she'd had enough of the wrong kind of excitement tonight to make her look more favourably on the routine aspects of PI work. I watched her, in tenderness and admiration. She was going to be very good, one of the two best PIs in Beckford. Her resourcefulness had been incredible in one so young. I remembered those stirrings of professional jealousy when I'd begun to realize just how good she was. Perhaps we'd always be touchy about each other's abilities. It could keep us on our toes, forge us into a formidable team.

I put a hand on her hair, kissed her. 'Look after me, John,' she whispered, her voice still shaky.

'I think it's been the other way round tonight.'

'I'd have gone anywhere if I'd thought you were in trouble. Done anything. . . .' It took a lot of getting used to, being cared about the way she did.

There was no sign of the cars. It was very late now, and the two or three cars that did pass the gates had the chunky, four-wheel-drive look of the sorts of cars that might belong to a vet or a doctor on emergency calls.

'Well,' I said, 'it looks as if we've either disabled their beautiful machines, or they've gone back to Windermere.'

I restarted the Volvo, and a little further along the Coniston Road we took the turn-off for Hawkshead, passed the village itself and drove on to Esthwaite Water, and the large, gaunt-looking house that seemed to watch over it broodingly.

'This must be the road from the ferry then?'

'Right. We've gone round the lake instead of crossing it.'

She shuddered noticeably as I drove on to the sloping and rutted drive of Four Winds, past the tall cypress trees and the high dense hedge, and I remembered her fear, the first time we'd entered the house, that we might come upon Durkin upstairs, lying dead. Perhaps she'd had some kind of premonition, because by then Durkin was indeed very dead.

The Granada still stood in the garage, the rear french window was still unlocked. I took her trembling hand and we crept into the dark silent house.

'Do we put lights on?'

'Perhaps just the one in the bedroom. It's at the back. Might be as well not to draw attention to our presence.'

She was almost quivering again now. 'You don't think he

brought him back here . . . Challis? Did it here and hid it somewhere . . . the body. . . .'

'No chance. Not when he had the whole of Windermere to sling
the body in. Now take it easy, Vicky.'

But her nerviness was catching, as we felt our way up the steps
in the darkness. The old house creaked now and then, as old houses
often did as they settled into a microscopically different shape with
the passing of daylight, and I felt an uneasiness that was as indefin-
able as it was almost certainly groundless.

It was a relief to be able to switch on the light in the bedroom
Durkin had used. To my practised eye everything in it looked
exactly as before, the rumpled bed, the overturned chair, the same
evidence of a hasty departure.

I opened the wardrobe thankfully. There were trousers, shirts, a
sports jacket, the track-shoes. Smiling at her, I dragged off my
damp clothing. There was no need for modesty, she knew what my
body looked like now. She touched my arm. 'Will you come to the
flat . . . when we get back?'

'Or you can come to my place. . . .'

It would seem like a perfect end to this long, fraught day. The
case was over as far as I was concerned, if I could contact Fenlon,
it would be solid police work from now on. But I didn't let my
mind dwell on it. We still had to get away from Cumbria. I'd
decided to rejoin the Coniston Road and make a loop that would
take us west and south, and then east to Yorkshire on the M62.

The clothes hung a little, as Durkin had been heavier than me,
but it was a hundred per cent better than being in damp ones. The
track-shoes were also slightly too big, but I compensated for that
by wearing two pairs of Durkin's socks. It was an incredible relief
to have footwear again, after the recent painful walk I'd made along
the house's uneven, gravel-strewn drive.

'Right,' I said, as I transferred the contents of my pockets from
the wet to the dry clothes, 'time for Fenlon. . . .'

There was a phone extension in the room, the model a heavy

old-fashioned one with an analogue dial. The purr of its tone was the best sound I'd heard all day, next to Vicky's voice carrying down to the *Veronica*'s saloon.

Just as I was about to dial out, there was a click on the line, and then the tone took on an odd, spaced quality. In a day of nasty shocks it was one of the nastiest.

'What is it?' she said, her face paling even as she spoke.

I had my hand over the mouthpiece, and I put a finger to my lips and laid the handset gently at the side of the base without breaking the connection. I quietly crossed the room, switched off the light, and drew the door ajar. Immediately outside, in the glow of a landing light now turned on, stood Doherty.

He reached into the room and switched back on the bedroom globes. 'I was right,' he called behind him, 'it's Goss. The bugger's everywhere. And the totty on the motor boat, by the look of it.'

He pushed past us and replaced the phone on its base. I grasped Vicky's moist hand and squeezed it, trying to transmit a reassurance I didn't feel. I'd got it badly wrong coming to Four Winds, like so many things I'd got wrong in the Durkin affair. It was clear now that it had looked to be as ideal a spot for them to sort themselves out as for us. The *Veronica* would have begun to seem too risky, but they needed somewhere to talk, perhaps even spend the night. They must have arrived minutes after us.

Challis and Speight now loomed into view at the door. Challis's face had reverted so completely to its normal look of benign shrewdness that it seemed scarcely possible to believe he kept a ferocious beast tied up inside him that he'd briefly unleashed on the *Veronica*. But Speight looked shrivelled and old, and once more couldn't meet my eyes.

'Hello, John,' Challis said warmly. 'I don't believe we've had the pleasure of the young lady's acquaintance.'

I made no attempt to introduce her. 'Let's sit down for a few minutes, Goss,' Doherty said, 'and have a little chat.'

'We'd sooner stand, if it's all the same to you.'

'Well now, John,' Challis said, 'you seem to have got to Four Winds all on your own. We thought you'd be with Bill and Chris, seeing as the rest of us were obviously looking out for you in the wrong place. All we need is a little chat, as Sean said.'

'We bumped into Chris and Bill on the way over,' I said flatly. 'They could be having a tracking problem.'

There was a look of contempt in Doherty's face, but it wasn't for me. I continued squeezing Vicky's hand.

'Trouble is, John,' Challis said, 'everything happened so quickly we never had a chance to come to an arrangement with you, the boys and I, so we'll just have to work something out now.'

'A deal? Is that what you're trying to say? I thought you worked out your deals with the baseball bat,' I said, against the sound of Vicky's indrawn breath.

Challis shrugged. 'We're businessmen. We know when we've lost the advantage. Now that you're off the *Veronica* and the lady's involved . . . things are a little out of control.'

'Just a little. . . .'

'What would it cost to make you forget everything you heard on the *Veronica*, Goss, in your hand and in the morning?' Doherty said bluntly.

'I thought I was supposed to be incorruptible. Those were Challis's words, not mine.'

I watched Doherty, wondering what I could see in his face beyond toughness. There did seem to be something else, something I couldn't interpret, some buried emotion perhaps that flickered with the weak strength of a candle flame, and belonged to the days when he'd been a grand broth of a boy who'd sung the old songs to Maureen's accompaniment, at the Irish Club, so Crystal had once told me.

'We'd set you up for life, John,' Challis said. 'You'd be able to go off with your girlfriend and settle comfortably anywhere in the world.'

I wondered if they could possibly be serious. The advantage *had* passed to me now. Challis was crazy enough to be able to kill people, but could the rest, even Doherty, allow themselves to be involved in the cold-blooded elimination of two more people?

And yet their only alternative, if I couldn't be bought, was certain bankruptcy. I watched Challis in silence, wondering if we had the remotest chance of getting back to the city, even if I finally, with a show of extreme reluctance, hesitantly agreed to take the pay-off. Would they all leave the arrangements to Challis again, as they had with Durkin, make themselves believe he'd spirited us abroad when, working to yet another secret agenda, he'd quietly made us disappear?

'I hope you're giving our offer careful consideration, John,' Challis said softly.

'What's going through my mind,' I said, 'is that you're a very skilful operator. A bit too clever for me. You see, I *believed* you when you said we were coming up here to talk things over with Maurice. It's made me wary of trusting you twice. Not without certain precautions.'

'Which would be?'

'That me and Doherty do the talking. And that you go and sit downstairs for ten minutes while he runs it past me in detail so I can get it quite clear in my mind.'

'Very well, John, I can agree to that. Spell it out for him, Sean. I think you'll find in the circumstances it's a very good offer indeed.'

His readiness to accept my terms so quickly seemed puzzling in a man who'd always liked to be in such total control, even to the point of killing people. I glanced at Doherty and seemed to detect surprise in his face too. I felt we'd both expected a lengthy silence from Challis as his mind worked through every possible angle: what was the *real* reason for wanting him out of the way, what secret agenda of our own might we put together in his absence? But he was smiling his old avuncular smile, the light from above winking on his heavy glasses. I didn't think I liked it. But he made for the door without further word, Doherty's eyes following him. Speight continued staring into space with unfocused gaze, back it seemed in the totally passive role he'd adopted for so much of the time on the *Veronica*. Vicky's hand still clenched mine, as if the force of her grip could somehow inspire me to sort out the situation. I gave her a faint smile, wishing I could put my arm around her, but feeling that simply holding her hand already gave an indication of a closeness that might possibly be used against us. When the door clicked shut and we could hear the faint creak of Challis's footsteps on the old staircase, Doherty turned back to me.

'What's on your mind, Goss?'

I watched him for some time in silence. 'I'm not buying it.'

'Why didn't you tell him that?'

'Because he's one of the most dangerous men I've ever met, and he can't be allowed to get away with it.'

'Look, Goss. . . .'

'I'll cut you a deal, Doherty. If you'll guarantee me and Vicky a safe passage to Beckford, I'll tell the police exactly what happened on the *Veronica*, and I'll give the same evidence in court. That way, Challis won't be able to take you all down with him. Not for murder one, three times over, at least.'

The hard green eyes rested on mine for long, calculating seconds. He'd not be involved in a murder charge, but he'd still be ruined; it could be, from where he was standing, that it was like being told he wasn't HIV positive, he just had cancer. He glanced sideways at Speight, but there was no help there. The time when he'd seemed to have some kind of authority had been all too brief, and in a delayed reaction he looked to have closed his mind on thought, as Denholm and Ackroyd had before him, because of the things he'd heard on the cruiser he was unable to cope with.

'Christ, Goss,' Doherty muttered, 'I wish to God I'd never clapped eyes on you.' The shillelagh Irish had been faltering all night, and was now quite gone, he simply spoke normal English with a similar accent to Maureen's.

'What would you have done if you hadn't? If Crystal had hired a deadbeat who'd have taken the money and done what he was told? Could you *possibly* have convinced yourself Challis had sorted it out, got a man like Maurice, who had ambitions to be an MP, to live on handouts for the rest of his life? Pull the other one. There'd have been a voice in your head, Sean, that would have started as a whisper and ended as a scream that would have driven you crackers.'

He turned abruptly away, his hands clenched, his face flushed. I supposed he was bound to be of Catholic upbringing, like Ferrara. And conscience was the Catholics' speciality, you were encouraged to confess and express contrition for your sins on a regular basis. It might have been twenty years since this two-fisted buccaneer had been near a confessional, but the programming would still be there, ineradicable, as it had been with Ferrara.

'He killed Maurice, Sean,' I said gently. 'The best friend you ever had, all of you, a good, kind, generous man. Even if he'd not made all that money, he was the type who'd have given you the coat off his back.'

'It'll slaughter us,' he almost whispered. 'You can't begin to get your mind round the money involved.'

'But you all made the decision to go in up to your necks. And you owe the money to Maurice's estate, so the debt can be cleared. You can make a new start; you wouldn't be the first entrepreneur to go bust.'

I still held Vicky's moist hand, but I'd almost forgotten she was there in the concentration I was giving to Doherty. I didn't think I was really getting through to him. He was too hardened now. He'd had the lifestyle for too long: the cars, the harp-shaped pool, the respect of the business community. A quarter of a century of toil and sweat. If he began again he'd be starting at less than zero, and even if he made another fortune he'd be an old man.

'If you were my husband, Mr Doherty,' Vicky suddenly said, in a quiet voice, 'I don't think I could bear to see you living with secrets that made you so very unhappy.'

The small, female voice was incredibly affecting in that silent atmosphere of what I felt to be near-despair. I wondered if it struck a chord, reminded him of the tender voices of other women from his past – a mother, a sister, an aunt – helping him to resolve other crises.

'We've got to sort it out, Sean,' Speight spoke for the first time. 'God, nothing's worth all this. I couldn't live with it and neither could you.'

I could only guess at the supreme effort he'd made to cast aside that mindless, almost comforting stance, to drag out once more the decent man from the Co-op I'd seemed to glimpse on the *Veronica*. He still looked old, his large, heavy features an almost alarming puce-like shade, but he spoke decisively. 'Why don't we sort it together, Sean?' he said. 'You and me, we're the only real friends left now. I don't count Ferrara and those other tossers. We'll be able to give each other moral support. We're going to need it.'

'What's that smell?' Doherty said then. 'Woodsmoke or something?'

I'd noted it myself as we'd talked, but abstractedly. I'd had a vague impression Challis must have lit a wood fire, as the night was now decidedly cool. There was a sudden crash, the sort of crash a large piece of furniture such as a wardrobe falling over might make. I ran to the door, pulled it open. The whole of the ground floor was engulfed in smoke and flames. The crash had been a section of the lower bannister falling into the hall.

'Dear *God*!' Doherty cried from behind me. 'He's trying to kill the lot of us now!'

SEVENTEEN

'He must have used petrol!'

'He carries spare gallons in his cars. . . .'

Even as we gazed down, horrified, what could only be described as a ball of fire seemed to leap up the stairs from the intermediate landing to our own. The flames in the hall were now a steady roar, broken by the cracking sound, as loud as fireworks, of wooden furniture rapidly igniting. The intensity of the heat seemed to dry the moisture in my eyes, to choke me. Doherty slammed the door shut. 'We've got minutes,' he said grimly, 'if we're lucky . . .'

He grasped a straight-backed chair and began to smash out the glass in the long, square-shaped, bay window. Speight took hold of a footstool and I one of the small bedside cabinets, and we began to do the same.

'The framework'll have to go, too,' Doherty gasped, hammering at the spars of wood, 'we need to throw out the mattress.'

'We can't tie blankets, Sean, ' I said, 'there's nothing on the bed but a duvet.'

'It'll have to do.'

Fear seemed to have honed our reflexes to electronic reaction. Vicky, her pupils white-edged with shock, tore the duvet off the bed and began grappling with the heavy mattress. The roar of flame, the explosions and the shattering of glass grew steadily louder, but the large window was rapidly reduced to a hole in the wall, as the framework had been old and brittle.

'For the love of God, don't anyone open that door!' Doherty cried, glancing down into a back garden lit by the fire raging through the ground-floor rooms. 'Not with the draught we'll have now.'

We each took a corner of the sprung double mattress, carried it to the window, and dropped it broadside down to the ground, where it bounced and then flopped about a foot from the wall, on to what was fortunately a flowerbed.

Then Doherty grasped the duvet and drew it together in his big hands. He leant over the window-sill as far as he could, with the duvet held by each of its top end corners. 'Hold my legs, one of you!'

Speight crouched behind him and held his legs. 'Right, miss . . . Vicky,' Doherty shouted sideways, 'you'll have to climb out and hold on to the duvet by the edges. It won't give. Help her out, John.'

I drew her trembling body towards the window. The gathering roar of the fire was like the inexorable advance of a flow tide. With Doherty half-hanging over the sill, plus the length of the duvet, it meant the final drop was reduced to about ten feet. 'When you let go,' I said into her ear, 'try and push yourself out a little so you'll hit the mattress cleanly.'

I kissed her quickly on the cheek, helped her scramble out through the window, and held one hand while she got a firm grip on the edge of the bunched duvet with the other. Then, both hands gripping the duvet, the knuckles bone-white with strain, she began to lower herself to its end, her passage, to we who waited, our faces streaming with tension and heat, seeming painfully slow. Finally, and remembering to push herself out from the wall, she dropped to the mattress. It was a good clean fall, and she scrambled to her feet almost immediately and moved to the side. From above, she seemed foreshortened, like a child in the glow of a bonfire.

'Get right away from the window!' Doherty cried. 'The panes could go any minute. Come on Joe.'

There was a sudden great crack from the bedroom door, but it was a stout one and held. I took Speight's place, holding on to Doherty's legs, as the other climbed out nervously and began to lower his bulk down the duvet, with Doherty unflinchingly taking his weight, the muscles of his legs seeming metal-hard in my hands with the strain. But Speight had none of Vicky's youthful agility, and two-thirds the way down the duvet he lost his grip and fell heavily to the mattress. Badly winded, he lay sucking in breath before crawling off the mattress towards the lawn. As he did so, the window below suddenly blew out, showering him with shards of glass. He was lucky to be facing away and so save his face and eyes, but his back had to have been badly torn. He dragged himself across the lawn like an animal sprayed with shot.

'John!'

'No! You've done your share. I'll take the duvet.'

'Don't talk rubbish, man, I'm heavier than you.'

'How would *you* get down?'

'I'll hold on to the window-sill and drop.'

'You'll break a leg. Let me. I'm younger than you and I work out. I can take your weight, don't worry.'

'Will you cut the blather and *go*!' He hesitated, despite every second counting, and his eyes met mine. The hard look had gone, to be replaced by an almost wistful sadness. 'If there are any chances going, you've got to deserve them more than me, the frigging pig's arse I've made of my life.'

There was another ominous crack from the door. The next one would almost certainly signal a blow-out. There was a crashing sound beyond it, as if a further section of the bannister had fallen.

'You need something to hook your legs on to,' I said. 'If I go.'

'The dressing-table. . . .'

It was solid and Victorian, and had been pushed aside when we'd been smashing out the window. We dragged it rapidly into place so that he could hook his legs into the knee-space as he leant out once again. The heat was now increasing beneath the bedroom floor, and a thick plume of smoke had sprung through in one of the corners.

I got out fast, and with all my training on the wall bars was soon down the duvet and dropping to the mattress. I'd dropped from greater heights on to harder surfaces, several times. Speight was lying against the trunk of a tree at the end of the lawn, and Vicky, who had been worryingly lost to sight, now suddenly appeared round the side of the house, carrying an extendable metal ladder. 'I remembered seeing this in the garage,' she gasped, 'and it was obvious the last one out wouldn't be able to use the duvet.'

There was no time to admire her incredible presence of mind. 'Sean!' I cried, above the endless roar of flame and the gunshot cracking of timber. 'I'll get this ladder up to you.'

I laid it against the wall and adjusted the extension until it rested on the window-sill. He looked on as I did so, glancing behind him with rapid, bird-like jerks of his head. But as he was on the point of climbing out there was a sudden thunderous explosion. The door had finally given. He was caught by a displacement of air so powerful that he lost balance and pitched to the ground, where he landed half on and half off the mattress, which we'd dragged to one side. He lay motionless then, his head against one of the stepping stones that provided a path across the flowerbed.

'Joe . . . Vicky . . . help me get him away from the house!'

Vicky was at my side in seconds, but Speight lay slumped beneath his tree, clearly out of action. Even so, with the reserves of strength that seem to arrive in life's emergencies, Vicky and I managed to drag him, as carefully as we could because of possible internal injuries, into the middle of the extensive lawn. He was unconscious, but breathing. The whole house was now engulfed in fire and smoke, the ochreous flame flaring out through every window, the noise and heat swirling around us in the darkness. Leaving Vicky with Doherty, I crossed to Speight. He glanced up at me, grimacing with pain, a bloodstained hand pressed to his chest.

'I think ... I've started ... some kind of heart attack, John,' he gasped.

'I'll get help, Joe, right away. Are you badly cut?'

'Don't ... think so ... the blood ... makes it look ... worse than it is.'

'There's a phone in your car ... yes? Give me your keys, I'll get the emergency services.'

'Right ... jerkin pocket. It's the Merc. ...'

It was as if he felt his heart would fail completely if he stopped clutching his chest. I eased the keys from his pocket with difficulty, and set off round the side of the blazing house and along the tree-lined drive. Halfway down, the glare of the fire reduced by the foliage, someone spoke. 'Goss? Is that you, Goss? What's going on?'

It was the voice of Chris Denholm. He emerged from among the cypresses. 'It took me a while to get my car going again. When I got here. ...'

'Challis torched the house,' I said bluntly.

'God almighty! What's happened to the rest? Have they bought it?'

There was enough light to see that his face dripped with sweat, and he was a twitching bag of nerves, but that was normal for him. Yet there was something about his sudden presence that made me uneasy. Why had he been standing among the trees, why not come and see for himself what was going on, lend a hand?

'I've got to get the emergency services,' I said. 'Fast.'

'I'll come with you. I've got a carphone.'

He stepped closer, suddenly lost his footing on the drive's uneven surface. He lurched against me, and as I instinctively stepped back to brace myself, I fell over something immediately behind my legs. As I hit the ground, whoever it was who'd been crouched there pulled himself over my legs and said, 'Right, Chris!'

It was Ackroyd. He'd been able, because of the noise of the fire, to creep up behind me unnoticed. I saw the familiar baseball bat, that Denholm must have been holding behind him, rise in the air and begin its downward arc towards my head. Blind instinct made me hunch my pinned body and jerk as far to the side as possible, so that the bat missed my head and thudded into my upper left arm just below the shoulder. The intense, searing pain brought tears to my eyes, but the fear was worse than the pain. An instant numbness set into the arm that I knew would leave it out of action for minutes. I also knew that a blow to the head could mean disablement, that two or three could turn me into a vegetable. But Ackroyd had my legs pinned, and he was a heavy man.

As Denholm raised the bat again, another body seemed almost to fly through the air. She knocked Denholm sprawling, and when he tried to scramble to his feet she landed a foot squarely in his crotch. His scream of pain was better than listening to Schubert. She then did certain deft and rapid things with her hands to the sides of his face and neck that made him flop down heavily again, in a daze so close to unconsciousness as made little difference.

She then swung round to Ackroyd, who gave a yelp of panic and scrambled off my legs. I leapt up and armlocked him round the neck with the arm that still had feeling. 'I'm not a man who deliberately inflicts pain, Ackroyd,' I muttered, 'but make one wrong move and it'll give me a great deal of innocent pleasure to kick you senseless.'

He became as still as a man under general anaesthetic.

'Vicky, if there's a clothes-line or some garden cord in the garage, would you bring it?'

'It'll be a pleasure. . . .'

She was back in a couple of minutes, holding a coil of thin rope, and with her two hands and my one we tied the wrists and ankles of both men and left them propped against trees.

'I don't know how to thank you,' I said, as we made for Speight's Mercedes out on the road. 'You probably saved my life. Again. Twice in one night.'

She shrugged, grinned in the glow of the courtesy light spilling from the car door. 'Norma says you can't do enough for a good boss.'

'Where did you learn that karate stuff?'

'I did once tell you I was taking lessons in self-defence, but you were very sniffy about it. You didn't really think I'd go into decoy work without having the rudiments, did you?'

'If we're going to be an item, and we ever have words, you must swear a solemn oath you'll never use that stuff on me.'

'As long as you stop using my motors as battering-rams.'

I keyed out the emergency number, rapidly requested the fire service and medical help, but didn't ask for police back-up. They'd be on to it quickly enough anyway, and I wanted to speak to Fenlon first.

I cleared the line. 'Vicky,' I said, remembering what Miles Rainger had once said to me, 'I can't think of anyone I'd sooner have at my side in a tight corner.'

'I'd not need a tight corner.'

We kissed, briefly and passionately, and then I began to key out Fenlon's number. 'Did I ever read people as badly as I read Challis and Co,' I said, shaking my head wryly. 'People are supposed to be my business, for God's sake. Denholm and Ackroyd were supposed to be the men I could eventually rely on to do the sensible thing, because of being in the professions. I was certain Doherty and Speight were the hard men, who'd always look after their own skins. And Challis was the man I felt I could trust. He might bend the rules, but only because he seemed to care so much about Durkin. And it's all the other way round. Doherty and Speight come through with a conscience, Denholm and Ackroyd try to kill me, and Challis tries to wipe us all out. One of life's little ironies. Let this be your first real lesson in the perversity of human nature.'

Fenlon didn't answer. It could be he wasn't there. His wife would be able to relay a message, but I knew she muted the bedroom phone in order not to wake her small son, and the hall phone could take time to pierce her sleep.

'But what had they got to gain – Denholm and Ackroyd?'

'Your guess is as good as mine. Maybe they thought they'd have the most to lose. Speight and Doherty are businessmen who'd have some kind of chance of making a comeback, but it's unlikely Denholm and Ackroyd would ever practise again in their fields of expertise. Total meltdown. Perhaps they arrived after Challis had cleared off, realized that everyone's car was here except Challis's, including your Volvo with its dented wings, and put two and two together. Told themselves it was a *fait accompli*, that there was nothing they could do, not that they made the slightest attempt to try. We'd all gone, so they could leg it back to the city and sit tight. The police were going to have God's own job piecing it all together with none of us alive. And then I come loping round the corner. I don't know. In their right minds they'd not have acted as they did, but too much has happened too quickly, and they had to act first and think second. It'll all come out in the wash, that's for sure. Come *on*, Enid, pick up the phone. . . .'

'Yes, pick up the bloody phone,' she said, 'we want to get back to *Yorkshire*.'

I smiled ruefully. We'd be lucky to be home by this time tomorrow. I knew from bitter experience how long the fall-out could last from a mess like this. A fire, badly injured men, certain arson. She had my own distaste for paperwork and humdrum detail, but during tonight she was going to find out she'd have to learn to live with it. Yet I didn't disturb her naïve assumption that inside an hour we'd be speeding down the A65 to food and wine and the rest of the night in bed together. And only wished I didn't know how long it was going to be before we'd be allowed to do just that.

'Bruce? John . . . I didn't think you were in.'

'I wasn't. I've just walked through the door. I've been round at your place again. I've been trying to decide what to do. Thank God you rang; what's going on?'

'A hell of a lot, but I'm going to have to give you the edited version. . . .'

EIGHTEEN

'Hello, Brian.'

'Good morning, sir.' He suddenly gulped and turned away for a moment, then slowly brought his eyes back to meet mine. They were red-rimmed and moist, and it looked as if he'd been crying again. My presence must have been a brutal reminder that it had all begun with me, that if I'd not been involved he'd not have known the man he loved so deeply and desperately was now dead, not simply hiding, which he could probably have coped with, even if suspecting he might never see him again.

'It's a bad business, Brian. I'm very sorry.'

He began to blink, and was unable to speak for a few seconds. 'She's ... down below, sir,' he managed to get out, in a strangled tone. 'The other ladies are just preparing to go. . . .'

The mirrored lift took us down to the pool-room, where the wives of the friends, including Cecily but not Guinevere, stood on the point of departure gathering their jackets and bags. They nodded in my direction, Maureen and Dora giving me rueful smiles. They were as expensively turned out as ever, but not now with that flawless, almost aggressive finish I remembered from before: the brand new dresses, the perfect helmets of hair, the detailed make-up.

Crystal stood among them, in a simple cashmere sweater and a dark woollen skirt, her streaked hair looking as if she'd done little more than draw a comb through it. There was also a fine line of grey showing along the roots above the temple. Her hazel eyes rested on mine almost without expression, and there were dark shadows beneath them that glistened slightly. She was an attractive woman who'd fought a successful battle against the ageing process, but it had required time, money and effort, and it was as if she no longer had the stomach for it. It reminded me of Léa in Colette's *Chéri*, who had neglected her own sumptuous looks so dramatically when she and Chéri had separated, so that she had seemed like some almost unknown, middle-aged woman when he had tried to return to her.

'Bye then, girls. See you next week.'

'Bye, Crystal love.' They all kissed and embraced her, even Cecily, as they moved to where Brian waited at the lift. When they'd gone she said, 'Come and sit down, Johnny, I'll get Neil to bring some coffee.'

'I'm sorry, Crystal. . . .'

It sounded pathetically inadequate, as condolences to the recently bereaved always do. She nodded bleakly, then picked up a phone and pressed a key. 'Coffee for two, Neil, and for Christ's sake remember the demerara sugar this time.' But there was almost a weariness in her tone, and it held none of its old asperity. She gazed vacantly out over the gleaming pool. 'I'm gutted, Johnny,' she said heavily. 'Poor bugger. I can't get my head round it. It's like someone turning off the sun. We'd have had our twenty-fifth in two or three years. I first took up with him when I was twenty; we were married in six months.' She smiled faintly. 'He was such a cocky devil, so full of it. He could hardly afford a gallon of petrol for that rust-bucket he drove round in, but he always knew he was going to be a somebody one day. He kicked off selling tins of food, you know, that had dents in – he could pick them up for pennies. And then crockery and candles and tablecloths and jewellery. Bankrupt stock, line ends – they'd always give Maurice first refusal because he made them laugh while he was screwing them rotten.

'The old ladies loved him. He made them feel special. He always had a rock-bottom price for them. But there were so many of them he still made a profit. He couldn't go wrong somehow. And then, when we bought that dump we made into a minimarket, we both worked day and night, I don't think we had a holiday for three years. He'd be here, there and everywhere buying stock, and I'd run the place. It sort of carries you along, you don't seem to feel tired, know what I mean?'

'I know what you mean, Crystal.'

'They were good days, Johnny. You only seem to realize how good they were when they're gone. Nothing ever seemed as much fun afterwards. Even this lot. . . .' She waved a hand to indicate the pool and the house, and the things that had gone with them: the parties, the cruises, the shopping sprees.

'What's . . . going to happen about the bank debt?'

'I had him round, your solicitor pal, Jeremy Green. You were right, he's one clever bloke. He said he couldn't see any problem in suing the others for their share. There was nothing in writing, but the statements showed there was an agreement to act together. He spoke to the bank. If they all tip in now as they should have done in the first bloody place I'll be all right because Maurice never took on what he couldn't cover. Even so, it's blown a big hole in our money, silly fathead. . . .' She shook her head in sad exasperation.

I nodded sympathetically. The only silver lining to this particular cloud seemed to be that she'd be spared the shock of knowing that Durkin had been planning to leave her for Guinevere, that being a man of honour and in a hurry, he'd taken one risk too far in an attempt to double his assets.

'Anyway,' she said, 'your Jeremy rang me just before the girls came. He'd been in touch with the others' solicitors. No one wants to make a case of it. They're going to pay up. They've acted right in their bloody heads for once, it could only cost more still if we went through the courts.'

'Even Challis?'

'Even that murdering swine,' she muttered between clenched teeth. 'He's already in such serious shit he can do without another pile. I just can't get it together, Johnny, I've known Ray Challis since I was *nineteen*. I even went out with him for a bit before Maurice arrived on the scene and gave me the old come on. Well, there was no contest then, was there.'

'I . . . think that was a big part of the trouble, Crystal.'

The lift door opened and Neil came into the room then, the best eau-de-nil china rattling insecurely on a silver tray. He still sniffed, but in a rather more restrained manner, as if out of respect for the dead. He put the tray on a side-table, and stood sullenly before it for Crystal to check that everything was in order, including the demerara sugar.

'It'll break them,' she said, when he'd gone. 'Every one of them. They'll have to sell up. And Joe and Sean are so poorly it'll be a long time before they'll work again anyway. That's why the girls were here.'

'To . . . ask your help?'

She picked up her cup and saucer, and walked to the great floor-to-ceiling windows that overlooked the pool and the wooded slopes across the valley. 'When everything's sorted out I'm think-ing of buying the Mamma Patti restaurants from Patti so she can pay off that clown's share of the debt. And then we girls will run them together. They turn a good profit, and one day we might consider branching out. We all worked our fingers to the bone helping the men to get going, and Dora and Patti both know a lot about the accounting side. And we're not afraid of working again.' She turned round to me, her eyes suddenly glinting, spots of colour in her pale, unmade-up cheeks. 'The men have made a total arse of it, Johnny. All those years of slogging hard work gone for nothing, chucked away. Well, it's our turn now, and if we manage to get a few bob to one side it won't be going on frigging futures and currency deals, you can bet your last pound on that. We'll have to let it all go, the cars and the houses and the staff, but every one of us came from sod-all, and we can handle it.'

I realized then what else was different about Crystal, apart from the air of neglect and the bruised-looking eyes which were the obvious signs of the devastating effect on her of Durkin's death. It was now gone, that former impression of an almost permanent discontent that both she and the others had always seemed to give; gone, I suspected, for good.

Despite her sadness about that remarkable man she'd married, there seemed now in her eyes something of the animation, eagerness almost, of those days when she'd worked so hard but never felt tired, carried along by that surge of optimistic energy Durkin had seemed able to inspire in everyone he'd ever met. Crystal was returning to roots I felt she'd never stopped fretting about getting so far away from.

'I wish you every success, Crystal.'

'It's our turn now, Johnny,' she said again.

I remembered her obsessive preoccupation with the condition of her pool on that first day, her frank advances to a man she'd just met, her determination to get me into her bed. She had different goals and objectives now, and I knew quite certainly that I was being jettisoned as an object of desire, along with everything else – the cars and the clothes and the cordon bleu cooking – that had failed to satisfy her restless discontent. And perversely, human nature being what it is, I couldn't restrain an irrational sense of rejection because I was no longer of the remotest sexual interest to a Crystal intent on reconstructing a life when work had been more fun than fun.

'I've definitely decided on a supermarket trolley, by the way, done in flowers. . . .'

Her mental leaps were as hard to accommodate as ever, but after a few seconds I remembered that following the complete success of the greyhound sculpted in flowers that had graced Durkin's father's funeral, Crystal had considered that when the time came for Durkin himself to go a supermarket trolley would seem appropriate. It didn't seem funny any more.

'But . . . there's no body. . . .'

'We'll have a service just the same. They'll sort it all out at Delaney's Death with Dignity, it's happened before.'

She moved then from the window to the magnificent white-wood edifice of her desk against the side wall. 'Here you are, pet, I got your bill the other day.' She handed me a cheque for £5,000.

'But you don't *owe* me anything. That wasn't a bill I sent you, it was a statement of account. It showed a balance in your favour, and if you agreed it I was going to send *you* a cheque. You gave me a retainer for five thousand, don't forget.'

'Take it, Johnny. You forgot to charge for the hassle. Getting nearly burnt to death and that carry-on on the boat. No one could have sorted it out like you did, even if it did have to end like this.'

I felt that the lining to the cloud of losing Durkin was brighter than I'd thought. He'd gone now, and I doubted she'd ever really get over it, but she couldn't bring him back, and his going had provided the means for her to give purpose and direction to her life again.

'Well, thank you very much, Crystal. It's been a pleasure working for someone I could get along with so well.'

She put her hands on my shoulders, and there seemed to be a faint reminiscent wryness in her eyes now, as if she, too, thought of those times when her desire to sleep with me had seemed so all-consuming, a desire which had now evaporated but which she half-wished she still felt. 'She was a lucky kid to nobble you, wasn't she,' she said, 'that Vicky Barker. . . .'

He was standing at the bar, a cigarette cupped defensively in his left hand.

'If the camel-crap cigars didn't work,' I said, 'what's it to be next – nicotine patches?'

'Don't start. Enid bought me some once and I told her the only way they'd do any good was if she stuck the bloody things over my mouth.'

I nodded. 'Awkward. You need your mouth such a lot in your line. You'd be all right in a monastery.'

'My old dad couldn't give up the fags,' Kev told us, placing a clinking gin and tonic in front of me. 'Thirty a day habit. Then he got broncho-pneumonia and the doc said it was nothing but the fags. Never touched another after that. Not that it did him much good – he was dead in three months.'

'I'll bear that in mind, Kev,' Fenlon said heavily, grinding out his cigarette in the ashtray as if he'd lost the taste for it.

'Had you considered snuff?' I said. 'My mum remembers her granny taking it, to get herself off the clay pipe. Kept it in an Oxo tin.'

'Wouldn't touch it if I were you,' Kev said. 'Bad as cocaine for doing your nose in. My Uncle Bobby, he took it all his life. Got as he hardly dare blow his nose in case it came away in his hanky.'

'You know,' Fenlon said, 'the only reason I come in here is because of the sympathy and advice.'

'That's what friends are for, Bruce,' Kev said, who had never been noted for an ability to detect irony.

'Life is a tale told by an idiot,' Fenlon muttered, as Kev moved down the bar. 'And there goes the idiot.'

'I've just been up to see Crystal Durkin,' I said.

'How's she taking it?'

'Badly. But she's a survivor.' I told him what she planned to do. 'Can't wait to get back to work. She's never really got much out of life since they made it.'

I couldn't help smiling at his expression of genuine bafflement. It was a concept well beyond his reach that anyone who had a pool, servants, six cars and access to the very best food, drink and sex money could buy could ever be any other than permanently on cloud nine.

'Funny woman.'

'What's the form on Challis?'

He shrugged, seemed dispirited. 'That's one tough, cunning bastard you swung on to us, pal. He's hired the best criminal lawyer in the area, and you can be sure he'll retain the best barrister.'

'But for God's *sake*, Bruce, you'll have me, Speight, Doherty, the forensic evidence on Tessa and Sukie. . . .'

'You can forget Tessa. He took whatever he hit her with away with him. The car he was in that night's disappeared.'

'Disappeared?'

'He reported it stolen weeks ago. You ask me, he left it where it *would* be stolen, and it's such an expensive machine it'll be the other side of Europe by now. Well, you know. And from what we can gather there's nothing conclusive about Sukie's death either. No one saw him go there; he used gloves to kill her; you can be sure he's burnt everything he was wearing. They couldn't even find a hair at the SOC. Speight and Doherty are very sick men and a good counsel can twist that carry-on on the boat any way he bloody well likes.'

'I can't believe I'm hearing this.'

'There's no hard *evidence*, John. And from what you told us I don't think he actually admitted anything, even when he went off his head.'

Frustration began to knot my insides in the old familiar way. He *hadn't* really admitted anything, despite a screaming outburst that had seemed totally conclusive. And in the case of Durkin there wasn't even a body. 'But Four Winds! The fire. . . .'

'Did anyone *see* him do it? The next *we* know about Challis the sod's back home and in bed, saying he thought you were all following on behind. He's admitting nothing, and don't forget those other two were lurking about – Ackroyd and Denholm – and it helps nobody that Denholm had two empty petrol containers in *his* car's boot.'

'Oh, God! If Challis was to walk after all this. . . .'

'John, you know what a pile of dog meat a first-class counsel can make of a case where there's barely a shred of evidence that isn't circumstantial.'

I felt weary with disappointment. Get benign, twinkling Challis in front of a jury and they'd find it just as impossibly difficult to make an accurate character assessment as I had myself. With a top-ranking barrister and no hard evidence they could quite easily give him the benefit of the doubt, even if they had misgivings. I'd been involved in too many court cases.

'However,' Fenlon said, 'there's always Windermere Wally, isn't there?'

He was smiling faintly. I watched him for a moment in silence. 'Go on.'

'Well ... we all know damn fine Challis dumped Durkin in Windermere, but the lake's eleven long by a mile wide. In other words, don't even begin to think about it. But the night Durkin went missing, Windermere Wally saw something being tipped from a boat down in the southern end. He's some kind of a lake freak. Roams round it winter and summer, camps out, studies birds and water-rats, all that crap. Beard down to his dick end. But his mind's sharp enough, and he saw everything through infra-reds. He thought it was someone tipping rubbish and he considered reporting it, but didn't bother in the end.'

'*Fantastic!*'

'When he read about the case he came forward. He didn't get the name, but he can describe the cruiser and it fits the *Veronica*. But – get this – he can pin down where the boat was anchored to within ten square yards. They're sending down a diving team tomorrow.'

'Rotten *sod*! You really had me going then for a while, didn't you, and I was stupid enough to let you.'

But Fenlon had always taken a great deal of pleasure in trying to send me up, and it was an act he was continually refining.

'We're nearly there, John! With a body, we can nail him to the floorboards! In fact if his defence are right in their heads they'll get him to change his plea. Guilty, but one tin short of a six pack, the usual cop out. It'll all come to the same thing – Challis inside a cell, either barred or padded. Well *done*, old pal.'

We caused a minor stir in the early evening calm of the bar parlour by our whoops of delight, that near-hysterical crowing common to most men, whether they've scored the goal of the match, or seen a triple killer brought to justice. Part of my elation came from the feeling that I'd finally redeemed myself from the shambles of the Rainger case, which had always seemed to cast a long shadow over our friendship, even though Fenlon had never referred to it again. Durkin had been a genuine team effort: I couldn't have done it without Fenlon's input, he couldn't have reached a result so rapidly without the short cuts I could take that were denied the Force.

And neither of us could have done it without Vicky.

'It's just about in the bag!' I told her gleefully, striding into the living-room of her flat. 'Bruce is over the moon. I have here two bottles of Dom Perignon, suitably chilled, the makings of a tasty meal, and this. . . .' I handed her a cheque, made out for £1,000. 'Bonus.'

She looked at it impassively, then let it slip from her fingers to the table. I realized then that in my excitement I'd overlooked her lack of pleasure when she'd opened the door, the fact that she'd not thrown her arms round my neck as she usually did.

'Vicky? Something wrong?'

She turned away without speaking, almost as if she was unable to speak. I touched her arm. 'What is it, Vicky?' I said gently.

She suddenly gave a single, gulping sob. 'Why didn't you tell me?' she said, in a wavering voice. 'Why didn't you tell me about you and Mum?'

I felt myself redden, thinking for a second she meant me and Louise as lovers. Then I realized she couldn't – Louise never told her when there was a man in her life. Which had to mean she'd found out that Louise had used a little manipulation to get me to give her a trial at the agency. Which, with her touchy self-reliance, would be all that was needed to upset her again.

'She . . . worried about you working for Girl Talk. She thought it too dangerous.'

She turned to me, her moist harebell eyes meeting mine in a

puzzled glance. 'I don't know what you mean. I'm talking about you and Mum, John; I'm talking about your affair with my *mother*.'

I flushed again. I'd been right first time. I couldn't get it together. Louise had told me she never discussed her menfriends with Vicky, and I'd been certain she spoke the truth. 'I don't know *how* you know I went to see your mother once or twice, but. . . .'

'I passed the house one night a few weeks ago, and there was a Mondeo outside!' she almost cried. 'And I wrote the number in my diary because if it was a man she was seeing it was a precaution, just in case. That's how we are about each other. I was looking through my diary yesterday . . . I suddenly realized the number was yours.'

'All right, Vicky,' I said calmly, 'all *right*. Now take it easy. I'll admit it, I did go to Louise's. But that was because she wanted me to try and find you a job with the agency. We agreed not to tell you because we both know how little you like accepting favours.'

'John,' she said, in a low, shaking voice, 'I went to Mum's last night. She's got your number on her phone-pad. Not just the office, but your house and carphone.'

'Well, for God's *sake* – I gave her my card with all three on.'

'She's *different*! I've never seen her as happy. I *know* there's a man involved. She always pretends to be so self-contained, but she's smiling too much, she sings to herself in the kitchen. It wouldn't mean a lot to anyone else, but it's been me and her against the world and she's not been like this since—'

'Look, Vicky—'

'That night I passed by the house and your car was there, there was a light in the bedroom but none downstairs. John, it was nearly *midnight*!'

There was no answer to that, and I didn't attempt to find one. We stood for the best part of half a minute watching each other, the sounds of the flat slowly seeming to magnify, the juddering of a refrigerator, the staccato clicking of a digital clock, the rustle of curtains against an open window.

'Oh God, John, how *could* you! How *could* you!'

'Now, hold on. I knew her before I knew you. And when I got to know you, I didn't even think you liked me very much. Louise and I ... it was more friendship we wanted, we were both a bit lonely. And then all at once it was you and me. And since then, it's just been *you* ... well, you *know* it has.'

Her eyes suddenly brimmed with tears. 'I can't bear it,' she said, in a voice that was like a moan of pain. 'I can't *bear* it. Not both of us. Not Mum and I and the same man. Oh *God*!'

I put a hand on her shoulder, which she abruptly brushed off. 'Vicky ... Vicky ... it was one of those things. I barely knew you when Louise and I—'

'It's *horrible*!' she cried. 'It's too horrible to even think about. You *knew*. You knew when you slept with me you'd already slept with Mum. How could you do that? Can't you *see* how revolting it is? Oh, *John*.'

'I just didn't *think* about it that way. It was simply a coincidence. She was a friend, but you and me, well, you *know* it's more than that. We've got a future. . . .'

'It's not *possible*, John, not now. Can't you see that? It would be like some frightful, incestuous *ménage à trois*. Can't you see how horrible it is? What if you shared me with your own father?'

'You're comparing an apple with an orange,' I said flatly. 'My father was lucky, he had a long and stable marriage. Your mother wasn't, but she's only human and she wanted a little male company. And how can you talk about a *ménage* when it was all over between me and Louise the night you and I slept together? And don't forget, it was only through meeting Louise that I got to know you properly. I can't *change* any of it, Vicky, there's nothing I'd like better than to run it back and put a new tape in, but I can't.'

I touched her arm again, too briefly for her to shake my tainted hand free. 'What I felt for Louise doesn't begin to compare with what I feel about you,' I said, in a low voice. 'Why don't you think it through for a few days? I can see it's been a shock, but is it really so terrible?'

'It is to me,' she said, in a voice little more than a hoarse whisper. 'It wouldn't matter how long I thought about it, I couldn't ever accept it – you and Mum and then you and me, not in a million years.'

'Oh, Vicky.'

'I've only ever loved two men.' Her eyes glittered with tears in the early evening sunlight. 'One was my . . . my father, the other was you. He . . . he seemed to . . . to have a lot of what you have. He was kind, generous . . . fun to be with. But . . . but when you're very young you . . . you can't see the difference between charm and . . . and genuine qualities.'

She rubbed the back of a hand over her streaming cheeks. 'When he left Mum I knew I'd never be able to trust a man again until . . . until the qualities seemed genuine. And . . . and yours were. Oh *God*! I can't explain it properly, but . . . but, after you and Mum, it's as if you're more a father now, not a . . . not a lover. I just couldn't live with it.'

The euphoria that had peaked at the George had drained off as rapidly as water from a handbasin, and I could sense the onset of one of the almost disabling depressions that had dogged so much of my life. It seemed I'd never known genuine happiness until I'd met Vicky, the only woman who'd ever cared so much about me that it had seemed nothing I could ever do would affect the way she felt.

Except take her mother to bed.

I gazed down bleakly at the travel-bag near my feet, open on the misting bottles, the redundant cartons of Italian food, the fresh baguettes in their plastic sleeves. I was supposed to find it horrible, sleeping with both mother and daughter, but I couldn't. I wished it had never happened, but I could feel no guilt or even distaste. The hard truth was that I cared for them both in different ways, and had liked making love to them both – Louise for her tender sensuality, Vicky for her gauche and touching inexperience. But I was in my thirties and more or less mature, and I'd had a settled home-life with loving parents, and she'd gone through the trauma of a broken home and seeing the only other man she'd ever loved walk away, and, affected as I was by her bitter unhappiness, I knew I'd never be able to analyse or fully understand a mind that found my actions so difficult to accept. But I was going to have to live with it.

I told myself she was young, disturbed, in shock, that one day she'd be mature enough to be able to handle it, would gradually begin to get my brief affair with Louise into focus and accept it as the unfortunate coincidence it was.

I knew I was simply clinging to wreckage.

'Do you . . . still want to go on working with me?'

She shook her head, brushed tears almost angrily from her eyes. 'I'm sorry, John, the sooner I start learning to forget you the better.'

A week later, I drove to Louise's little cottage above the woods. They'd been very bad days. I'd got so used to having Vicky about, taking her with me on the round of errands, traces, client meetings, giving her jobs of her own to tackle, helping her with costings and reports. She'd become a part of the team.

It didn't help that Norma was so annoyed with me. The two women had developed an incredible rapport in the time they'd known each other, enhancing the myth about John Goss's stinginess and crabbiness to almost Homeric proportions, and Norma had made it obvious she was delighted about a relationship we no longer bothered to conceal.

'But it's what she's always wanted,' Norma had said, 'to work in a really professional agency for someone like you.'

'She's changed her mind.'

'She can't be going back to decoy work.'

'I suppose so.'

'But that's short-term. She knows it is. These men, out for pick-ups, they only want the young ones.'

'It's her decision, Norma. She can't face the humdrum, and you of all people know how much of that there is in this job.'

'You've had a bust-up, haven't you?'

'Oh, Norma,' I sighed, 'leave it.'

'John, what have you *done*? She's brilliant. You'll never find another as good as Vicky, not in this town.'

How could I tell her the truth? She was from a different generation, and you only had to catch those old black and whites her kind had gone to see, to be aware of the different moral codes they'd lived by. Norma was one of my two closest friends, she was understanding and compassionate behind the brisk persona she showed the world, but she went back, and I couldn't bring myself to tell her that I'd slept first with Vicky's mother and then with Vicky herself, and that Vicky couldn't hack it.

I pulled in outside the cottage. I'd thought long and hard about this, I'd seemed to do little else away from work. I felt that the amount of sleep I'd had over the last week barely added up to one decent night. But I'd reluctantly had to accept there was no point in trying again with Vicky; there had been no door left ajar that simply needed one or two good pushes, it was firmly shut, locked and bolted. Whatever the implications of my sleeping with both mother and daughter, which were beyond my layman's brain to accurately assess, she was never going to have me back.

And it was at about 3 a.m. on one of those long nights that I eventually remembered why I'd taken up with Louise in the first place. There'd been no women at all in my life since Laura Marsh, and before Laura there'd been Fernande Dumont, and I'd sworn I'd not get involved with anyone again on a similar level of intensity. Nor would I had Vicky not brought such genuine feeling for me into the equation, a bright, attractive *jolie-laide* who'd been carrying a torch ever since the Rainger fiasco.

But Vicky and I had unravelled too, just like the other relationships I'd put too much emotional expenditure into, a roulette wheel that seemed to throw a zero each time I raised the stakes. And lying sleepless, I'd begun to yearn again for Louise's calm smile and small talk, the friendly presence that I'd once felt was like that of a nurse who expertly cleans the wound and gives you something to deaden the pain.

I walked slowly along the short path, past the rhododendron, its violet blossom now browning a little as the season drew on. I wondered if she'd invite me to stay the night. Wondered how I'd react. All I really wanted was Louise's intelligent conversation, her smiling eyes on mine as we ate one of the little scratch meels she was so good at rustling up, to go with the good red wine I had in my bag. I wasn't here for lovemaking, though I'd provide it if I did stay, and try not to think of Vicky. Her daughter. It was said that women often traded sex for warmth and affection; what I had in mind was a role reversal.

'Hello, John,' she said, with a smile I remembered so clearly because I'd seen it so recently in her daughter's face. 'Come in.'

'I'm sorry it's been so long, Louise, I've been badly tied up with the Durkin case. Well, I'm sure you've seen the papers.'

'Yes,' she said, 'I've seen the papers.'

I wondered if I detected an odd flatness in her tone.

She led me into the little crowded room, with its mix of furniture, old and new, that had probably gone with a division of the divorce spoils. 'Gin?'

'Please.'

She went off to the kitchen, returned with a gin and tonic for me, what looked to be a dry sherry for herself. She was as relaxed as ever, in a long-skirted dress of indigo cotton, her tawny hair taken straight back and tied with a ribbon.

'Things are quieter now, thank God,' I said. 'I missed the evenings we spent together.'

'They were fun.'

'I wondered if I might take you to dinner. We could drive out to the Devonshire Arms, if you like.'

'If you don't mind, John, not tonight. I'm not really geared.'

'I should have rung, I suppose.'

There was something different about her. She'd always been

composed at first, in the defensive habit of the single years, the animation and the laughter only coming later with the drinks and the talk, but there seemed this evening an extra sliver of reserve, so small as to be the difference between one shade of white and another.

'Perhaps we could make a firm date for dinner,' I said. 'I really would like to repay your hospitality.'

I'd take her to a really good restaurant, push the boat out with some of the money Crystal had pressed on me. She deserved it, a woman living frugally on a single salary, deserved the flowers and the candles, the fluttering attention, the bottle rattling in its pail of ice. Just so long as I could lick my wounds in her calm, fragrant presence.

'I'm . . . afraid that won't be possible, John.'

Our eyes met, and I felt my cheeks beginning to tingle with the same flush Vicky had aroused. Was it possible Louise now knew about my later relationship with her daughter, had she too pieced it together as intuitively as Vicky? I couldn't believe Vicky would have told her, she couldn't bear to think about it let alone discuss it.

'I see. Is there something wrong?'

'I'm afraid I can't overlook what you've done to Vicky, John,' she said evenly. 'I feel you betrayed the trust I put in you.'

My flush deepened, my eyes fell guiltily from hers. So she *did* know. I could think of nothing to say. I had to accept how bad it must look from where she was standing: that I'd simply used Vicky, taken advantage of my position as mentor and guide, a one-night stand because I was too tied up with Durkin to spare an evening with my mature and established lover.

'Louise, I—'

'I thought you'd take care of her. You seemed such a sensible type, so level-headed. You had such a good reputation.'

'Louise, it's not what you're thinking.'

'I don't need to think about it, it's what I can *read* . . . in the papers.'

She was losing me. I watched her for some time in a puzzled silence. 'The papers?'

'I suppose it's nothing to you. I suppose you've become quite used to it over the years,' she said, her voice now more cold than cool. 'Houses on fire, people getting badly injured jumping from windows and young women risking their lives in flimsy boats on very large, deep lakes.'

'Louise, you can't believe—'

'My Volvo, John. She said she'd dented the bumper parking badly. But when she returned it I could tell there'd been a lot more replaced than just a bumper. It was a bumper and two wings – the garage confirmed it. It had obviously been in a collision.'

'But . . . but I covered the cost. I settled with the garage direct.' I realized how fatuous the words sounded the moment they were out.

'That's beside the *point*!' Her voice took on a higher, steelier note. 'You exposed her to such *risk*. I ask you to try and talk her out of decoy work because of the possible danger involved and you take her into danger ten times as bad. How could you be so *thoughtless*!'

I watched her ruefully. It had nothing to with me taking her daughter to bed. I was involved in two separate hang-ups here. Her face, with the triangular top lip, the gap between her front teeth, the bluntish features, seemed almost to merge into Vicky's, as Vicky's had once seemed to merge into hers. But Vicky's near-hysteria had been replaced by Louise's studied iciness and contempt, and there seemed little difference in the pain I was getting between the daughter's kicking and the mother's.

I sighed. 'Look, Louise, I didn't *ask* Vicky to follow me to Windermere that night. That was her own idea. I tried, believe me, to keep her away from the sharp end.'

'It won't do, John. I know she's got a mind of her own, but she's so much younger than us, and it's our duty to protect her from herself.'

'I'm not her *father!*' I couldn't help bursting out. 'I'm just a guy finding her a job of work, for God's sake.'

She turned away, almost abruptly, and began absently smoothing the lace cloth that covered the dining-table. I wondered if this was another twisted strand in the relationship, wondered if by becoming Louise's lover and taking Vicky under my wing I had somehow in Louise's mind, however sensibly she tried to rationalize it, become as responsible for Vicky as she was. I supposed you had to be a woman to grasp the full nuances of this complex and inadvertent triangle.

'You don't know what it's like to have children,' she said at last, in a low voice. 'No one can imagine what it's like until you see your own baby at your side for the first time. You think the worry will go one day, about their fragility and their illnesses, and then it gradually dawns on you you'll be worrying about them for the rest of your life. I've no husband, John, and my parents are both dead. I have a sister in Sydney and a brother in San Diego. Vicky's all I've got. And I can cope, I'm my own woman, I've lived alone longer than I was married. But I can't see how I'd begin to face life without her, and when she was up there with you, crashing cars and jumping out of burning houses I knew I nearly had to.'

I sank on to one of the dining chairs, drained the rest of my gin. I could have done with another, if not several. 'You'll not change her, Louise,' I said bluntly. 'She's sharp, she's one of the sharpest women I've met, and she likes to be in the thick of things. She doesn't go looking for trouble, but she'll never back away from it if it gets between her and what she wants to do. You're right about children, I don't know what it's like to have them. All I know for certain is that she's her own woman now too, and she'll live life her own way.'

'I'm aware of that,' she said in a softer tone, meeting my eyes again, 'and I know there's not a great deal I can do. But I'll do what I can, even so. And I'm asking you not to give her any more work.

If I'd known what your work sometimes involved I'd not have asked you in the first place.'

I wondered when Vicky would tell her she'd already quit, was back in the untroubled waters of taking men like Ferrara into hotel rooms.

'Very well, consider it done,' I said, unable to keep the brusqueness out of my voice. I was picking up the blame for everything here, for sleeping with both of them, for exposing Vicky to danger. There *was* a Goss version, but no one seemed to want to take it into account. They hardly ever did. I couldn't help adding, 'Don't think it'll make a button of difference to the way she lives her life.'

'I think it might. She'll not be around someone who seems to attract trouble. I'm sorry, but after all the recent publicity I couldn't help looking back at the reports of your other big cases in the *Standard*'s library. Miles Rainger, Laura Marsh, and now this frightful Durkin business. You're like the boy in the Omen films.'

'Let me tell you something,' I said angrily, 'each of those cases gave me two options – an easy one and a hard one. I could have walked through all three, accepted them exactly as they seemed, and society might have been left with unsolved crimes, people killing people and getting away with it. And I couldn't take the pretty route because it's just not the way I am. And Vicky's the same, and you'd better accept it if you don't want to make yourself very unhappy.'

'Oh, I do,' she said. 'I do accept it. And that's why I want you out of her life. She'll attract quite enough lightning all on her own without sharing the incredible amount that seems to go for you.'

'Guinevere?'

We were about to pass on the steps leading to the bank chambers where several firms of solicitors rented office space.

'John! Hello! How are you?'

'I'm well. And you?'

She wore a navy suit and a lavender-coloured blouse. She was as pale as Crystal had been, the pallor emphasized by the clothes, and had similar smudges below her eyes. 'I'm well, John. As well as can be expected. . . .'

'I just need to pick up some documents. If you'd care to wait a couple of minutes we could have a coffee somewhere, if you like.'

'I would like.'

She looked pleased, gratified even. I picked up the papers, and we walked the short distance to the café-restaurant opposite the town hall.

'I'm very sorry about Maurice, Guinevere.' The words had begun to sound even emptier with repetition.

A cafetière was placed between us; she waited to speak until the waitress had gone. 'It's been dreadful,' she said simply. 'I never thought I'd know such unhappiness and pain. It must seem impossible for you to understand, never actually knowing him.'

'I once knew someone as unforgettable,' I said. 'His name was Miles Rainger. The world seems a different place when men like him and Maurice are around.'

She pressed the plunger on the cafetière absently, her eyes passing without focus on to the busy square. 'I've been looking into the question of a divorce from Chris,' she said. 'That's how I came to be in Barclays Bank Chambers.'

'I see.'

'From what I can make out we're going to be rather more penniless than before Chris was qualified and we had two small children. I decided I'd prefer to be penniless on my own.'

'How will you manage?'

She smiled faintly, running a hand through her fair, wispy hair. 'Did you know that Crystal will be the only one left with any real money, and that she's talking of buying the Mamma Patti chain and bringing in the wives to run them?'

I nodded. 'I was up at Maunan the other day.'

'She probably told you she considered the men to have made an arse of it.'

I also smiled. 'A total arse. The wives were just leaving some kind of meeting when I arrived. I didn't see you, though.'

'I wasn't there. Patti told me about it later. I . . . went to see Crystal myself. I asked her, very humbly, if I could be allowed to join the team too.'

Her dark-blue eyes rested on mine, and I remembered the pool parties where Guinevere had looked on at the activities of the *nouveaus* with a disdain that seemed to go with an old money background, remembered how intensely Crystal had disliked her, more it had often seemed because Maurice had been keener to simply talk to her than strip off her knickers.

'I'd not have minded being a fly on the wall.'

'Crystal admitted to being "gobsmacked" – I quote. She'd not asked me because she'd thought I'd not want to know. Told me it would be long days and very hard work, and I'd have to turn my hand to everything – serving, cooking, admin. I think she thought I'd be grabbing my bag and heading for the lift, but I told her I did the housework, the gardening, the cooking, brought up two children and worked part-time as a doctor's receptionist when Chris was studying for his accountancy exams, and that no one could tell *me* about hard work. We reached a kind of wary respect for each other in the end. She used to think I was a snob – partly true – and I used to think she was an airhead – also partly true – but we're beginning to revise our opinions.'

I nodded. 'It's easy to get her wrong. She often got herself wrong. But inside Crystal there's an unrequited businesswoman, and I think this is the chance she's always really wanted. The tragedy is that it came about because of what happened to Maurice, but that's how things so often work out in life, I'm afraid.'

Her face became expressionless in the milky light from a cloudy summer sky. I put my hand over hers. 'Oh, John,' she sighed, 'I do miss him so terribly. He had such a career before him. I knew he'd make his mark in public life, I just knew. And so did he. He was *so* excited. I think he was happier than he'd ever been in his life. He'd achieved so much already, and then he suddenly realized he'd barely scratched his potential.'

I remembered her once telling me, as the music played and people snatched at the champagne cocktails and shrieked with laughter, about a Maurice that only she knew, who'd discovered a world beyond the pools and the cruises and the girlfriends. Remembered also a scepticism I'd not been able to overcome.

'I owe you an apology,' I told her. 'I have to admit that I found it difficult to believe in a reformed Maurice, especially when I first found out about the Tessa King murder.'

She nodded slowly. 'I always sensed it, that you couldn't really accept that he'd begun to change. I didn't mind. I knew the truth and I just enjoyed talking about him to someone I could trust. I wanted to talk about him so much. I was so proud of him, I cared for him such a lot. I really couldn't give a damn about the old girl-friends. I don't think I'd have bothered too much if there'd been any new ones after we were together. I knew he'd always need me, and if I only got two-thirds of him, or even a half, it was always going to be better than a hundred per cent of anyone else.'

She sipped a little of her black, unsweetened coffee. 'Do you know, John, you're the first person I've ever told about Maurice and me, and now you'll be the last.'

I heard a good many sad words in my job. They were among the saddest.

'He was everything you told me he was,' I said. 'I never heard a wrong word about him from anyone, except a man eaten up with bitterness and envy, and that's what made the case so difficult. He was trying to increase his assets when he died, exactly as you said, to do the square thing by Crystal and fund his new life with you. His only mistake was to try and do it too quickly and to cut in the others. But he always knew not to gamble more than he could afford. The others didn't.

'He perhaps made one other mistake,' I added. 'He was too successful and he made it look too easy. He was a big man in every way, and the others tried to be too much like him. It's . . . a man's thing, I'm afraid.'

And one man had tried so hard, and failed, that he'd not been able to bear for Durkin to go on living.

'Time for the women now,' I said. 'To quote Crystal again.'

Our eyes met in a wry smile as we prepared to go. We stood outside the restaurant for a few seconds before parting, she to retrieve her car from the multi-storey, me to plunge back into the city on my round of solicitors' errands. 'Well,' she said, 'if you're ever in a Mamma Patti just ask for one of us and I'm sure there'll be a free chicken nugget and chips in it for you.'

'I'll bear it in mind. Best of luck, Guinevere.'

'Goodbye, John, it's been so nice knowing you.'

I watched her walk away, crisp and businesslike in her dark suit. The goodbye had been quite final, and I felt I knew why. Any further meetings with me could only arouse painful memories of the new Durkin that only she and I knew about. I wondered if Crystal had sensed in Guinevere something of the same powerful love and admiration for Durkin she'd always at bottom had herself, wondered if it had in some way been one of the reasons she'd let her join the team. Perhaps she'd sensed there'd be someone to mourn that remarkable man with her in the way she mourned, a smaller, closer sisterhood inside the bigger one, as they filled their long hard days ensuring the survival of the Mamma Pattis. Even though they'd be mourning quite different men: Crystal, that cocky, big-hearted barrow boy who'd set his heart on making a million, Guinevere, the charismatic public figure who, with her guidance, would fast track to that palace on the Thames.

It seemed odd to envy the dead, but I couldn't help feeling a kind of envy for a man who'd be mourned so intensely by such women as Guinevere and Crystal. Because when I died, the way things were going, it seemed unlikely I'd be mourned at all.

CENTRAL 18.2.99